WASKAGANISH

WASKAGANISH

a novel by

Sandra Cohen-Rose

Editions Corona Publishers

ISBN 978-1-989653-01-2

Edited by Allister Thompson

Cover photo of Waskaganish by Colin Rose

Back cover photo of Sandra Cohen-Rose by Laszlo

CONTACT ME. I love hearing from readers. Drop me an email telling me your thoughts about *Waskaganish*. Email: **cohenrosesandra@gmail.com**

Like my Facebook page
https://www.facebook.com/sandra.cohenrose

"An object is useful when it either affects the senses pleasurably in the present moment, or when, by foresight, it is expected that it will do so at some future time....This function of utility is peculiar to each kind of object, and more or less to each individual. Thus, the appetite for dry bread is much more rapidly satisfied than that for wine, for clothes, for handsome furniture, for works of art, or, finally, for money. And everyone has his own peculiar tastes in which he is nearly insatiable."

Brief Account of a General Mathematical Theory of Political Economy by William Stanley Jevons
Journal of the Royal Statistical Society, London, XXIX (June 1866), pp. 282-87. Read in Section F of the British Association, 1862.

CHAPTER ONE

As she stepped away from old French doors overlooking Montreal to her burled amboyna Art Deco bedroom dresser, tears glistened like gold in Hannah Epstein Star's amber eyes and trickled down her forlorn face. Today, October 12, 1980, would be forever etched in Hannah's memory as the day ten years of promises came to a jarring stop.

From an embossed leather jewellery case, she removed a worn silver box containing her favourite necklace. Slowly, she ran the creamy white pearls through her fingers, each satiny bead an *aide-memoire*, before placing them around her neck. Today, against her dark widow's attire, they were a cherished reminder of her past, when anything was possible.

Hannah had considered wearing her necklace with the precious blue diamond pendant, a wedding gift from her father. Distraught, she did not have the strength to go to the bank and remove it from her safety deposit box. In her frazzled state, she also feared misplacing or losing this priceless, lasting reminder of her father. The necklace was also a fond memory of the sweet story he had told her of how he acquired it.

She tried to comfort herself by picturing Jonathan stepping forward to join her, as he had at the last funeral she attended. That was after he had been delayed in Waskaganish by a blizzard.

Today, Jonathan would not be delayed. He would be transported on time, in a sealed, plain pine coffin. Robert Steinman would be

1

beside her, as he had been at the last funeral. Also joining her would be her closest friend Helen and her husband Jeff Bloom, and Avrum Wood.

*

Farther up Montreal's iconic Mont Royal, about two kilometres from Hannah's modest Tudor-style house hovering over the city, sat Robert Steinman's stately, cut-stone Georgian mansion. Reclining on his bedroom lounge chair, Robert was taking his telephone messages. He had not slept well and did not feel himself. Was he coming down with the flu?

Just after the death of his wife, twelve years ago, he had been experiencing chest pain walking up hills on cold days. A treadmill test suggested a narrowed coronary artery. His physician, Dr. Joseph Meyer, advised him to see Dr. Jeff Bloom, who referred him to Hannah, a dietitian-nutritionist, for nutrition advice. Subsequently, they occasionally saw each other at social functions, where he often gravitated through the crowd toward her. Their unusual exchanges invariably caught Hannah by surprise.

Though free of chest pain, and his cholesterol was within normal range on diet alone, without any operation or medication, as he approached his fifty-fifth birthday, he was concerned about other health problems. Recently, he was plagued by erectile dysfunction and more colds and flus than usual. Dr. Meyer said, "It's nothing a vacation in the sun won't cure, or a stable relationship with a sympathetic woman."

Late last night, he had driven in from Dorval airport following an exhausting flight through heavy rain and thunder from Waskaganish, a small Cree community, two thousand kilometres north of Montreal in Northern Quebec at the junction of the estuary of the mighty Rupert River where it flows into James Bay. Since childhood, Robert had been coming with his father to Waskaganish, Cree for "little house." Previously known as Rupert House, it was one of four Cree communities on the eastern littoral of James Bay.

The Steinman family had first visited Waskaganish in the mid-1800s, shortly after arriving in Montreal from Poland, and became involved in the fur trade in partnership with the Cree Trappers Association. After acquiring considerable wealth, Jacob Steinman

2

built a sprawling white clapboard house by the Rupert River. From it, he conducted his business in this close-knit community. The fur trade was now a minor part of Robert Steinman's business interests.

When they arrived in this strange land they marvelled at how the roots of stunted black spruce clung desperately to the hard rocks. Their survival was dependent upon abundant species of lichen, slowly leaching nutrients from solid rock. Robert recalled as a boy pushing aside Spanish moss — a form of lichen — draped over spruce branches as they tried to stay on the narrow, slippery paths leading from the river.

Little did they appreciate what lay below this land, stripped of its soil by multiple glaciations, with barren rocks that are a part of the Canadian Shield, exposing the ancient craton forming the heart of the North American continent.

This time of the year, sixteen years ago in late October 1964, he and his wife had arrived home from New York with much to be thankful for. A deal he had struck with a young geologist, Avrum Wood, had set into motion a plan that promised to take his Waskaganish business dealings in a different direction, one he hoped would make him a very rich man. He felt satisfied and fulfilled.

Anxious and in a quandary, he paced the room. Today he had a funeral to attend.

CHAPTER TWO

Summer 1876, Eagle, Wisconsin, USA

To understand what led to Robert Steinman's thankfulness and contentment in late October 1964, one must step back to 1876 – the year Charles Wood, a flaxen-haired young man wearing worn denim pants and a sweat-soaked shirt clinging to his lean, muscular body, wiped rivulets of sweat off his face as he struggled to dig a well through the loose gravel of the glacier-deposited Kettle Moraine close to his farmhouse.

Under the gravel, he confronted a layer of hard, yellow material. About to give up for the day, he struck a stone possessing a unique, sunny sparkle and transparency.

After dinner, he pulled the stone out of his pocket and washed it in the old kitchen sink.

"It's beautiful! It is special. The best stone you've collected," proclaimed his wife, Clarissa, who was expecting their first child. Happily eyeing the crystal, she continued to wipe the dishes.

"You're right, it's my best find. It could be a topaz or a diamond." Charles was no doubt contemplating its worth, since he struggled to pay his bills. He cradled the sunny-coloured crystal in his hand for some time before placing it in a jar with some other stones he had collected.

Two years before, in 1874, Charles and Clarissa had settled on this ramshackle rented farm in Eagle, Wisconsin after fleeing Poland for the United States in the wake of the latest restrictions placed on Jews. Charles left behind the prosperous family furniture business, a life of elegant ease, and his long Polish-Jewish name.

*

A few dry seasons and crop failures left the Woods destitute. To feed themselves and their two young sons, Clarissa reluctantly took their treasured sunny crystal to Jack Boynton, a jeweller in Milwaukee.

"Could it be a diamond?" inquired Clarissa enthusiastically.

"There's no way. Diamonds don't exist in North America. No one has ever found a diamond in North America," Boynton replied authoritatively.

"I see. Then what could it be?" inquired Clarissa, clutching her purse.

"I'm not sure what it is, but it looks like a topaz. I can give you one dollar for it. Is that okay?" He took the dollar from the cash register and placed it on the counter.

"I was hoping for more."

"You can take it to other jewellers and see if they will give you more."

He was about to withdraw the dollar when Clarissa hastily placed it in her large purse. "I'll take the dollar."

*

Two weeks later, Clarissa returned to Mr. Boynton's store carrying more stones. As she looked around at the displays of jewels, a short young man came forward.

"Hello. I'm Drew, Mr. Boynton's son. May I help you?"

"Yes, I'm the lady who brought the topaz to your father about two weeks ago. I have more stones to show you." Clarissa nervously placed a small box on the counter.

The young man's eyes lit up and a broad smile spread over his face. "Oh, you're the lady who brought the diamond?"

5

"Diamond! I was told it was probably topaz. Where's your father?" exclaimed Clarissa, frantically looking around.

"Out of town for the day. May I see the stones you brought today?" He appeared to have no idea there was a problem.

"I will return when your father's here." Disappointed, Clarissa quickly removed the box from the counter and left.

"The stone I sold to Mr. Boynton was a diamond! Mr. Boynton's son told me. I knew it was special," proclaimed Clarissa to Charles while placing her purse on the table and removing her coat. She was distraught and tired from the long, bumpy buggy ride home.

The next day, after a sleepless night, Clarissa returned to Mr. Boynton's shop. "I heard from your son that the stone I sold you was not a topaz, as you said. It was a diamond. You said diamonds can't be found in America. So how did this one get here?"

"I don't know. It's a mystery to me. It's a mystery to everyone," Mr. Boynton said, trying to avoid Clarissa's steely gaze.

"I want to buy it back. I will offer you one dollar and fifty cents." She briskly removed from her purse a dollar and fifty cents.

"I can't do that," he replied decisively.

"This is not the end of this. I'll be back." Clarissa stormed out of the store.

*

"We'll sue Mr. Boynton. We were given false information and sold it as topaz." Charles was convinced they had been duped.

With the money from the sale of the stone, they consulted the local lawyer, John Stern, and told him the story.

"I understand that Charles was digging on his farm when he found the stone. Is that correct?" asked Mr. Stern, looking directly at Clarissa.

"That's correct," replied Charles without hesitation.

"Now, one technicality. Do you own the land the stone was found on?" Mr. Stern said with the precision of a prosecutor, leaning back in his chair and waiting for the answer.

"No. What difference does that make?" Charles was visibly irate.

"A lot. If you don't own the land, you don't own the stone. I can't help you. I'm sorry." Mr. Stern closed the folder he was writing in and stood up.

"This is ridiculous. I found it." Looking desperate and at a loss for words, Charles removed his and Clarissa's coats from the coat stand.

Clarissa's parting words were, "We'll go to another lawyer."

The second lawyer also told the Woods they had no claim to the diamond. With nothing to show for their efforts to reverse the sale of the diamond but more debt, they struggled on. Next season brought a bumper crop.

*

Charles and Clarissa eventually settled on their own farm and raised four sons. Charles related the story of the stone so often that it became a legend.

"My sons are my jewels, and I wouldn't want it any other way. We are so fortunate to live on our own land," Clarissa repeated each time he told the story.

"You're just saying that to make Dad feel better. I wish we'd recovered the stone and sold it for what it was worth; then we all wouldn't have to work as hard." George, their eldest son, resented having to get up early to labour on the farm before school. All he wanted to do was study.

"Physical work is good for the soul." Clarissa was proud of her son's determination to study medicine.

"One day you will be well-educated and able to afford many diamonds," Charles added confidently.

"Like your grandparents in the old country. When we got married, as a wedding gift my parents gave me a necklace with a deep blue diamond pendant." Clarissa could still recall her pride in wearing the exquisite necklace.

Charles looked toward the coloured photo on the top of the small bookshelf. "There it is in a hand-coloured photo. You can see how blue the diamond was, and even the unusual gold chain."

"What happened to it?" asked George.

"We sold it to a man for a generous amount. His family was fleeing to Vienna, and we needed the money to come to America," Charles declared unapologetically.

*

October 31, 1964, Queens, New York, USA

Queens, New York is fifteen hundred kilometres east of Eagle, Wisconsin. That was where Charles Woods' oldest grandson, Donald, and his father George made their home. In less than one hundred years, the family had gone from struggling on the land to becoming respected professionals.

Reading the weekend, October 31, 1964 *New York Times*, Donald Wood suddenly got up from his comfortable high-back wing chair, walked over to his father, George, who was relaxing by the fireplace, and said, "Will you read this headline, Dad."

"What do you know? There was a robbery in New York's Museum of Natural History. The robbers took all these jewels, including the Eagle Diamond. The one granddad found in Eagle, Wisconsin in 1876 — eighty-eight years ago. He was living on a farm, struggling to squeeze enough money out of the land to survive. Now here we are living a posh life in New York."

George continued to read. "It was one of the biggest diamonds ever recovered in the continental United States. They say it was sold to Tiffany's for eight hundred and fifty dollars. Later, one of the richest men in the world, J.P. Morgan, bought the Eagle Diamond and donated it to New York's Museum of Natural History, where it's been until it was stolen."

Looking up to see if he had Donald's attention, George added, "Now it's missing. Most of the other stolen gems were found. It's still missing. Apparently, some brazen young men took it."

"That's quite a haul," replied Donald, astonished that such a robbery could take place at the museum.

"Sounds like your son, Avrum. I wouldn't blame him. Who knows where he is or what he's up to when he should be studying? You were more lenient with him than his four older siblings. He was obsessed with the story of the Eagle Diamond you've related to him over the years." George, now approaching seventy, was close to his grandchildren.

"He still is obsessed with the Eagle Diamond. I think it's one of the reasons he wants to be a geologist," said Donald, wondering where his son's obsession would lead him.

"It was a riveting story. My parents even went to court over the diamond and lost. Have you spoken to Avrum recently?" said George with concern. He knew his grandson was headstrong and at times too smart for his own good.

"That's crazy. But—" bellowed Donald, knowing full well his son's compulsive temperament and determination.

"But what? You don't want to think about it? Before you know it, he'll be asking for bail or knocking on your door for a place to hide. He's done crazy things before," said George.

Looking up at the hand-coloured photo on the mantle over the fireplace of his great-grandmother wearing a necklace from which hung a deep blue diamond pendant. Donald turned to George. "Now, if Avrum could get his hands on that magnificent necklace, what a feat that would be."

CHAPTER THREE

Four days before Robert Steinman had returned from Waskaganish, Dr. Jonathan Star, an internist at the Montreal General Hospital, was preparing to leave for that same village.

"This letter just arrived for you, Dr. Star." Mary smiled as she handed Jonathan a white envelope postmarked October 1, 1980.

"Thank you, Mary. I'll be away for a few days. I have a clinic in Waskaganish from October 6th to the 9th. I'm leaving tomorrow. The current epidemic of gastroenteritis in the community has escalated," said Jonathan as he rose from his desk chair.

"I recall you were there about four months ago, just when I started in your office. I understand it's north of Montreal. How far?" Shortly before Mary started her position in the medical department, she had immigrated to Canada from London.

"It's about two thousand kilometres north of Montreal, on James Bay. Let me show you." He spun the colourful globe sitting at the corner of his desk and enthusiastically pointed to its exact location. "There it is."

"I see." Mary spent a moment looking closely.

"I'll be leaving the office early today. Take my messages. I'll take care of them when I return. If there're any immediate problems, call Dr. Olsen. By the way, Mary, do you know a good jewellery store to purchase pearls?" Jonathan appreciated Mary's elegance and quiet charm, along with her soft English accent and efficiency. The office was in good hands.

"I believe that little shop on Mountain Street, it's just above de Maisonneuve — the one with the fancy windows — has a wide selection." She was no doubt recalling the dazzling array of jewels she saw in the display window when she passed by.

"I know the place. My wife always pauses there to look in the window. Thanks for reminding me." Jonathan often got frustrated waiting for Hannah when she stopped to look in the window. In fact, when she was with him, he often tried to take an adjacent street to avoid Mountain Street.

"Hannah is a lucky lady. Pearls are so loved."

In the past year, Hannah had been busier than ever with her consultant dietitian-nutritionist practice. Much to Jonathan's chagrin, she had increased her workload by becoming a part of a weekly radio show. He despised seeing her associated with what he considered a bunch of low-lifes. The muscle-bound exercise man and hustling super salesmen lacking scientific knowledge and ethics, were the epitome of everything he loathed.

*

Alone, Jonathan hastily slit open the envelope with his penknife. His hands trembled as he read the letter from Rebecca Stone.

A small package containing a pair of caribou leather gloves had arrived a few days earlier. He was surprised and flattered Rebecca had remembered his birthday, as well as his fondness for gloves. Three months ago, after not hearing from her for fifteen years, she had written him. She had found his name on a list of visiting internists at the Waskaganish Medical Clinic, where she had recently taken a position.

Along with the almost daily letters, the gift set off a flood of emotions. Jonathan became obsessed by the idea of purchasing her a gift of pearls for her birthday, which fell about a week after his. Buying a pearl necklace for Rebecca was no doubt subconsciously a decision based on his wife's admiration for pearls.

CHAPTER FOUR

Clothed in a long, hooded cape to shield her from the pouring rain, Hannah, a portrait from a previous era, ran down the hill, through the Sulpician Seminary, past the remains of the oldest structures in Montreal. She was late.

Dodging a car, she scurried across Sherbrooke Street. In the lobby of the late 1940s streamlined-modern office tower waiting for the elevator, she flung off her hood. Hannah was a striking woman with a halo of golden hair.

Once off the elevator, she immediately greeted the congenial radio studio receptionist. "Good morning, *bonjour,* Julie."

"Good morning, Hannah. I'll let you in." Then, noticing Hannah focusing on the shiny granite counter with its large baskets of goodies — cakes, cookies, and chocolates — she added with a mischievous grin, "They're gifts from our sponsors. It saves me from buying lunch."

Hannah smiled as she proceeded through the labyrinth of corridors into the studio area.

Mike Mason's voice boomed through the corridors from recording studio three. "Eat all the fat you like and lose weight, and feel really, really great! I'm your exercise and fitness expert, Mike Manson. Listen in every Monday to get the latest on food and fitness from the experts."

Hannah's pulse quickened. She thought, *What is Mike thinking? Why does the station have to tolerate such absolute nonsense?*

Rushing into studio one, where the morning show was broadcast from every Monday morning, Hannah seated herself in the most comfortable chair, the one Mike usually grabbed first. The host of the weekly food and fitness show, Franklin Funkingstein, was seated directly across from her. He stretched out his super-tall scrawny frame, slicked back his mop of snow-white hair, and continued scanning his notes.

"It sounds like Mike is back with a vengeance," said Hannah, placing her papers on the table.

Franklin slowly looked up from his notes.

Hannah continued, "In the two weeks he's been away, he seems to have forgotten everything we've been discussing for the past six months. In the show's promo, he's ranting on about eating fat to lose weight. No wonder the public is totally confused about what to eat."

Before Franklin could muster an answer, Mike jogged into the studio, wiping the sweat off his forehead and roared, "Hi, Big Boy."

"Hi there, Mike. God, it's late. We've got to get this show on the road," said Franklin, swirling around in his swivel chair. "How was your trip?"

"Mind-boggling. Lots of bare, beautiful bodies on the beach."

"Yah. So, what's on for today?" asked Franklin, looking anxious to get started.

"Well, I asked Dr. Mace to be on the show today," replied Mike, flexing his muscular, tanned arms.

"Today?" exclaimed Franklin, obviously unaware there was going to be a guest.

"Really?" Hannah questioned.

"What the hell! You're sitting in my chair," roared Mike as he was about to sit down.

"I'll stay here so you can sit next to your guest, Dr. Mace," Hannah calmly replied.

She never agreed with Dr. Mace, whose research was funded by various pharmaceutical companies. He believed that it didn't matter what you ate as long as you exercised. *Mike invited him,* Hannah thought, *let him deal with him.*

"Boy do I hate you, more than ever," screamed Mike, flopping into the chair with the broken back. Totally agitated, he leaned forward as the music started, tapping his left foot to the beat.

Hannah said nothing. She was used to his irrational behaviour, but today he had hit an all-time low. Any trace of his charismatic smile and superficial kind-heartedness had disappeared.

The show was on the air. The theme song blared.

You're a macho man, who wants to be grand

You're a macho man who wants to be grand

But you don't understand

You don't understand

What to eat and how to exercise to be the head of the band

You're a macho man.

As the music faded, Franklin hollered, "Goood morning, everyone. As usual on Monday, we have our fitness expert Mike Manson and our dietitian-nutritionist, Hannah Epstein Star, with us today. So, what's new? What do we have today?"

Franklin rightly looked anxious as Mike continued to squirm in his chair.

"Have you heard about the fidget factor, NEAT — non-exercise activity thermogenesis?" questioned Hannah. They had no idea, not even a clue what Hannah was talking about, but wouldn't admit it.

On radio, a few seconds of silence can seem like an eternity. Hannah began to explain how fidgeting can burn calories when Franklin called for an advertisement break and beckoned in Dr. Mace.

"Hello, Dr. Mace," announced Franklin. "Dr. John Mace, our guest, is a physician with a big following. What would you like to discuss today?"

"Fat and exercise," he said smugly, removing his jacket. Next to exercise man Mike, he looked insipid and weak. His black hair dangled down to his surgically carved nose, below which sat his gargantuan mouth.

He and Mike ranted on for the remainder of the show. Every time Hannah tried to rebut, Mike and Dr. Mace, an advertisement, or a caller shut her off. The show ended giving the impression that it doesn't matter how much fat you eat — just exercise.

CHAPTER FIVE

If Hannah had taken the main road, as she did at times when she was returning from the radio show so she could do some shopping, instead of cutting through the Sulpician grounds, she just might have encountered Jonathan returning from the jewellery store where he had purchased a pearl necklace. On the grounds, she saw no one. That was one of the reasons she enjoyed this park-like path. Though surrounded by busy streets, it was a tranquil oasis.

She was annoyed. The radio show, which she usually enjoyed, was disturbing today. It was the first time she had witnessed Mike's dark side. What was he capable of? He certainly had the brawn to cause physical damage. A few months ago, he came into the studio with a black eye and cut lip. He said with a grin, "You should've seen the other guy. No one gets in my way."

Besides the show, she was bothered by the idea of Jonathan leaving for Waskaganish alone — without her. As usual, he had not asked her to join him. The previous time, when she bemoaned how she would have liked to have gone with him, he retorted, "Well, you never asked to come." This time she was determined to ask him.

Hannah's heart pounded as she passed by the remains of the oldest structures in Montreal, two circular stone towers built in the late seventeenth century, part of an old fort on the Sulpician seminary grounds used to protect Mohawks who had been converted to Catholicism.

From her childhood, when she lived close to the Semiahmoo Indian Reserve in British Columbia, Hannah had a deep, lingering attachment and empathy for the Indigenous people. Her classmates treated them as outsiders, as they did her, because they did not attend church or social functions with their colleagues.

Pausing for a moment at the statue of Saint Joseph and his son, Jesus, Hannah's stress heightened. Each time she saw the paternal figure lovingly holding his child, she felt an urgent need to replace the child she had lost shortly after her marriage to Jonathan, a union promising love, respect, and security. Irate, she was eager to return home.

Sheets of black rain fell continuously. Montreal rarely seemed so dreary. Hannah reminded herself that bad times pass. The sun would shine again. Six months ago, she, along with many of her close community, were totally engrossed and upset by the prospect of Quebec independence. Now, at least for the moment, the province would remain part of Canada.

What the Quebec separatists refused to acknowledge or discuss was the constitutional rights of the Indigenous people. They had signed treaties with the United Kingdom, not with Quebec. If it separated, they could not be forced to join Quebec. Without the native lands, Quebec would be left with a small fraction of its original land mass.

In the past four years, Hannah had felt more alone than ever. Her brother, Daniel, and his wife, Alice, who used to frequently visit from Toronto, proclaimed they would never set foot on Quebec soil after its efforts to separate. Most of her friends had left Quebec in the aftermath of the November 1976 election of the separatist Parti Québécois. They said they would not tolerate a province where they felt like second-class citizens. It was not that they could not speak French; they just did not want to be forced to work in French.

There were those in the Jewish community who recalled the political climate in Germany prior to the Second World War. Hannah shivered at the thought. But she recognized that Jewish Quebecers were not being singled out for discrimination.

Separatist terrorism of the 1970s spawned the exit of large numbers of the younger members of the substantial Montreal Jewish population. They followed the departure of the wealthy corporations and jobs to Toronto or other North American cities.

Hannah noticed, on entering the medical building housing her nutrition office, that daily there were more blank name spaces on the directory. Being shared owners of the building, if the doctors had not left Montreal, they never would have moved out of the building. A five-minute walk from her home, it was a convenient location. It was also a friendly place to work. Now a good number had followed their friends and left Quebec.

Mrs. Rosen, a dowager from a prominent Jewish family, lamented to Hannah that none of her four children were in Montreal. No longer could she go for a cup of tea in the afternoon with her daughter or to play with her grandchildren when she felt up to it. Now the trips from New York, Toronto, Miami, or San Francisco had become too arduous for her family. When their busy schedules allowed them time away, they paid her brief visits. She thought the next time they would all be together would be at her funeral.

*

Once home, Hannah flung off her cape and hung it up on the oak hallstand. Watching the water dripping onto the Moorish patterned tile floor of many shades of blue, installed by the previous owner, she settled on the wood bench next to the door, struggling to pull off her wet leather boots.

Hannah was so intent on her thoughts that she failed to notice the mail carefully stacked on the entrance table. She walked straight ahead through the book-lined, high-ceilinged parlour to the adjacent sunroom.

Gazing pensively out the window, trying to relax, she leaned heavily on the back of her favourite chair, an oversized, stuffed armchair upholstered in a lively cotton lawn fabric. Its green and yellow swirling pattern, designed in the late 1800s by William Morris, appeared to cheerfully defy the army of accumulating dark grey clouds.

In the late afternoon of this particularly gloomy day, sitting at her desk sipping her hot Darjeeling tea, Hannah became absorbed in writing her weekly food and nutrition column. The telephone rang three times, and she slowly picked it up.

CHAPTER SIX

Upstairs in his office overlooking the busy street, Jonathan heard the telephone ringing and then being answered. Hastily, he closed his office door, went to his desk, and reread the latest letter from Rebecca Stone.

From his black leather briefcase he removed a bundle of letters from Rebecca, addressed to Dr. Jonathan Star at the Montreal General Hospital and postmarked from July through October 1980. He sealed them, along with today's missive and the receipt for the pearl necklace he had just purchased, in a legal-size brown envelope, on which he scribbled *Waskaganish*, hiding it in the back of the lower drawer of his desk.

Rebecca's letter today was unusually short, merely a few lines written in small script, like she was in a hurry. She mentioned that the gastroenteritis epidemic was difficult to suppress and that they were looking forward to seeing him at the clinic on Tuesday.

Downstairs, Jonathan found Hannah sitting distraught, her head resting on her hand.

"What's happened? Is something wrong?" asked Jonathan as he put down the catalogue he had been leafing through. He knew something was amiss. Hannah always greeted him with a grand hello and a radiant smile.

"It's too bizarre to talk about." Anxious and upset, Hannah pushed her golden hair back from her face and stood up.

"You don't want to talk. Why?" Did she know about the letters or maybe the pearls? The jeweller could have called for any number of reasons.

"I'm thinking. It's absurd. Nancy from CBSB radio just called to tell me they no longer need me on the show. They can handle it. After all, I initiated the food and fitness program and donated my time." Hannah had always been secure in her knowledge and abilities as a dietitian- nutritionist. She had never been rejected before. It was a gigantic blow to her ego. She was totally distraught.

"Why did this happen?" asked Jonathan, relieved her anxiety had nothing to do with him.

"They gave no reason, and I never asked, though I really wanted to. Although I suspect Mike Manson, the so-called exercise specialist, couldn't stand my objection to his absurd claim that eating a lot of fat is the key to weight loss and all his other crazy, unscientific ramblings." For Hannah it was outside her realm of comprehension how such nonsense could be allowed on a radio show.

"The radio station has to keep him happy. He's one of the program sponsors. He helps pay the bills. That's how he got on the show. What do you think? He has no credentials." Jonathan saw this happen every day. Everyone was becoming complacent.

"Then, to make matters worse, today he brings in as a guest Dr. John Mace. He has a weight-loss medical clinic. He agreed with everything Manson said." Hannah could visualize Dr. Mace sitting smugly across from her, smirking like a Cheshire cat.

"He no doubt was happy to be asked by Manson to be on the show to flog his weight loss clinic. He might also be paying to be on." Jonathan had seen this before.

"True." Hannah looked drained and tried to be resigned to the problem.

"Forget them. Who needs this kind of aggravation? It's bad for your reputation to be associated with those scumbags. They have no respect for the truth. They used you to give some credibility to that Manson character. He's dangerous. Be thankful it's over." He felt sorry for how Hannah had been used. He had no idea that she had also been abused.

"But I feel responsible. I initiated the show to bring sanity and truth to the food and fitness jungle. Now I've helped create another monster. I've opened the door to more misinformation."

"You tried. What else can you do? Everyone wants to be able to eat cheesecake and lose weight. In your column, continue to speak the truth." Everything was black-and-white for Jonathan.

Jonathan's remarks confirmed Hannah's decision not to ask the producer why she was let go. In reality, she did not want to know. This was not the first time, nor would it be the last, that she would not seek out an answer to a perplexing dilemma.

Leafing through his camera catalogue, Jonathan resumed focusing on telescopic lenses. He had recently purchased a new lens for his Minolta camera, and he could hardly wait to use it in Waskaganish to continue his explorations of the geological formations in the area. As an amateur geologist, the tracings left by glaciers 10,000 or more years ago in the Hudson's Bay area were now his focus.

With the raging epidemic of gastroenteritis, it was a difficult time for the thousand Cree inhabitants of Waskaganish.

"Tomorrow I've got an early flight to Waskaganish. I must go pack a few things." Jonathan fought to hide his anxiety.

"I wish I could come with you. I know the epidemic is bad. There are even infants dying from the polluted water added to their formulas, when really they should be on breast milk." Hannah knew she understood the situation and shared Jonathan's concerns. She longed to see Waskaganish and to share Jonathan's experience, be a part of his life.

"Hannah, believe me, it's best you stay here. I'd be concerned all day while I'm at the clinic."

Thoughts of visiting Waskaganish brought back memories of her childhood near the Pacific Ocean and fishing with her friends Jimmy, Charles, and Lorrie for the scant remaining salmon in the Campbell River in British Columbia.

In the early twentieth century, before the European settlers came and cut down most of the forests and erected sawmills polluting the nearby Campbell River, Hannah was told the salmon in the river were so abundant, you could scoop them up with your hands.

Her friends were the grandchildren of the few remaining Salish who had survived the killing and looting and the abduction of women and children as slaves by neighbouring Indigenous groups. Smallpox and other epidemics brought by the Europeans to the Indian reserve resulted in the demise of many of the remaining Salish people.

Hannah understood explorers had altered the lives of the Cree living in the James Bay area. Three hundred and twelve years earlier at this junction, explorers established Rupert House, the home of the Hudson's Bay Company, and brought white man's diseases, food, guns, and alcohol, as well as the missionaries.

*

Feeling rejected and defeated by Jonathan and the radio show producers, Hannah walked over to the window. There she consoled herself by focusing on the familiar rows of tall, spiralling poplars defining the upper perimeter of the Sulpician seminary. Beyond, the rich, tangled tapestry of buildings and rooftops extended the Saint Lawrence River, a constant reminder of Montreal's roots as a seaport. The river, which had brought the first inhabitants to the area, had become a nautical superhighway, one of the world's greatest waterways. Slightly distorted by the window's aging panes of leaded glass, this familiar vista afforded Hannah an illusion of adventure and escape. The kind of exploit a trip to Waskaganish might offer her.

Lying in bed with the rain pounding down, she could not sleep. She got up to get a glass of water with thoughts of finding her diaphragm but dismissed the notion. When she returned to bed, Jonathan put his arms around her, and they made love.

*

Next day, after watering her ailing avocado plant, Hannah remained in the sunroom for several minutes, trying to make some sense of recent events before returning to the dining room to join Jonathan at the antique solid oak refectory table, easily seating ten people.

Quickly scanning the births and the obituaries in the Gazette, Hannah flipped to the "Antiques for Sale" section. She tore it out, folded it in four, and placed it in one of the drawers built into the old table. A century earlier, in these very drawers, nuns had stored one of their few personal possessions, their individual place settings of china and cutlery. After Jonathan left, Hannah planned to search for past treasures.

On weekdays, Hannah and Jonathan usually arose and ate their breakfast at a time suited to their individual schedules. Today was an exception. Hannah had awakened early to prepare Jonathan's favourite hot cereal, a blend of steel-cut oats, rye, and spelt flakes, cooked with plump, dark, muscatel raisins, sliced McIntosh apples and freshly ground cinnamon. The aroma permeated the house, reminding her of a sweeter, simpler time, a time when they were first married and ate all their meals together and anything was possible.

"I must be on my way. Do you know where my brown leather gloves are?" He thought he had left them on the table.

"Last time I saw them, they were in the front closet with your coat."

He quickly zipped up his parka and placed his gloves in his pockets. "Well, I'm on my way. While I'm gone, relax and enjoy yourself. Now you don't have that time-consuming radio show to do, you can concentrate on your writing. It's the best thing you can do. Tell the truth, the way it is."

"It's funny, I always hate to see you leave. I wish I could come with you," Hannah pleaded. To her chagrin, he was more adamant than she had ever seen him that she should stay in Montreal.

"Hannah, I'll only be gone for three days. I'll be back by Thursday night. This will be the last time I go up north until spring."

Hannah noted a deep concern in his grey-blue eyes. "Take care of yourself. As you've told me, it can be dangerous in Cree country."

"I will. Don't worry, promise me," Jonathan said, wrapping his arms around her lithe frame. Her amber eyes betrayed her vulnerable, downhearted spirit.

Holding his backpack and one small bag, he lingered at the door before walking out to the waiting taxi.

How does one escape the reality of bad moments and memories? Some turn to food, others drink or drugs. If Jonathan were home, he would take her in his arms, make love to her, and transport her to another place where nothing could go wrong.

Hannah recalled a trusted physician friend telling her, as he always told his patients, "When in distress, get away, take a trip. The world will look different when you return." But Hannah, like many people, could not always get away. At these times, she escaped through her writing or her collectables and antiques. These allowed her to mentally time travel.

Her favourite period was from 1890 to just after the Second World War. In this fifty-year span, Hannah could touch the past but still see the future taking shape. Cars became everyday means of transportation; airplanes soared overhead, as did skyscrapers. Women got the vote, cut their hair, and shortened their skirts. Every time period had objects of interest and was reflected in Hannah's home. Once again, she scanned the antiques and household goods-for-sale columns of the newspaper. Possibly there was something she could enjoy, something to help her see all the beauty in the world, and not the pain, something carefully crafted by an artisan, which she could hold in her hands, allowing her to embrace the aura of another era.

Looking up from her cup of freshly brewed Darjeeling tea, Hannah was overtaken by anxiety. Observing the days grow shorter as the sun dropped lower in the sky, she knew summer would soon be a warm memory in Montreal, one of the coldest metropolises in the world. Another cold winter and another year would pass as her biological clock ticked down. Next year she would be forty-five years old.

At seven in the morning, Hannah climbed up the small marble step into the bathroom. Moving her hand over the cool, moist, arched, chrome faucet, she smiled. Watching the water flow, she recalled how she and Jonathan often joked about their phallic faucet.

For some time, her pale, lithe body lay beneath the surface of the warm water. She trusted that the extraordinary powers and benefits many ancient cultures attributed to bathing were true.

Until the last minute before Jonathan left, she was hoping he would ask her to accompany him to Waskaganish.

CHAPTER SEVEN

At six in the morning, with little traffic on the road, Jonathan's taxi sped along. In no time, he looked up to see he was at Montreal's Dorval Airport.

He had planned to rest on the flight to Waskaganish, but he was unsettled and excited. With a busy practice in Montreal, in the past he had questioned why he was taking the tiring trip to Waskaganish Medical Clinic. Recently, besides the possibility of seeing Rebecca, which he found hard to acknowledge, he had another reason to return: his geological curiosity. He might be on to something big. His recent research confirmed his suspicions. Reading about the discovery of the diamond-bearing kimberlite pipes in Russia, he wondered if they could exist in the cratonic Canadian Shield.

Was the heavy excavating equipment he had seen on his last visit to Waskaganish, which he had assumed was part of the James Bay Hydro Electric Project, actually a mining operation?

Dawn was breaking when Jonathan's airplane landed on the runway at Waskaganish. Climbing into the four-wheel drive truck, he noted the stocky Cree driver awkwardly lighting a cigarette was missing the index finger on his right hand. He also had an unsightly crescent-shaped scar across the right side of his face.

Scrutinizing the driver puffing on his cigarette, he tried to picture how different the Cree territory must have been before Europeans established the first Hudson's Bay Company trading post at Rupert House in the latter half of the seventeenth century.

Jonathan had read that a charter granted the Hudson's Bay Company a monopoly over the region drained by all rivers and streams flowing into Hudson Bay in northern Canada. At the time, it was hard for him to imagine this made the Hudson's Bay Company the largest private landowner in the world. The area of the Hudson Bay watershed, known as Rupert's Land, comprised fifteen percent of North America's acreage.

"While you go to your room to drop off your bag, I'll go for some smokes," said his driver, stepping out of his truck.

Returning with his backpack, Jonathan was now wearing Rebecca's gift of caribou leather gloves.

"Did you notice the tall, fit fellow who left the store?" His driver beckoned toward the store as he stepped up into his four-wheel drive.

"I did. What does he do?"

"He's a trapper, Yvon Jacob. Mighty fine one. Ladies' man, about forty years old, part Cree, part white, bad-tempered bugger. I think that's why his lady doctor friend dropped him. When he's about, he rides around in this big, fat, black four-wheel drive like he owns the place. I think it belongs to Steinman. He does some jobs for him. Don't know what."

"I see." Jonathan thought he must be the guy Rebecca mentioned in her letters.

Once in the truck, Jonathan asked, "Tomorrow afternoon, are you free to pick me up?"

"Sure."

"Could you pick me up, say around three?" asked Jonathan.

"Will do," the driver replied briskly.

"We'll be going to the same place we went last time. It's about three kilometres west. To that clearing." Jonathan could visualize the exact location. He was eager to return.

"I wouldn't go in there. Stay away," said the driver, putting out his cigarette.

"Why?" Jonathan was startled by this response to a simple request.

"A few nosy visitors to those parts never came out alive," the driver said grimly.

"You know I've been there before. It looks pretty safe to me." Jonathan felt he was talking to deaf ears.

The driver repeatedly insisted he should not go near those parts.

Entering a square, utilitarian building, Jonathan went directly to the first-floor medical clinic. In the entrance, he was drawn to the melodious voice of Rebecca Stone bidding goodbye to a Cree patient. Jonathan spoke English in the clinic, the Cree's second language, rather than French, due to their historic contact with Hudson Bay Company. He intended one day to master Cree, the most common Indigenous language in Canada.

He hastily hung up his parka and settled into his assigned room. On the floor next to his desk he placed his backpack. Stretching out his legs, he reached down to pull his shoelaces tighter. After checking the time on his Rolex watch, a wedding gift from his in-laws, he left the small room.

At the main desk, as Jonathan reviewed his heavy patient schedule, he turned around to find himself face to face with Rebecca.

"Hello," he muttered in total disbelief. She was right before him

"Hi, I'm so happy to see you," said Rebecca, placing a chart on the desk.

"Me, too. In fact, as soon as I settled in my room, I was going to find you." Reaching forward, he kissed her on each cheek, an old Jewish European custom adopted by Montrealer's. Her face was flushed.

"I thought maybe you weren't coming." Rebecca appeared anxious as she undid the top button of her cardigan

"Oh, because I delayed my trip?"

He had, at Hannah's request. She had beseeched him to stay until after the Jewish high holidays, Rosh Hashanah and Yom Kippur, which celebrate the Jewish New Year and the day of atonement.

Though he had resisted at first, since they meant nothing to him, he was pleased he had stayed. Hannah had gone out of her way to prepare some of his favourite dishes.

"But it's good you came later," Rebecca, quickly adding, "because it's gotten a lot busier in the last few days. It's the gastroenteritis epidemic. Can we speak later, after clinic?"

Thirty-eight years ago, Rebecca's fifteen-year-old Cree mother from Waskaganish had died of hemorrhaging during her birth. Her father's identity was never revealed. Rebecca was told he was killed during the Second World War. A childless aunt had helped raise her.

For elementary and high school, Rebecca was sent to Montreal to live with a second cousin, graduating with a scholarship to McGill University, where she majored in anthropology, prior to studying medicine. Jonathan admired her determination and pride in her Cree heritage.

After her medical residency and failed marriage, she travelled through Europe and then worked in Africa and South America before returning to Canada. A year ago she took a position in Chisasibi, a village on the eastern shore of James Bay about 270 kilometres north of Waskaganish. On one of her visits back to Waskaganish, she met Yvon. He introduced her to a world she never knew existed in Waskaganish, one of wealth.

Picking up or returning a patient's chart at the desk, Jonathan caught passing glimpses of Rebecca going in and out of the examining room.

"I thought I could change things, but the health of my people is getting worse by the day," Rebecca remarked, preparing to leave for the day.

She paused a moment. "But I'm disturbed by the apathy of many of my people. While the government has to modify its policies, the native people also have to accept greater responsibility. Money is not enough. What you say reinforces my own beliefs; without change things will get worse. Come on. Let's go and have that chat we promised each other. You'll see my latest project, my house. It's just been finished."

"Yes, it's been far too long," replied Jonathan, trying to submerge his excitement.

Shortly after leaving the clinic, walking past a sprawling residence perched close to the Rupert River, Rebecca caught a glimpse of its owner, Robert Steinman, entering the house with a group of men, including Yvon. Since his wife died twelve years ago, Robert Steinman had been seen more frequently in Waskaganish.

"I see Robert Steinman's house is all lit up. All sorts of people are coming and going. I wonder what's going on." Jonathan looked back at the house, trying to get a better picture of the activities.

"It's often busy." Rebecca had recently been working long hours and been too occupied to notice. It had been a while since she saw Yvon visiting. With Robert Steinman's house and hers being on the same gravel road, she would have spotted him. Through their shared interests, notably in collecting native artefacts, travelling, and the economic development of Waskaganish, Rebecca and Robert had become friends. She had recently become involved in his business dealings too.

"You're shivering. Are you cold?"

"A little. It's the damp. We'll be there soon." Then she turned to him and added, "I just saw Yvon going into Robert Steinman's."

"My driver pointed him out when we stopped to drop off my bag. He has quite a reputation." Jonathan thought he wasn't exactly the kind of man he had imaged Rebecca would get involved with.

"I know. He drives around in one of Robert Steinman's trucks."

After walking quietly for a few minutes, Rebecca turned off to the left. There, on the shore of the Rupert River, arising from its mundane surroundings of boxy, utilitarian, mostly run-down buildings typical of Waskaganish and Robert Steinman's old clapboard residence, stood a pristine log house.

"This is it," Rebecca said with pride.

CHAPTER EIGHT

$\mathbf{A}$ welcome rush of warm air greeted them as Rebecca quickly unlocked the tall wooden front door. After removing their boots, she reached over and took Jonathan's parka and backpack, hanging them alongside her things in the entry closet. She smiled as she placed the caribou leather gloves on the shelf.

Walking through the house, Jonathan noticed that in some rooms the log walls were left exposed, while in others they were plastered over to a fine finish. Above the plush sofas in the great room hung photographs and paintings from Rebecca's travels. Also prominently displayed were her treasured argillite and soapstone sculptured pieces. Dominating the room was a gigantic, circular stone fireplace, which extended up through the fourteen-foot ceiling. Its intense heat indicated someone had been to the house and lit it before they had arrived.

"Make yourself comfortable, I'll be right back."

Jonathan continued to look around. He wondered how she could afford such an extravagant house. It certainly was not on a clinic physician's salary.

He was drawn to a photo of Rebecca placed on the wall at the far end of the room. He recognized it as one he had taken of her standing in front of Roddick Gates at the main entrance to the McGill University grounds. He remembered her asking him specifically to take her photo in front of the gates, since she told him they were a gift from Lady Amy Redpath Roddick in memory of her late husband, prominent physician Sir Thomas George Roddick, Dean of Medicine in the early 1900s. Rebecca admired Lady Roddick, not only for her literary achievements, but also for her dedication to the Canadian Indigenous community.

With the wind in her hair, Rebecca appeared so young and carefree. Stepping back from the photo, he noticed it was slanting to the right, as if she had recently hastily hung it. Pulling it much too far to the left, he was taken aback to find a small safe behind it.

Rebecca returned to find Jonathan fixated on the deep orange glow from the fireplace. She was now wearing a soft deerskin wraparound skirt with a fringe along the bottom and an exquisitely embroidered off-white blouse over which her dark hair hung to her waist. As she walked, her skirt clung to her thighs and the fringe swayed. Her clothes reminded him of the ones she was wearing on the cool fall day they met while waiting in line at the medical library. He could still recall her buttery-yellow suede leather jacket, with the intricate beading at the cuffs.

"May I take a photo of you in front of the fireplace?" requested Jonathan.

"A photo would be nice."

"I'll get my camera." From his backpack he removed his camera, along with the small box holding the pearl necklace, placing it in the back compartment of his camera case.

"I see you're still interested in photography. What about your interest in geology?" said Rebecca as she straightened her skirt and smoothed her hair back.

"Photography continues to fascinate me. Geology as much as ever. There're interesting rock formations right here. Did you notice? Did you ever hear anything about mining in this area?" Jonathan was anxious for any information she could give him.

"Why do you ask?"

"I thought I saw signs of mining activity." He was sure he had seen them and was eager to hear what Rebecca had to say.

"You did? It would be a boon to the area," Rebecca replied introspectively.

Jonathan sensed there was something Rebecca was not telling him. He knew from her letters that she had regularly visited Waskaganish before accepting a position at the clinic. The time she was seeing Yvon, they must have wandered around the area. He knew Rebecca liked to hike and explore. How could she miss the clearing in the woods he had found?

Pleased with the three photos he took, he settled back to savour his wine. Watching Rebecca position the puffy feather-filled pillows behind her back, he noted her small form and her sparkling earrings.

"Your earrings really glimmer in the light." Jonathan could not get his mind off the idea of diamonds being mined in the area. He was looking for clues everywhere.

"I'm surprised you noticed."

"They light up your face like diamonds." How could one not notice? They were large, clear stones with the sparkle of real diamonds.

"They are diamonds," acknowledged Rebecca. "They're not blood diamonds," she hastily added, remembering his disdain for diamonds mined in war zones and used to finance conflicts.

"I thought you got them on your travels in Africa." In her letters to him, she had mentioned being in Africa. He assumed they'd be less expensive there, since it was the world's largest producer of diamonds.

"Oh, no. Would you like more wine?" She refilled his glass.

"This is great wine." It was reminiscent of wine he had when travelling in Europe.

"I brought it back from Provence a few years ago. I've been saving it for a special occasion."

Memories of the happy gleam in Hannah's amber eyes as they ambled through vineyards hanging with ripe red grapes, fields of lavender, sunflowers, and olive trees spoke to him of Provence and the woman he had promised to love and cherish.

"You're quiet. I remember when you could drink anyone under the table," Rebecca noted thoughtfully.

"I rarely have even a beer these days." To Jonathan those days seemed another lifetime ago.

"Why not?"

"Just my life. Don't ask me why. How about you? What do you do when you're not working?" Jonathan was wondering what there was to do in this small Cree community. He was also still hoping for more information about the source of her diamond earrings.

"I travel a lot. But when I return to Waskaganish, I know I'm home. There's a special quality to the light. It's unlike any place I've been."

Jonathan admired her passion. But had she truly come to terms with the rampant suicides, domestic violence, drug and alcohol addictions, and chronic degenerative diseases, all signs of social disintegration of the proud Cree? In their turbulent lives, the merciless weather seemed scarcely a footnote. Why was she anxious when he mentioned the idea of mining in the area?

Rebecca returned with an enormous platter of food, including smoked trout, walleye, salmon, and bannock. "Let's sit at the table."

"This looks like a native feast," proclaimed Jonathan with zest.

"You're just hungry." Rebecca passed him a plate and napkin.

"I remember when you used to make bannock." Jonathan detected the lingering aroma of baking bread.

"I still do, when I have the time. I find it relaxing. My aunt taught me the traditional recipes she used for bannock. In place of the wheat flour the Scottish settlers originally used, we often use corn flour and even some ground vegetable roots. We also add all sorts of different berries. Blueberry bannock is still my favourite. Traditionally, we cook it on wooden rods positioned over the open fire."

"Did you make this?" He loved the familiar smell of baking bread.

"I did. The blueberries I picked at Smoky Hill. I also picked cloudberries for jelly." Rebecca silently watched him devour his food with the same gusto as in their student days.

He had been hungry. Now, after eating, he leaned back in his chair and relaxed.

"Don't you miss city life?" It was hard for Jonathan to believe she did not.

"Not at all. I know it's there if I ever want to visit, or decide to return, for that matter," Rebecca assured him.

"I'm still somewhat surprised you chose to return to Waskaganish." He continued to wonder what was here for her.

"This is my home. I feel particularly attached to this area. Muskuuchii hills, a biodiverse reserve about a hundred kilometres south of Waskaganish, has a special meaning for me, and for many of the Cree people. My aunt and her family have always lived near this mountainous area, a source of spirituality. It is a sacred place to the Cree people."

Jonathan recalled the legendary abundance of game, particularly moose. During the 1800s, when beaver, a staple of the Cree diet, disappeared from Cree territory, many Cree suffered starvation and poverty and were saved from death by the bounty of Muskuuchii. Beavers were slaughtered for the skins to make the popular beaver hats and trees cut down. This resulted in the disappearance of the wildlife and consequently of the traditional Cree pursuits and way of life.

"It's frightening and heartbreaking to see the changes in my homeland. What will be next? But we can't do anything tonight or tomorrow. Tonight we should relax. Let's sit by the fire."

"As I confessed in my letters, when I heard you had gotten married during your obstetrics rotation in Toronto I was—"

Before he could finish, she added, "Yes, I heard you were upset. But at the time I had little choice. I was pregnant. Unfortunately, I lost the baby at three months. I was devastated. My husband gave me little comfort. In fact, he said he thought it was for the best. He never wanted children then, maybe later. After that, our marriage disintegrated."

"I'm sad to hear it." He reached forward and took her hand. It was small and soft.

"I noticed you were disturbed when you saw Yvon outside of Robert Steinman's house." Jonathan remembered his driver's words and contemplated what he could be up to.

"I wonder where his jealously and bad temper will lead him?"

"Could he get violent and be dangerous?" It was a major concern Jonathan had carried since he first heard of Yvon.

"I hope not. I don't even want to imagine or think about him." She had witnessed his temper tantrums. That was one of the reasons she broke off her close relationship with him. Yet she still saw him and conversed with him.

"The driver also mentioned a controversial Catholic priest in the area. Why's he controversial?" Jonathan wanted to hear Rebecca's take. All he had heard made him sound a bad fit for the Cree community.

"I just hear rumours. He's polite to me. The Catholic church has a lease on the plot of land next to his church with his residence. It's just to the north of us here. You saw it ahead of us as we walked by. Well, a patient told me he tried to run him over when he was a teenager. He was riding his bike on the church property. He said he chased him off. He was lucky, he said. He jumped from his bike. I don't think he respects the people here. He once said that if the Cree were given compensation under the James Bay treaty, they wouldn't work."

"Does he have many people in his congregation?" If he had a small congregation, as was rumoured, why would he stay?

"No, not many people go to the Catholic services anymore. There's the Anglican church, the Pentecostal, and the Baptist churches, and also a group of mostly young Cree intent on getting back to their roots, the spirituality of their forefathers." Her family had always gone to the Anglican church. Her family was buried in the Anglican graveyard.

"There doesn't seem enough people here to fill all the places of worship."

"There's resentment against the Catholic and Anglican churches because they ran the federal residential schools. Children as young as six years of age were uprooted from their families and culture for the

35

whole school term. I understand they weren't given a break to go home from September to June. The children were lonely and often poorly treated, often strapped. We're just beginning to hear all the horror stories," Rebecca related with a sadness only those who had seen the devastation it had caused could understand.

"We were strapped at school all the time. I remember well. It was common practice. Things have changed everywhere. Other abuse? No one ever talked about it, but who knows? You do hear horror stories occasionally." Jonathan recalled the red welts he had on his hands for days after being strapped.

"To be fair, at the residential schools they did get enough education to learn English and deal more effectively with the government when it came to negotiate the James Bay and Northern Quebec Agreement. It helped establish the Cree School Board. I could talk about this all night. All I'll add is Yvon went to a Catholic residential school. He was abused there. It could be the reason he's so bad-tempered." Rebecca thought about how lucky she was to have escaped going to a residential school. She wondered what she would be like now if she had. She felt sorry for Yvon and all the others who were sent away to the residential schools.

"Now you've finished your house, what's your next project?" Jonathan asked with a grin.

Rebecca laughed and added, "You'll be the first to know."

"You've a lot of space here for one person." Jonathan was thinking she no doubt wanted a family.

"You're right. Sometimes you seem to see right through me," she said with a wide grin.

"I should go. I have an early morning clinic, as I imagine you do." The wine was taking effect. He felt mellow.

"There's a heavy rainstorm. Why not stay? Leave when it stops," Rebecca implored.

CHAPTER NINE

In the calm of Rebecca's home, Jonathan felt mellow and content and far removed from problems such as those of his last patient, Maria Jacks, who lived in a one-bedroom house with fifteen other people. During the long, cold winters, their bodies generated so much humidity in the house, toxic mould festered behind the walls. He had seen this deadly mould shut down hospital operating rooms. It was the kind that left people like Maria ill with severe headaches, respiratory problems, and ear infections. Under the 1975 James Bay and Northern Quebec Agreement, the government was obligated to provide adequate housing. To date, this had not happened.

Bending forward to refill his wine glass, their hands touched. Rebecca's dark, soulful eyes and shiny ebony hair shimmering and moving like a continuous hypnotic wave evoked long-buried memories. He was drawn to her like a moth to a bright light at night.

There was a silence erasing time and place. They both savoured the moment like children do the final gooey, sweet sticky lick of an ice cream cone on a hot summer day. Hand in hand, they walked to an adjoining room dominated by a high, four-post, canopied bed.

A warm glow from huge circular globes of two electrified antique Gone with the Wind lamps on either side of the bed reflected the room's multiple shades of white.

A gust of excitement overtook him as he ran his fingers through Rebecca's silken hair and embraced the curves of her small torso, pressing his moist lips to hers. Like a deer in heat, she waited and submerged herself in his passion. Penetrating into her soft cavity, the promise of life was planted. Then calm and tranquillity returned. The music had stopped.

*

At six in the morning, Jonathan awoke with a startle to the sound of his wristwatch alarm and the howling wind. Rebecca turned over in bed.

Pulling himself away from the warmth generated under the folds of the snow-white down duvet, he felt like he had been on an odyssey in a foreign land. Reluctantly, he reached for his clothes. He had to leave immediately if he was to drop by his room to shower and change his clothes and be ready in time for his early-morning clinic.

"I'll see you later. I've got an early clinic. Happy birthday, Rebecca," Jonathan said softly, carefully placing the long silver box containing the golden string of pearls on her bedside table. Beside a book, a necklace matching her diamond earrings caught his attention.

Bundled up in his parka, gloves, and boots and holding his backpack, he closed the heavy wooden door and walked outside. The cold, dark air engulfed him and spoke to him of reality.

Jonathan was a cautious, careful man, one who did not like to complicate his life. His plain gold wedding band let interested women know he was married and off limits. Yet this did not deter certain women's attraction to a tall, lanky, boyish-looking physician. Today, for the first time in his marriage, against his better judgment, he had acted out of passion rather than reason.

Now he knew the relationship was over. He would talk to Rebecca tomorrow and make that clear. All he wanted was to return home and thrive on making Hannah's life happy. That, he realized, would include starting a family.

Walking away from Rebecca's house, lost in thought, he barely noticed the rain was falling in icy sheets. Looking up over the rim of his glasses, bright headlights in front of him blinded his vision. He jumped to the far side of the road to dodge a large, speeding black truck.

*

Before Rebecca knew Jonathan had changed his clinic days, she had made plans for her birthday. Since she often practiced weekends, she had taken the day off. Jonathan was hoping to catch up with her later.

Looking around the clinic waiting room, he noted a number of patients were standing or sitting on the floor when there were plenty of empty chairs. Then he realized the girth of many of the grossly obese patients was so wide, the chairs could not accommodate them.

Trying to deal with the ever-increasing number of patients with diabetes, high blood pressure, clogged arteries, gout, and infections was frustrating, particularly when his advice often fell on deaf ears.

It was still raining when Jonathan's driver arrived. He pulled up his parka hood and stepped into the truck.

"Hi there," hailed Jonathan.

"Hi. Like I said, I wouldn't go near that clearing." The driver looked frightened.

"Don't worry, I'll be fine. You don't have to wait for me. I think I'll walk back. I need the exercise." Jonathan thought, *What, possibly could go wrong? I get lost.*

"Okay," the driver said reluctantly, shaking his head.

Even with his rubber hiking boots, Jonathan found that the soggy moss and igneous rocks, interspersed with murky, deep pools of water from the rain, made it difficult to navigate. Every few steps, he found himself stumbling. As the wind picked up and the rain became heavier, he realized it was not a good day to be roaming outdoors, let alone taking photos. But the weather forecast was for continued bad weather, and tomorrow he would be leaving. His determination propelled him forward.

The well-worn trail to the area he had walked through only a few months before appeared to have disappeared. He pushed the brambles aside, determined to make his way through the black spruce of the boreal forest. Not to lose his direction, he followed the flow of the Rupert River, the waves of which were churning about a hundred metres away. Looking between the stunted trees, he could see the turbulent water splashing the shoreline.

For thousands of years in this unforgiving yet astonishingly productive land, the Cree survived by hunting bear, moose, and geese, fishing, and picking an array of wild berries. Since the Europeans' arrival, white flour, sugar, and various other staples had been added to their diets, some to the detriment of their health.

Ten minutes into the forest, he still saw nothing of the interesting rock formations he was looking for or the clearing. Close by, he could hear hunters' gunshots echoing through the forest. A reminder that it was moose-hunting season. He should be careful.

Heavy rain and high winds made it increasingly difficult to find his way. He thought of his driver's warning. Could it have been a combination of the foul weather and treacherous terrain that caused the demise of visitors like him unfamiliar with these hazards?

After walking another ten minutes, Jonathan emerged from the brush into a clearing and was shocked by what he saw.

CHAPTER TEN

Hannah was washing her hair when the telephone rang. The answering machine could have taken a message, but as was her habit, she ran to get it. She was hoping it was Jonathan; she had not heard from him since he left for Waskaganish.

Jonathan always said, "Leave the phone; pick up your messages at your leisure. That way your work won't be interrupted." He knew how important Hannah's writing was to her and how frustrated she was when at the end of the day upon his return all she could say was, "I've done nothing all day, absolutely nothing but answer the phone." It seemed to Hannah that every insurance and mutual fund salesman had them on their radar.

Anxious, Hannah picked up the telephone on the first ring.

"Is this Hannah, Hannah, Star?" said the caller in a distinct American accent.

Hannah at once recognized the caller as Avrum Wood. "Yes," she automatically replied before she could give much thought as to why Avrum, an associate of Robert Steinman, would be calling her.

"This is Avrum, Avrum Wood. I need to talk to you. May I come over?" he said from his car phone.

Shortly after, Hannah guardedly removed the chain from its latch and opened the door with one hand. With her free hand, she unwound the heavy white towel holding back her wet hair. Matted strands of long, damp, golden hair, like drooping wheat after a rainstorm, fell down onto the shoulders of her light-blue denim shirt. She grabbed them together and pushed them back from her face.

Peering out, she saw Avrum Wood, a tall man in his mid-thirties, with dark blond hair combed back from his clean-shaven face. His deep-set hazel eyes looked like they were housing a secret. To Hannah, Avrum always looked and acted secretive. She had often questioned what he had to hide. She wished she knew more about him, but he generally never opened up to her.

"May I come in? As you know, we've met before. I'm a friend and associate of Robert Steinman," explained Avrum.

Hannah had no idea why Avrum would be visiting her, but since it was early in the morning, she instinctively knew it must be important.

"Mr. Steinman, Robert, would have come himself, but he's in Waskaganish. He phoned me to call on you," he said, removing his black leather gloves.

In spite of the radiant morning sun streaming through the eastern windows, making the house unusually warm and welcome, her visitor stood solemnly with his coat on.

"May I take your coat?" asked Hannah. Though she thought, as he slowly unfastened its plain, round buttons, he felt more comfortable wearing it.

"Yes, thank you," Avrum said after a moment's thought. Then he added, "Please, don't bother to hang it up. Just place it on the chair."

"Do sit down. You look like you could use something to warm you up. I have hot tea on the stove. Would you like a cup?"

"Yes, hot tea sounds good," he replied gratefully.

As he sat down, there was a hesitancy and sadness in his manner. His sombre mien extended to his clothing, from his dark grey suit, light grey shirt, and patterned grey tie to his grey socks, which sharply contrasted with his shiny black leather shoes.

"Would you like milk or sugar?" Hannah asked with a smile.

"Plain will be fine," he said without hesitation.

"Excuse me for a minute." Hannah left the room, returning a moment later with her hair clasped back by a barrette.

"Now we can talk. Sorry for the delay. I always find any time of the day a cup of tea is heart-warming." She carefully placed the two cups of hot amber tea on the coffee table and settled comfortably back in her chair.

"I understand, you are wondering why I'm here first thing in the morning, barging in. I have some bad news." Avrum paused and looked down into his splendidly flowered teacup, then directly at Hannah. "Last night in Waskaganish, apparently, there was an accident. There was a terrible storm, with howling wind and icy rain. Your husband was out in it. A hunter returning home early this morning found his body in the long grass at the roadside. I'm so sorry. The cause of his death is not clear. Mr. Steinman's office is making the arrangements to have his body flown to Montreal."

"How could this happen? What would he be doing in the woods, near the road?" Hannah found herself numb and confused.

"I understand how shocking this is for you. I have few answers. Please accept Robert Steinman's and my condolences. What can I do for you? Would you like me to stay? Phone anyone for you?" There was genuine concern and compassion in his voice.

"No, no thank you," Hannah muttered.

"Are you sure there's nothing I can do, anything," Avrum insisted.

"No, yes, I'm sure." Hannah's throat was dry, and she felt a lump forming. She had to be alone to get her bearings.

"Then I won't keep you. This is my card. You can reach me at any time. Please don't hesitate." Avrum handed Hannah his card.

He lingered a moment, then, seeing he was not wanted, gathered up his coat and let himself out. By the time Hannah looked up, he was gone. She had not even heard the door close.

Paralyzed by the news, a clammy chill crept over her. It was impossible to believe. There must be a mistake. Yes, a mistake, she told herself over and over, as she desperately searched for an escape from this impossible reality. Walking from window to window, she

43

focused on what she understood. She believed — and rightly so, she had no reason to doubt — that Jonathan was the most careful, cautious person she had ever met.

As she was lost in her thoughts, the doorbell rang. She peered out to see a policeman.

He had little to add to what Avrum had told her.

After his confirmation of Jonathan's death, Hannah told herself she must be strong. She must keep going until after the funeral. Then it would be her time. Now it was his. The ability to postpone her emotional needs had been nurtured as a child.

Being thirty-eight and healthy, Jonathan had no funeral provisions. Hannah knew he would prefer the simplest arrangements, cremation.

When Avrum called, she specified a dignified Jewish burial. Cremation was against her faith. Hannah had read in a book of Jewish law that the living could overrule the deceased's desire for cremation. Hannah was grateful Robert Steinman had volunteered to take care of the arrangements. She trusted him to do the right thing, although she questioned why he was so generous and concerned. How would she repay him?

Settling at her desk, with her vintage sterling silver Waterman fountain pen Hannah wrote in her diary.

October 12, 1980

Death defies definition

It leaves you desolate and defeated

Devoid of words

Only tears

Are abundant

Nothing will make the pain go away

Jonathan was the only child adopted by an elderly childless couple who died prior to her marriage to him. Hannah was unaware whether he had any relatives. Mary, his secretary at the hospital, assured her she would pass the sad news along to the staff.

Her older brother, Daniel, could not be reached. No doubt he was out of the country. At fifty-two and a member of Mensa, an elite group of people whose IQ was in the top two percent of the population, he was pensioned off from a thriving pharmaceutical company. Most of his time was spent travelling. An inheritance from his grandmother on his mother's side, the amount of which he never disclosed, contributed to his leisurely lifestyle.

All Hannah could recall from her last conversation with him was his offhand remark, "Do you know as you get older there's a reduction in the fat pads on the bottom of your feet? I know. I can't walk on the stones at the beach like we used to as children." After he hung up, Hannah laughed to herself. Imagine having nothing but the fat pads on your feet to be concerned about. Then she felt sympathetic. The soles of his feet could be bothering him.

It was best he could not be found. He hated to be inconvenienced, as much as he despised the slightest pain. No doubt he would remind her in a condescending manner of his intellectual prowess, inferring he was above such bourgeois events as a funeral.

Hannah's father had died suddenly of a brain hemorrhage eight years ago, at age sixty-nine. Her mother was the same age as her father when she died a year later of a heart attack. Today Hannah missed her parents.

Even if her mother was alive, Hannah doubted she would have come to the funeral. When her husband died, she did not attend his funeral. She simply said she did not like funerals. Nor did she like sick people. If one spoke to her about bad things, she considered it bad luck. She never mentioned the Nazi concentration camps where many of her family were killed. It was as if death and misery were contagious and had to be quarantined. She only wanted to be exposed to beauty, beautiful people, precious jewels, and fine art.

What made her feel that way, Hannah did not know. At some time in her life, had she been traumatized, or was it the early death of her own father? He had died of cancer when she was ten years old. Hannah only found this out recently from a death certificate she had acquired. Her mother had always told her he was killed in a motorcycle accident. Hannah appreciated cancer was— is a taboo in certain parts of British society, as are death and dying, despite being the only certainty in life.

Before marrying her father, in the early 1930s her mother had studied art in Paris. It was a time when the city was still basking in its fame from the 1925 Exposition and home to droves of artists and artistic expressions.

During the Second World War, her father fought for the Canadian army. By the time he returned from overseas, Hannah was a young woman. During his five years away, for a child an eternity, all she had to remind her of him were photographs. She cherished a small black-and-white photo taken on the sandy beaches off the coast of Bournemouth, in England. With towering rock cliffs in the background, he was smiling down on her from above her Silver Cross pram. Under the fringe of the pram's silk sunshade, she was smiling back as her small fingers pulled on the single string of smooth, round corals she wore around her neck.

Later, Hannah was told the corals were to ward off evil spirits and promote good health. She still occasionally wore the colourful necklace, hoping it would perform its magic.

Closing her eyes, she imagined how blissful their world must have been before the Second World War disrupted their idyllic lives. In 1939, they were fortunate to leave Bournemouth on the last ocean liner out of England before the war. While they avoided the Nazi bombing and the possible invasion, they left behind their families and luxurious lifestyle.

After the war, in Canada her father's dreams dissolved as he fought to eke out a life in a new society. Dressed in black brogue shoes, dark grey flannel trousers, white cotton shirts, silk ties, and grey fedora hats, clothes brought with him to Canada before the war, he appeared a handsome, congenial, outgoing businessman. But hidden behind his deep-set, aquamarine eyes was turmoil. He often said, "After seeing men all around me die like flies, I'm happy to be alive."

Today she missed the comfort only family can afford.

CHAPTER ELEVEN

On the morning of the funeral, Hannah awoke before her alarm clock went off. Enveloped in her covers, deeply distraught and reluctant to face the day, she lay motionless. Through the parted curtains she caught glimpses of the sun.

As Hannah lowered her grief-stricken body into the comforting, lavender-scented warm bath, she consoled herself with the thought that while trees and people were here for a number of decades, the sun was sure to outlive her.

Today she had chosen lavender bath oil for its purported medicinal properties, inducing relaxation, reducing headache pain, and easing symptoms of depression. At eight o'clock she reluctantly lifted herself out of her soothing cocoon. Seeking to extend her bathing experience, she methodically dried off her entire body and then smoothed over it a generous layer of velvety rich body cream.

Comforted by her familiar surroundings, Hannah slipped into a set of exquisite black lace lingerie she had purchased years ago in a small boutique in Paris and kept carefully folded in white tissue paper in the back of her armoire. She had planned to wear them on a special occasion.

Taking her pearl earrings from a small glass dish on her burled amboyna Art Deco dresser, she sadly realized this was the only jewellery Jonathan had ever given her. Ritually, she placed their gold pins through the holes in her earlobes, securing them with their gold backs. Then, hesitantly, from her jewellery case she took a slightly worn silver box, lifted the lid, and closely scrutinized the choker-length string of pearls it contained. Running the pearls through her fingers under the bright table light, she wondered about their value, as she had done many times.

Though it was twenty years since she had purchased them, she could still recall the dark-haired young salesman with the unexpected light blue eyes, pleasing smile, and French accent, acquired in Morocco, who had helped her choose them.

Coyly, obviously trying to impress her with their beauty and value, he slipped the most expensive string of pearls around her neck, carefully fastening the clasp so as to not catch her long hair. Without wavering, he boldly told her how they matched her skin, the whites of her eyes, her teeth, her beauty. A happy, contented feeling engulfed her as she inspected them closely in the mirror. It was a few minutes before she asked him to remove them.

The pearls she chose from the vast spectrum of shades and sizes of pearls he presented, even though they were the least expensive of the selection, to Hannah appeared unusually beautiful. She often imagined the young man had made a mistake and placed the expensive pearls in her box. She loved them and the sweet memory of the act of purchasing them. Wearing them, she always felt special.

She went back to the shop several times. He was never there. On subsequent visits, his uncle, the owner, told her he had only helped out during his summer break from school; he had won a scholarship to an American university, where he was at graduate school.

*

Fastening her close-fitting black woollen jacket and straight, midcalf woollen skirt, she caught a glimpse of her silhouette in the long armoire mirror and was satisfied with her clothing choice. Though both black woollen pieces had been purchased separately, together they formed a suit. To complete her attire, she pulled on her tall black leather boots, which disappeared under the hem of her calf-length skirt. These comfortable boots were well suited for walking across the often-muddy mountainside cemetery where her husband would be buried.

Without hesitation, she completed her outfit with a gold chain bracelet from which hung a single charm, a small compass set in whalebone.

At her desk in her diary, she wrote:

October 10, 1980

We are born alone and die alone. If God had meant us to live forever, he would have made us out of stainless steel. If ever a man was made out of steel, it was Jonathan. He was so strong. Nothing stopped him. Oh, how I wish I had a child of his to hold and love.

Checking the stove was turned off, from the front closet Hannah took her long fall coat and her large-brimmed black felt hat before securely locking the front door.

*

Once seated, Hannah looked over the array of yarmulkes and fashionable hats. More mourners than she imagined filled the room, many from the medical community. Jews consider attending the funeral of a deceased fellow Jew a mitzvah a blessed deed.

Every seat was taken in the funeral home's small chapel. Hannah was pleased her friends Helen and Jeff had come early. When Avrum arrived shortly after, she was taken aback by his genuine concern and comforting words.

Just as the service was about to start, to her left she caught sight of Robert Steinman cutting through the crowded room. Hannah and Robert had conversed at the occasional social event, which Jonathan rarely attended. He said he had better things to do with his time than waste it on meaningless chatter. Today, dressed in a closely-fitting, Italian-cut charcoal-grey suit, he appeared fit and healthy. Apart from some additional silver strands in his dark brown hair and a few more character lines on his face, adding to his aura, he retained distinguished features and an athletic figure that set him apart from other men of his age.

Striding gallantly toward Hannah, he took her hands and kissed her on both cheeks before lightly embracing her. He was beside her, just as he had been six months earlier for the funeral of a mutual friend when Jonathan had been delayed.

"Hannah, you have my deepest condolences. You know I'm here. If there is anything, I can help you with, anything." For a man of Robert's status, used to dealing with diverse situations, his demeanour seemed anxious.

"Robert, that is very kind of you. Thank you so much. I appreciate everything you've done. I don't know how I would have managed without you." Hannah was grateful for his kindness but taken back by his grave sadness and unease.

Before Hannah sat down, Robert added, "Rebecca flew down with me. She sends her condolences. I believe she's already seated. She was tired after the flight. She had a late emergency last night. A very sick patient to contend with." This was true; she had also told Robert she had felt obliged to come to the funeral, but she could not face Hannah. Robert, having seen her with Jonathan, understood the dilemma.

Hannah found it strange that Rebecca never came over to give her condolences in person. She thought she must be feeling out of sorts. Looking toward the back of the small chapel, she could see Rebecca sitting silently engrossed in her own world of sorrow. She was flushed. Her braided hair, which usually hung to her waist, was twisted around her head to form a crown. At her throat hung Jonathan's gift of golden pearls.

*

Robert had first encountered Hannah, unknown to her, at the Montreal General Hospital when he overheard her arguing with the chief of surgery, Dr. Allan McDuff.

"Why do you want to do a gastric bypass on an eighteen-year-old boy? Has he been given diet and lifestyle advice?" she said defiantly.

"No, but he wouldn't listen. He's grossly overweight. Don't interfere. This is none of your business," McDuff curtly replied.

"He needs a chance to talk to someone about his diet and lifestyle and problems. Maybe I can help him," said an undaunted Hannah.

Her passion and determination were Robert could not forget.

Clever deals and hard work had made Robert Steinman an extremely wealthy man. Though his parents had died and left a fortune,

Robert had only inherited the family residences, which included the Waskaganish residence and the fur trade business. The majority of the estate was left to his younger sister, who had never worked a day of her life and against her parents' wishes married a lazy, good-for-nothing fool who could not hold down a job. The few insiders, lawyers, and accountants who were privy to the nature of his inheritance found it strange, because in Jewish law it is usually the eldest son who receives the lion's share of an inheritance. They postulated Robert was so successful, there was no need to secure his future with a rich inheritance.

As a difficult, rebellious teenager, just before the summer of his fifteenth birthday, Robert was accused of having a sexual encounter with his thirteen-and-a-half-year-old sister, Mildred. Shortly after, Robert was sent to Waskaganish for the summer and then off to a private boarding school in Vermont.

Mildred blackmailed the family, threatening to report the incest to the authorities if her demands were not met.

As Robert's fortune grew — no one was sure how he acquired so much wealth — Mildred's inheritance declined. Her husband, a gambler, had lost most of her money at the crap tables. Until barely three months ago, when Mildred died of breast cancer, Robert had lived with her allegations and threats.

CHAPTER TWELVE

During the Shiva, Judaism's weeklong period of grief and mourning with relatives and friends, Avrum had joined with Hannah's closest and dearest friend, Helen Bloom, to help ease her pain. She was growing accustomed to his aloofness and formal manner, making him appear older than his thirty-five years; it stood in marked contrast to his young face surrounded by a mop of dark blond hair.

On the eighth day after the funeral, quietly reading, Hannah recalled the words of novelist Mark Twain: *Truth is stranger than fiction. It has to be. Fiction has to be possible and truth doesn't.*

Hannah could not relax. She felt at odds with the world. She picked up the telephone after three rings; "Hello, yes, this Hannah Epstein Star... You'd like me to do a weekly nutrition TV show with your host... I understand. I'll have to let you know."

Now, Helen's call had disrupted Hannah's thoughts on what she was going to do about the TV show offer. "Let's get together for lunch. I'll bring it over," said Helen.

"Okay."

"I'll see you at noon. At your place."

"See you."

Helen, a social worker prior to her marriage to Jeff, was now content to be a full-time homemaker and mother to their two children.

Being a part of the wealthy Steinberg family, Robert's cousin, she and Jeff could afford to be strong-willed and opinionated.

Jeff refused to order medical tests and procedures he deemed unnecessary. Unable to convince other cardiologists of the merits of limiting angiograms, a major source of income for the department to those with a proven indication, he quit doing them. This reduced the cardiology department's workload and income.

When fewer tests and procedures were ordered, cardiology residents also complained their clinical experiences were being jeopardized. They said they went into cardiology to do high-paying, high-tech procedures, not simply talk to patients.

Consequently, Jeff was removed from clinical teaching on the wards. It gave him more time to pursue own interests, which, like Jonathan's, included photography.

Shortly after noon, Helen arrived loaded with two bulky brown paper bags labelled in fancy red lettering: *Hot and Fresh Gourmet Delights.*

"Come in. Give me those bags. Did you invite some others to join us?" Hannah looked surprised at all the bags Helen was holding.

"No. It just looks like a lot. I hope you're hungry." Helen was concerned for Hannah, who had always been slender but looked like she had lost weight.

"I've not had much of an appetite. I feel miserable," replied Hannah, taking the bags into the kitchen to open

"You must eat. I understand it happened in Waskaganish?" Helen was waiting for the complete story.

"Yes, Avrum Wood came by the house to tell me, and also, of course, the police." Hannah wished she had more information. She was waiting for the police report.

"Oh, how I wish I'd been here for you. We came as soon as we could." Helen and Jeff, who travelled frequently, had been out of town when Jonathan died. They returned home the day of the funeral. Since the funeral, they'd had little time to talk.

"I feel so badly. Just before Jonathan went to Waskaganish, I received a phone call from a woman assistant at the radio station. She told me they didn't need me any more on the nutrition and food show." Hannah hated to admit to Helen that she felt totally rejected.

"I know how much you usually enjoyed doing the show. Oh my, I know how much it must hurt."

"Well, the entire time before Jonathan left, I talked constantly about how distressed I was about being let go. I think by the time he left he was exhausted by me. He didn't know how to deal with it." Then a dark thought passed through her mind: maybe that was the reason he never even entertained the idea of her accompanying him to Waskaganish.

"I'm sure Jonathan understood. He was a really smart guy. He knew how disappointed you were. Merely the way CBSB told you the news was upsetting." Helen comprehended such problems.

"No one wants to be the carrier of bad news. You know how you're rated by who's sent to inform you. The method is another question, in person, phone, or by post," Hannah said tentatively as she picked at her food. She lost her appetite talking about the situation; the more she analyzed and talked about it, the more disheartening it became.

"You could tackle this thorny issue in your writing. Who and how news is related depends on your perceived importance. If you're in the upper echelons, the head of the company or someone close to him informs you in person. Like how Avrum Wood, Robert's personal assistant, came to your house to inform you. I'm sure Robert would have come himself if he could," said Helen with authority.

"It was good of Robert to be so considerate. He really didn't have to go out of his way for me." Hannah was thinking there must be more to this story than she knew.

"If you're way down the pecking order, or if it's rather an unethical business, you're informed by phone. That way there is no record. The informer on the phone can even be anonymous. In the case of the radio station, a woman was assigned to relate unpleasant information to another woman." Helen was trying hard to articulate her answer.

After a pause in the conversation, Hannah looked up and announced skeptically, "Now I have another dilemma that just came up. I should say decision to make. The last thing I need."

"What is it?"

"I've been offered a weekly nutrition TV show with the host of CFTV. As usual, I pick and prepare the topic for the show."

Helen looked like she was searching for words then finally replied, "I thought you liked being in the media?" Then she added, "How much are they paying you?"

"I hate to tell you…nothing." Hannah understood it was a good opportunity to educate the public and build up her credibility and the popularity of her newspaper column.

"Nothing. Are you sure you heard correctly?"

"I'm sure. They rattled off how much they loved me on CBSB and my newspaper column and looked forward to me joining them. They'd see where the show takes us."

"I see."

"Most of all, I feel the timing is really bad. You have to look super relaxed and jolly on TV. I'm not up to it and all the other craziness that comes with the territory." Hannah gazed out at the first snowfall. "I must find out what happened. How Jonathan died."

"You mustn't torture yourself. What good would it do to try to retrace Jonathan's steps looking for an explanation? Let the authorities do their job."

"I suppose. I'm expecting the final police report any day. Then maybe I'll have some answers." Trying to come to terms with Jonathan's death was more difficult than she could ever imagine, particularly since the cause of his death was unclear.

"Keep me posted," said Helen as she said her farewells.

After Helen left, Hannah struggled to convince herself that everything had a reason. As her mother often said, "There is a universal plan. Things will fall into place."

CHAPTER THIRTEEN

With her bowl brimming with hot oatmeal covered in blueberries, pine nuts, hemp seeds, and milk, Hannah sat down to eat her breakfast. Most mornings, this was her breakfast of choice. If in a rush, she would pour a bowl of shredded wheat, puffed rice, or wheat, or Grape-Nuts, the only cereals on the grocer's shelves containing whole ingredients without added sugar.

She deplored the wasteful overpackaging of dry cereals, no doubt costing more than the contents and as nutritious as a slice of white bread, amply sprinkled with sugar. When the 1970s Coates Cereal Report alerted the world to the low-nutrient content of refined, high-sugar cereals, the cereal manufacturers responded by adding vitamins.

Hannah also abhorred the way cereal producers aimed their advertisements at children, often claiming the addition of a few added vitamins to the mix made them nutritious. They understood brand loyalty formed in children gave them customers for life.

A day shy of two weeks since Jonathan's death, while reading over the American Express account, she noticed a purchase for pearls made on October 6, 1980, at Spears Fine Jewellers. She realized that was the day before Jonathan left for Waskaganish. Had he planned to give her pearls?

Would they be found in his home office? They were not amongst his personal effects returned to her from Waskaganish or in his office at the Montreal General Hospital. Returning home, Hannah found no pearls amongst his belongings in his home office.

Next day, at the library researching her paper, "Diet, Ethics, and the Media," for an international conference in New York in August, unable to concentrate, she grabbed her papers and headed for Spears jewellery store.

Hannah usually lingered to ponder the dazzling display of diamonds, rubies, emeralds, sapphires, and pearls in the display windows. It was one of the most impressive gem collections in North America. Walking past them, she approached the counter.

"*Bonjour,* may I help you?" said an elderly gentleman.

"*Bonjour. Oui.* I think you can help me. My husband passed away recently, and I'm trying to sort out the accounts. I notice on our monthly American Express statement of October 6 there is a debit for a pearl necklace from your store on the account of Jonathan Star for $262.50. I haven't seen them. Do you know if they were delivered?"

"*Un moment.* Allow me to check my books. I'll be back shortly," he replied in a Parisian accent.

Impatient, Hannah did not attempt to reply in French or even look around.

"*Oui,* I located the receipt. In fact, a tall young gentleman purchased the pearl necklace. He took them with him. They were—" He stopped abruptly and looked up at Hannah. Then, searching for the right words, he added, "They were the last necklace of that particular golden shade I had in stock."

Hannah remembered seeing golden pearls somewhere, recently, but could not recall where.

"*Merci.* Good day," said Hannah.

"If I can be of any further assistance, let me know. *Bonjour,* Madame."

What was he going to say? No doubt he sensed a problem, one he had faced before.

CHAPTER FOURTEEN

Being late to pick up the research medical ethics committee's protocols for the next meeting, Hannah threw her long camel-hair coat over her Ralph Lauren tweed trousers and deep cornflower blue cashmere sweater and headed for the hospital.

As the sole woman on the committee of physicians, she presented a female perspective. A recent study of the long-term effects of abortion on women's mental health generated diverse responses.

Scanning the ethics protocol to be discussed at the next meeting, she looked up to see the distinguished figure of Dr. James Quince, a fellow member of the ethics committee, appear from out behind a file cabinet.

"Why, hello," said Dr. Quince.

"Hello," Hannah responded.

"I'm so sorry for your loss. Accept my sincere condolences on the tragic passing of your husband," he said with sincere compassion. Then he added, "I've missed you on your radio show."

Hannah did not have the heart to tell him she was no longer a part of the show.

"Well, since you mentioned it a few weeks ago, I have been trying to catch it. Though last time you weren't on." He paused, laughing, and added, "I understand why."

Wearing his usual classic three-piece English suit, he looked more a diplomat than a retired surgeon. It was said when he was a resident, he changed his whites twice a day. Also rumoured was that he had them specially starched and ironed.

Hannah was aware of how ridiculous the show had become since she had left. Mike Manson was out of control.

"Are you going back on the show?" He looked concerned.

"No," Hannah replied. She was hoping maybe now he would go away.

Then, to Hannah's surprise he added, "I can see why you don't want to be on that show. The guy Mike Manson you're on with has no idea about metabolism, exercise physiology, or nutrition. What the hell's his background?"

"He never said." Hannah wanted to cut the conversation short and forget about Mike. As far as she knew, he had no university education. If he did, he kept it well hidden.

"You know, the Canadian Radio and Television Commission should look into this. No one has the right to mislead the public." Dr. Quince sounded really serious.

"Yet they do every day." Tired of complaining about the shabby media coverage of food- and nutrition-related topics, Hannah thought the only way to confront them was to fight back through her own newspaper column, and until her dismissal, through the radio show.

Dr. Quince was usually a man of few words. Those he gave away he weighed and measured carefully. She tried to picture him sitting in his office, sipping his morning coffee, listening to CBSB instead of reading his morning newspaper or a journal, while enjoying classical music.

*

Two weeks later, in the early afternoon, feeling warm and satisfied after a large bowl of homemade vegetable soup, including her favourite chanterelle mushrooms, accompanied by a chunk of dark, crusty bread, the postman brought Hannah a special delivery letter. It was the police report on Jonathan's death.

According to the report, *Jonathan Star arrived in Waskaganish around noon of October 6, 1980. He spent the day at the Medical Clinic. About six the morning of October 7, 1980, he was seen leaving Rebecca Stone's house. He spent the next day at the Medical Clinic, leaving around 3:00 p.m. At about seven on the morning of October 7, 1980, a hunter found his body in long grass at the roadside a short walk from the medical clinic. Beside his body was a lens cover from a Minolta camera. An autopsy revealed he died from a number of bullet wounds. Conclusion: Death occurred shortly after 4:00 p.m. on the afternoon of October 7, 1980, from multiple bullet wounds. This is an ongoing investigation.*

Hannah had heard about the bullet wounds. Avrum had said it appeared a hunter had accidentally shot Jonathan. Hannah had since wondered what had really happened and also who had taken Jonathan's precious camera, and if the police in that isolated, close-knit Cree community would be diligent in their search for the killer. In movies she had seen, it appeared the hunter only took one shot, not multiple shots.

Without hesitation, she went to Jonathan's desk and dumped the contents of his drawers on the table. Grabbing the metal letter opener, she ripped open the sealed legal-size brown envelope scribbled with *Waskaganish*. Out fell Rebecca's letters. Pushing back the tears from her face, Hannah recalled the words of the seventeenth-century poet and preacher, John Donne: "More than kisses, letters mingle souls."

It now registered that Jonathan must have been emotionally attached to Rebecca all through their marriage, the reason they could not plan a future, including children. The possibility of meeting Rebecca made him eager to go to Waskaganish. There were all sorts of opportunities he could have taken in other locations.

In a moment, ten years of marriage crumbled like a stale piece of wedding cake. Disillusioned, betrayed, and alone, Hannah felt angry and lost, in free fall without a safety net, asking herself, how does one mourn the loss of someone they never had? All she felt was deep anger and pain.

She wanted to escape, but there was no place to go to lose herself. She needed time to redefine and refocus her life.

CHAPTER FIFTEEN

A week later, early in the morning, dressed in her old, faded blue jeans and a loose white T-shirt, she flung open the door to Jonathan's room. Without a glance around, she left, went downstairs, and made a pot of Irish breakfast tea and French toast. Rather than leaving the tea in the teapot, where it would cool as it became deeply infused, she poured it into a bulbous black thermos pitcher, one of her collection from the 1930s. There the tea would remain hot all morning as Hannah drank from it at her leisure. Unlike the inside of her china and silver teapots, the glass lining of the thermos always remained free of stains. Those qualities, plus its pleasing form, made it more appealing to use than a teapot from her collection.

At the oak table, she spread on her French toast slices of sweet strawberries and daubs of thick yogurt cheese. This she savoured slowly while sipping her tea and reading the morning Gazette before hurrying down to the basement. A few minutes later, she returned with cardboard boxes, big green garbage bags, and string.

Jonathan's clothes were hung in a very orderly manner. Hating clutter, he systematically disposed of clothes, whereas Hannah found it hard to part with clothes. For her they were memories.

Amongst his personal papers, a gold certificate caught her attention. Engraved in an old English font was the name *Jonathan Star*, followed by a flowery statement of thanks for his contribution to the student award fund in commemoration of his tenth anniversary as a staff member of the university.

He could have, like his colleagues, chosen a gift instead of giving a monetary contribution to the student award fund. One gift offered was an exquisite long string of cultured pearls, so much more glamorous than the short string she had bought many years ago. She even imagined how happy she would be wearing the luminous pearls he gave her. He would not budge. His mind was made up. He was not going to accept any of the gift rewards the university offered. He was set on giving the money as a student scholarship.

Never having seen it before, Hannah imagined it arrived shortly before he went to Waskaganish. He must have quietly put it away without showing her. That was understandable, since she had expressed her dismay over his contribution. She did not give a substantial amount yearly to the university, or even that she begrudged the amount he gave. It was just that the contribution was an unusual, unnecessary gesture.

It was not that he did not give a substantial amount yearly to the university, or even that she begrudged the amount he gave. It was just that the contribution was an unusual, unnecessary gesture.

He could have, like his colleagues, chosen a gift. One gift offered was an exquisite long string of cultured pearls, so much more glamorous than the short string she had bought many years ago. She even imagined how happy she would be wearing the luminous pearls he gave her. He would not budge. His mind was made up. He was not going to accept any of the gift rewards the university offered. He was set on giving the money as a student scholarship.

At the time, she had felt robbed of something tangible to show he cared for or even loved her. Now it heightened her distress.

Hannah removed an official-looking certificate on crisp off-white parchment paper before sealing Jonathan's remaining boxes with masking tape and placing them in the closet.

Seated at her desk, she read the parchment paper certificate one more time. It was Jonathan Star's carefully preserved baptism certificate, confirming his parents were nominally Christian. Surely her mother would have burned it. Hannah found it hard to dismiss.

Jonathan inferred he was Jewish when they married, though his actions were more attuned to an atheist. He had been given a Jewish funeral.

In the following weeks, sleep often eluded Hannah; she hated to go to bed. Instead of a time of rest, tranquillity, and renewal, night had become a period of turmoil and anxiety. When Hannah could no longer fight her haunting thoughts and nightmares, she would turn to her paper on the Health Profession, Ethics, and the Media to be presented at the conference in New York City. It was the ideal venue for her to express her dismay and anger at the frequently shoddy media coverage of nutrition. Though the conference was still nine months away, she enjoyed the luxury of developing ideas at her own leisurely pace.

In the kitchen, Hannah put a kettle of water on the stove. From an old Royal Doulton tobacco jar, she carefully measured a spoon of Darjeeling tea leaves into a small, ornate silver tea strainer and slowly poured steaming hot water over them.

Sitting in her favourite armchair, slowly sipping the hot, deep amber beverage from an Aynsley bone china cup decorated with a seventeenth-century pattern of brightly coloured flowers and birds, she thought about her upcoming trip to New York. She imagined her stay at the luxurious conference hotel, the Art Deco Waldorf Astoria Hotel on Park Avenue. It would be her first stay at the hotel, but she had seen it in the movie *Weekend at the Waldorf,* which was filmed entirely in a hotel.

Flipping to the conference schedule, she focused on the presenter listed after her on the program, Kurt Garner, a film director who had trained as a physician.

CHAPTER SIXTEEN

To reach his present position as a respected film director and actor, and activist Kurt Garner had more than the usual series of contingencies. Since childhood, he had dreamt of following in the path of his Uncle Theodor, who until the mid-1930s, with the rise to power of the Nazis, was a part of the blossoming Vienna film industry.

He could still recall one of his last conversations with his parents before leaving Vienna on August 24, 1937. It was as they were eating apple strudel after a leisurely Saturday afternoon lunch on the patio.

"Now is the time to study. One day we might all go to America. There your English will be your passport to the new world," said his mother, Magda, as she pushed back her recently bobbed fair hair from her face to reveal her deep blue eyes, echoing the colour of her fine cotton afternoon dress.

His father, Bernard, a tall, upright man with an aristocratic air who was a part of Vienna's well-established, wealthy, assimilated Jewish intelligentsia, agreed. "Spending time in England will help open the world to you. You will be able to improve your English. Vienna is not what it used to be. Things are changing. You've seen the vicious attacks on Jewish shopkeepers."

"Kurt, you'll not be alone. You'll stay with your Great-Aunt Esther. She has no children and will welcome you like her own. We will come to visit," Magda assured him.

"You remember Aunt Esther. She had red hair. She was a schoolteacher before she retired to Bournemouth. It's a beautiful place on the south coast of England. They have an excellent secondary school she highly recommends," added Bernard.

In 1937, Bernard was preparing his family to leave Austria in the wake of increasing attacks and restrictions placed on Viennese Jews.

As the family had done before leaving Poland in the late 1800s, they had again found themselves in the process of disposing of all their non-portable possessions: their magnificent homes filled with artworks, antiques, and silverware, including Bernard Garner's prized oil painting of his late mother by the famous Austrian painter, Gustav Klimt.

The evening sun filtering through his study window cast an eerie shade over the impressive collection of gleaming diamonds Bernard had bought with the money he received from selling his possessions. Among the collection were four diamonds of an exceptionally intense blue. These were the most valuable objects he owed.

One blue diamond was set in a pendant. Bernard hesitated to add it to the collection. After wavering for a while, he sewed it securely, along with the other diamonds, behind the lining of a small, tanned leather pouch. Before snapping it shut, he inserted a spare pair of Kurt's wire-framed glasses in the belief that the glasses would disguise the true contents of the pouch.

"I see you've the pouch ready for Kurt," observed Magda.

"All is ready for him," Bernard replied confidently, trying to put his wife at ease.

"Before you packed it, did you remove the diamond from my necklace? It would make it less bulky to include the diamond without the heavy chain." Magda was trying to indicate she was ready to part with her cherished necklace.

"No. I hope that soon we will join Kurt in Bournemouth, and I will have the pleasure of seeing you wear it again." Looking up at Magda's face, his smile showed he was trying to visualize a bright future.

"It was a wedding gift from my parents. I remember my mother telling me that when her father purchased the diamond in Poland from a young couple going to America, as a memory the couple retained a hand-coloured photo of his wife wearing it on her wedding day."

"For safekeeping, among the few photos I packed for Kurt I've also included the photo of you wearing the necklace. So we will always have the photo, even if we have to sell the diamond necklace."

*

At the departure platform of the Vienna train station, Kurt, dressed in a brown-tweed suit, waited with his parents and Uncle Theodor for the overnight train to Le Havre. Carrying one brown suitcase, a rucksack, and the tanned leather pouch his mother had sewn into his right front trouser pocket, he was resigned to his parents' decision.

Reaching up to kiss her son goodbye, salty tears flowed down Magda's pale face. At thirteen, Kurt was already taller than his mother.

"Mother, don't worry, I will write you every day. It'll be an adventure. I'll tell you all the news." He mustered his radiant smile, which complemented his outgoing nature. Kurt had inherited his father's bright, optimistic outlook.

"We'll look forward to your letters. We also shall write. We may even start writing each other in English," said his father, fighting back his tears and reservations. Then he added, as much to reassure himself as to comfort Kurt, "We will all be together soon."

Once the train had pulled out of the station and Kurt could no longer see his parents and Uncle Theodor waving, he shed his jacket and tried to get comfortable. Firstly, he checked the right front pocket of his trousers to make sure his pouch was still secure. He was concerned about crossing three borders carrying its valuable hidden contents. On arriving in Bournemouth, he was to give it immediately to his Great-Aunt Esther for safekeeping until his parents arrived. They hoped to join him before the year was out, in December at the latest. Satisfied all was well, he sat back in search of words to submerge his pain and anxiety.

Arriving at the French-German border, the customs agent pulled him aside. "Do you have your papers?"

"Yes," said Kurt, focusing on removing his passport and great-aunt's letters of introduction and invitation from his jacket pocket.

"They seem in order. I understand you are going to study in England and stay with your great-aunt. Is this correct?"

"Yes, sir. I am," replied Kurt without hesitation.

"Have you ever been to England before?" the agent said, looking through the papers Kurt had given him.

"Yes, sir. To visit my great-aunt." Then, he was a small boy and had been with his parents. It was a happy family reunion.

"You only have a one-way ticket. When are you planning on returning to Vienna?" the agent inquired.

"At the end of the school term. We weren't sure when it ended, so we only got a one-way ticket," explained Kurt.

"Is this all the luggage you're bringing with you?"

"Yes sir, just my suitcase and a rucksack," replied Kurt.

"I see," said the agent, looking Kurt up and down. "You may go ahead." He stamped Kurt's passport.

Kurt rushed to board the train and find a seat next to the window. By the time he reached Le Havre, the better half of a notebook was filled with his notes and sketches. The ferry to Portsmouth gave him new vigour as he looked across the channel to the legendary white cliffs of Dover.

Lining up to go through the United Kingdom's customs, Kurt struggled to conceal his apprehensive and anxiety. He was relieved this was the last customs inspection of his trip. He was now used to the routine, which he went through with no problem, until just as the agent was stamping his passport.

The agent looked up and said, "Do you have anything in your pockets, money, gifts?"

"Yes. I have a few French francs my parents gave me before I left." Kurt pulled them out from the bottom of his trouser pocket.

"Is that all?" said the agent.

"Oh, also, there's also my glasses." Kurt carefully removed his wire-framed glasses from the pouch in his pocket.

"Okay, you may go," the inspector said reluctantly.

Great-Aunt Esther was waiting as he came out of the building into the sunlight. She greeted him with open arms. No longer did she have her bright red hair. Now in her seventies, her hair was snow white. "It's so good to see you. But my have you grown."

"I'm happy to see you. My parents send their love." Kurt felt relieved to have arrived in Bournemouth. He was also tired.

Everyone was being ushered forward to clear the platform.

"You can tell me all about your trip on the way home on the train. It looks like they want us all to move forward off the platform," said Aunt Esther.

They talked the entire way on the fifty-eight-kilometre train ride from Portsmouth to Bournemouth. Esther wanted to know all the latest news from Vienna. She did not realize how bad it was for the Jews and hoped his parents would join them very soon.

"I'm happy you arrived in time for Shabbat dinner. Tomorrow we'll go to synagogue together." She was excited about introducing her nephew to her friends.

"In Vienna, we never go to synagogue, except on the high holidays," said Kurt apprehensively.

"Here, it's different. There are many Jews who have lived in England for generations who are observant. We cherish our religious freedom. Enough for now. Let me show you your room. Change your clothes and wash up for dinner." Aunt Esther showed Kurt his room and left him.

Pulling hard on the thread until it broke, Kurt detached the pouch from the pocket of his travelling trousers. Along with a letter from his father to his aunt, he placed it in his clean grey trousers before leaving his small, sparsely furnished room.

Esther had set a full table for her most welcome grandnephew. Kurt was starving and in no time devoured the traditional dinner of gefilte fish, chicken soup, roast chicken, potato knishes, and carrots. After dinner, tea with apple cake was served in the parlour.

"I've arranged for you to go to secondary school close by." She had heard of its good reputation.

"My English is bad. I worry," replied Kurt, in English with a strong German accent.

"I'll help you. You'll do fine. I know," she assured him."

"Before I forget." Kurt handed Esther the pouch and letter.

"Yes, I'll keep it save for your parents for when they join us." They had written her to tell her to expect it, not elaborating on the valuable contents concealed in the pouch.

*

Kurt settled into his studies and his great-aunt's routine. He missed his old life, his family. His aunt reassured him his parents would be joining him on completion of their business dealings.

Toward the end of December, snow fell, a rare occurrence for this seaside town, known for its mild weather. Stepping outside, Esther felt her age weighing on her, as she did the financial burden of caring for the needs of a teenage boy. She had anticipated, as had Kurt's parents, that they would leave Vienna within a few weeks of their son's departure and join him in Bournemouth.

Unable to navigate the slippery sidewalk, covered with wet, slushy snow, as the temperature hovered around freezing, she decided to wait for Kurt to return rather than going out to shop for groceries. At four in the afternoon, it was pitch black outside.

"Why were you so late coming home from school? I was worried. Is everything going well at school?" asked Aunt Esther as Kurt walked in the door, soaking wet.

"Everything is fine at school. On the way home, I stopped by to see the jeweller, Mr. Epstein. I've been reading about diamonds. He said he's particularly interested in blue diamonds. Did you know he plans to move to Canada?" Kurt looked pleased.

"It's such a bad day to be out, so wet and damp." She appeared more concerned about Kurt's well-being than their poor financial situation.

"I know. But we need the money," said Kurt as he removed his wet, threadbare socks.

"I see. Your father in his last letter mentioned selling. He even gave me an idea of how much we should receive for them. Before we talk, get out of those wet clothes."

Next day, Friday, Kurt left school early and ran home to meet his great-aunt. As they arrived at Mr. Epstein's jewellery store, he was getting ready to leave.

"I was closing for the Sabbath. I close early on Friday," said Mr. Epstein. Looking at Kurt, he remembered the attractive young man wearing a wet coat, which appeared uncomfortably small for his lanky frame. "You were in yesterday?"

"Yes, I've returned with my Great-Aunt Esther." Kurt introduced her to Mr. Epstein.

"Do come in. Here, do sit down." He brought a chair forward. Esther sat down. He removed his heavy double-breasted gabardine coat. As he moved back behind the glass counter, into the shop walked a woman with a young girl.

"These are my wife and daughter," said Mr. Epstein with pride as he looked up at a tall, slender women dressed in a stylish calf length, wrap-around navy-blue woollen coat with a fox fur stole around her neck and a cloche hat of matching navy blue covering her hair.

"I won't be long." He beckoned to his wife and daughter. "Now let me see what you have, young man."

Kurt put the blue diamond necklace on the white satin-lined tray Mr. Epstein had placed on the counter.

"It is an unusual deep blue," observed Mr. Epstein.

The young girl of about three years old came over to the counter. She looked up from astonishing amber eyes surrounded by a halo of golden curls, which caught Kurt's attention, as they would anyone who saw her for the first time.

"May I take it into my office to look at it more closely? You may come with me," said Mr. Epstein, gesturing to Kurt.

On his return, Mr. Epstein said, "This is how much I can offer you." He wrote it on a white sheet of paper. "If you agree, I can give you cash. If you want to think about it, I understand."

Without hesitation, Esther said, "The amount is acceptable."

He went into the back, returning with the money in an envelope. "Please, count it." He then made out a receipt.

*

"I'll put it in the bank on Monday," said Esther as she hung up her coat on a large brass coat-hook in her cottage's small entrance hall.

"It's a lot of money. It's more than we thought we'd get for it, isn't it? Much more than Father had said we would get." Kurt was used to hearing about how people usually received less than they anticipated. Mr. Epstein's offer was confusing.

"It's quite a lot more." Esther was pleased by Mr. Epstein's generosity as she set the table for dinner.

"That's why you said yes, immediately, to his offer?"

"It is. A lesson one learns in life: when something is right, seize it, don't let it get away."

"He could have offered us less. Mr. Epstein is a businessman. He's in business to make money." Kurt was still trying to understand.

"You told me he was planning on leaving for Canada as soon as possible and will be able to take little with him. He appreciated blue diamonds are scarce. The price will go up. He could afford to wait."

Mr. Epstein had voiced a preference for the blue diamond in the necklace, rather than a loose stone. It was understood that his wife could wear the necklace inconspicuously when they left England, since they were allowed to bring a limited amount of assets out of the country.

Kurt and Esther had not considered the necklace's sentimental value.

*

For about a year, Kurt received regular letters from his parents and Uncle Ted, which he lingered over and read numerous times. Then they stopped. He never heard from them again.

On October 1, 1939, about a month after Hitler's invasion of Poland, which led to the obliteration of the Eastern European Jewish culture, Esther died following a short illness. For Kurt, it was a great loss. The Jewish community rallied to find him a family to stay with.

Initially, Kurt felt awkward and out of place living with Dr. Harold Roth, a physician and his wife, and three daughters, aged sixteen, fourteen, and ten. Like his family, their kinfolk had fled Poland in the 1800s. They were Orthodox Jews. Friday at sunset, everything stopped. No work was done until sunset the next day. The only exception was if Dr. Roth had a medical emergency.

His late great-aunt was not as strict. It was hard for Kurt not to write and to go about his normal routine on the Sabbath. At the synagogue, he met others from the continent who were often invited back to the house. He quickly became accustomed to the good food and company at the Sabbath meals.

At school, he had top grades and met a young girl who caught his fancy, someone he could dream about. Toward the end of the school day on the twelfth of May 1940, at the age of fifteen, British soldiers came to take Kurt away as an "enemy alien." Among the other German and Austrian internees from England who were boated to the Isle of Man were old Orthodox Jews, professionals, and other young men like himself.

Slowly, this traditional holiday island was transformed into an internment camp. Boarding houses and luxury hotels became detention centres. Internees took part in local farm work, ran their own newspapers, and even set up internal businesses. Kurt was happy to be taken under the wing of an English professor.

In June, Kurt was transferred to Southampton and forced to choose one of two ships leaving England. He chose the ship on the left. It ended up in Canada. Later he found out the ship on the right went to Australia. On the ship to Canada were thirteen hundred other internees, amongst whom were artists, doctors, scientists, open opponents of the Nazi regime, even those who had lived in Britain since they were infants. Kurt was interned in a camp in Farnham, Quebec.

Upon his release from detainee camp in 1942, at the age of seventeen, Kurt was placed with the affluent Steinman family in Montreal. He found a familiar thread from his old life of privilege in Vienna. After quickly settling into his new home, his first priority was to buy a safety deposit box for the worn tanned leather eyeglass pouch containing his fortune in diamonds.

He spent his first summer at the Steinman house in Waskaganish. It was another new adventure for Kurt, unlike anything he could have imagined. The environment, the food, and the people were foreign to him. He was particularly entranced by the young girls with their long, straight, shiny black hair. They were so different from the girls Kurt knew with their fair skin and bobbed curly hair.

One day walking through the village, Robert, the Steinman's son who was the same age as Kurt, with a mischievous grin said, "Do you want to meet them? I can introduce you."

"I was just looking. They're interesting."

"One is a close friend of mine, Yvonne Stone. I always see her when I come to Waskaganish. I will ask her to bring a friend over to the house tonight. Father has to fly back to Montreal for a day. He'll be back tomorrow. Only the housekeeper will be home," said Robert, running his fingers through his thick dark-brown hair.

"You really don't have to. I have a lot of reading I'd like to get done," replied Kurt in his distinct German accent.

Robert wasn't listening or just didn't care. Robert's invitations to the most impressive house in the area were readily accepted by the Cree girls.

At the end of summer, Robert and Kurt said their farewells and flew back to Montreal. It was their last summer of youthful freedom.

Robert and Kurt completed their final year of high school before going on to university. Robert pursued his business interests, ultimately with a young associate, changing the Waskaganish landscape.

Kurt practiced medicine for a while before settling in Los Angeles and fulfilling has dream of becoming involved in the film business. He wove his painful past and interest in social injustice into his films, yearning to make the world a more compassionate canvas.

When he eventually returned to Vienna, his home was gone, as was the Vienna railway station where he had bid his family farewell. They were destroyed during the war, as was his family — they were killed in the concentration camps. Not a trace of anything he cherished remained.

All he possessed of his former life were his memories, a few family photographs, an old battered brown suitcase, and a leather eyeglass pouch holding a pair of wire-rimmed glasses and a small fortune in diamonds.

CHAPTER SEVENTEEN

Hannah pulled on her tall leather boots and removed her long, sheared, sheepskin coat from the front closet, along with her sheepskin gloves, while waiting for Robert to come by the house to take her to dinner. It was an exceptionally cold night.

When they arrived at the small, intimate restaurant in Old Montreal, featuring fine French cuisine, it was bustling with the December holiday crowd.

Seated in a quiet corner next to the window, Robert, dressed casually in a navy-blue pullover and corduroy trousers, said, "Thank you for dining with me."

"It was good of you to ask me to dinner. I'm sorry I was busy the last time you called." Hannah had pondered what to wear to keep warm. She was happy that she had settled on a woollen mid-calf skirt with a cashmere cornflower-blue cardigan over a cream silk shirt. This way, she reasoned, if she got overheated, she could remove her sweater.

"I understand. I call at the last minute. I spend little time in Montreal as I'm travelling more than usual. I'm off again tomorrow until after the holidays. We were lucky to get a table. There is quite a crowd here," said Robert, looking around the room.

"You do travel frequently to Waskaganish? How is Rebecca? Is she still working hard?" Hannah had last seen Rebecca at Jonathan's funeral. She left right after the services.

"This time of the year I'm not going to Waskaganish. I don't go during the winter months. I'll return in the spring. The weather's too uncertain. Last time I saw Rebecca, she was still working hard. She should slow down." What he failed to tell Hannah was that Rebecca was pregnant with Jonathan's child.

"She seems very devoted to her work. You know I've never been to Waskaganish. Jonathan always said there really was nothing for me to do there." After seeing the letters from Rebecca to Jonathan, she understood why he hadn't asked her to join him on his trips.

"I feel an affinity with Waskaganish, the Rupert River, and Hudson Bay, the water. When I was young, I always went with my father during summer vacations from school. I also still have business interests in Waskaganish." Robert was obviously aware of why Jonathan never asked Hannah to join him there.

Though Hannah was curious about what these business dealings were, she was more interested in what he knew about Jonathan's death. "You were there when Jonathan lost his life?"

"I was. It was a stormy, miserable day. A day no one should have been out. A hunter, I believe, mistook him for a deer," he explained without hesitation.

Hannah had heard this simplistic explanation before. She felt guilty she had not gone to Waskaganish. Helen's haunting words held her back. *What can you do? There is no sense in you worrying about it.* Was there something Robert was not divulging?

He thought for a few moments. "In the past twelve years since my wife passed away, I've spent more time in Waskaganish. I also have had some new business opportunities there."

Then he paused and added, like he wanted to forget about Waskaganish, "Time goes fast. To think I first saw you by the hospital private pavilion elevators the day before my wife passed away. You were talking to the head of surgery, Dr. Allan McDuff. I was impressed with the way you stood up to him — something about an eighteen-year-old boy he wanted to operate on. Do you remember?"

"Very well. He wanted to do an experimental surgery on the boy to help him lose weight, a stomach reduction. I thought he should have been given the benefit of lifestyle advice first, which he had not received." Hannah never realized anyone was listening in on the conversation.

"Did you see the boy? What happened?" Robert had waited a long time to ask these questions.

"I did see him. He changed, lost weight. I was determined, and so was he." Hannah paused. "And he kept it off. I followed him for years. He's out in British Columbia now. Every so often I get reports from friends. If he is ever in town, he calls me."

"His success must be wonderfully rewarding." They were waiting for the dessert menu. It was getting late.

"It is. I am so happy you reminded me of him. It was one of the first ethical dilemmas I had with a fellow professional." She wished it were the only one. Since then, there had been many. "There are no controlled studies to show the effectiveness of stomach-reduction. Much of the medicine practiced has never been scientifically justified. After many years and thousands of joyous summer school breaks interrupted by the urgency of tonsillectomies, research showed having tonsils removed makes no difference to children's health."

"To think I lost my tonsils and suffered for nothing. I'm lucky, a school friend died during the so-called routine operation. I'm not sure what happened."

"No operation is routine. All have risks. I still have my tonsils. I couldn't stand the thought of the operation. Unlike new drug manufacturers, surgeons can devise a new operation and do it on thousands of patients without having done any controlled studies to prove the operation is safe and effective."

It seemed strange to be talking to Robert about her work. She wanted to know more about Waskaganish.

"During the holidays, I'll be in San Francisco, a warm place. It will be good for my cough. It's most annoying." Robert buttoned up his coat as they left the restaurant.

"Coughs sometimes take so long to get over. It's wise to take some sunshine." Hannah had noticed his cough but was reluctant to mention it.

After trips to see a medical specialist in San Francisco, Robert often flew to Los Angeles to see his long-time friend Kurt Garner, with whom he frequently collaborated on movies. Robert helped finance production. Together they were successful. Kurt also starred in other company's films — small art films, documentaries, or popular money-generating films.

"Will you stay in Montreal over the holidays?" asked Robert.

"I'll be at my country house in Austin, the Eastern Townships." Hannah looked forward to the change.

"I have a house in the area. It's strange we've never met out there."

"It seems as true in the country as the city, you can almost be neighbours and never meet," observed Hannah.

*

Over the next seven months, the infrequent times Robert was in Montreal, he would call Hannah. They would go for long walks along the Main, the original immigrant section of Montreal, still known for its smoked meat sandwiches. Robert's family had settled there in the late nineteenth century when they first immigrated to Canada from Poland. He talked about his grandfather and how they had lived opposite the Mount Royal Park on Esplanade. Hannah knew the street well. She and Jonathan had lived in the area when they first married. It was inexpensive and close to the major hospitals. She loved to go back and explore there.

If their ventures took them near McGill University, they would stop at a bohemian coffeehouse or a small cafe in the student ghetto. When spring eventually came, Robert in his carefully crafted Italian shoes, fine cotton shirts, and khaki pants, and Hannah with her hair casually pulled back in a long ponytail dripping to her waist, fitted blue jeans, and leather jacket, looked like two tourists.

Hannah contemplated her relationship with Robert. It was a friendship. Maybe it was all he wanted. He would send her flowers, kiss her goodnight, and seem engrossed when she talked, attentive to her every need. He never asked her to join him on his frequent trips.

CHAPTER EIGHTEEN

It was an unusually hot late August day as Hannah prepared for her trip to New York.

After putting the finishing touches on her presentation for the Health Profession, Ethics, and the Media Conference, she looked at the conference schedule once again, as she had dozens of times already. Turning to the now familiar photograph of Kurt Garner, the speaker directly following her on the program, she imagined meeting him when the phone interrupted her thoughts.

"Let's treat ourselves to lunch. How about Eaton's Ninth Floor? There're rarely good-looking fellows there," Helen said, laughing, "but you must admit the atmosphere is genuine and you can linger as long as you like, and there are no pushy waiters. We can simply order the buffet and chat."

"How about twelve noon?" Hannah thought; going early it would not be as crowded, and there'd be a greater selection at the buffet.

"I'll meet you in the lounge on the ninth floor." There was an express elevator directly up to the restaurant.

*

When Hannah arrived at Eaton's Ninth Floor Lounge, Helen was seated in the corner at one of the small round tea tables supported by blades of white Monel metal in the form of a miniature skyscraper. The use of expensive Monel metal, a nickel and copper alloy named after the president of the International Nickel Company, reflected the care and thought with which the entire Ninth Floor was designed.

Light reflecting from the recessed circular ceiling lamp onto the carefully polished glass tabletop cast a warm glow on Helen's face framed by her meticulously maintained, streaked blond hair, which ended at the wide collar of her pale grey Gucci suit.

"Hi. I can see you really like this place." Helen got up and embraced Hannah. It had been a long time since she had seen Hannah smiling so openly.

"It transports you to a different era," said Hannah, looking down at the carefully composed walnut and oak chevron-patterned parquet floor, abruptly stopping at the impressive glass and Monel metal doors leading to the dining room. "Even the floors take you back to the thirties," she added, sliding into the chair across from Helen.

Hannah took pride in telling everyone Eaton's Ninth was probably one of the world's best-preserved Art Deco restaurants.

"I think we should go in to eat before it gets too crowded." Helen stood up, looking around at the lunchtime crowd.

Walking behind their hostess to a small table covered with a white linen cloth, set with a bouquet of fresh daisies and silver cutlery, Hannah welcomed the cushioning quality of the floor. No longer did the clattering noise of heels resonate.

Hannah had once counted seven shades of grey and pink in the tiles. It intrigued her how the linoleum tiles harmonized with the rows of French Escalette marble columns to support the soaring thirty-five-foot ceiling.

"You look adventuresome," said Helen.

"It's this room, and I leave for New York tomorrow."

"This room is just like in those old thirties movies." Helen looked up at the large alabaster vases and ladies being served by waitresses in black-and-white uniforms.

"How exciting the world was between the two great wars. Women shingled their hair, shortened their skirts, and everyone danced the Charleston all night and drank cocktails. Women felt liberated. But most of all, there was such a flow of artistic talent," exclaimed Hannah.

Then she added, "At the time, due to Prohibition in the States, Americans flocked here for their alcohol and nightlife. Montreal was the largest wet city on the East Coast."

"My parents say there was lots of action. Even after Prohibition was lifted. Montreal was referred to as sin city. People came from United States and Europe to enjoy the nightlife and decadence until the mid-fifties. It was then our puritanical Mayor Drapeau cleaned up the city. Waging a war against immorality, he shut down the cabarets, gaming houses, and brothels found everywhere on the Main." It made the headlines of the local newspapers.

"Rumour had it these red-light establishments were owned by the Mafia," Hannah added as she got up from her chair. "Let's get lunch before the buffet gets crowded."

They were both pleased to sit back and enjoy their lunch, going back to the buffet for dessert, and watching the mingling crowd of locals and tourists.

"Men and women used to seem much more stylish." Hannah was recalling how women in the fifties always wore a hat and gloves at social outings.

"Well-heeled Montrealers continue to be stylish. You must see some mighty stylish, interesting men in your practice," said Helen, redirecting the conversation.

Hannah threw her head back and laughed. "Helen, today you're all full of questions. How come?"

"You seem to have a way of dodging my questions."

"I see stylish and mundane and garish men and women and children. Strangely, recently I've seen more men than usual. Men with big gold chains hanging on their hairy chests. I suppose they think it looks sexy. They also have manicured nails and coiffed hair. What a sight. I guess men think they are attractive regardless of how big their abdomens are or how many chins they have."

"They must be checking you out. Still, you must see some men who interest you?" Helen's mind was racing ahead to all sorts of scenarios.

"Last week, this absolutely magnificent tall man walked into my office. Then he sat down, and I asked him his address. He spoke slowly, in an irritating high pitch. I looked up, and the handsome man had completely disappeared. I think we so often worry about the way we look; we totally forget about the way we sound."

"I once met a fellow on a blind date. He was as plain as sin, but when he spoke, I was totally entranced. He was one of the most attractive men I've ever met." Helen looked up from her coffee and added, "I hate to bring this up, but did you consider the exercise fellow you did the radio show with attractive?"

"What made you think of him?" Hannah was trying to forget him and the show.

"His voice." Helen recalled how it stood in such marked contrast to Hannah's.

"Yes, he wasn't bad-looking. He could be charming and likeable, in spite of his lack of language skills. I liked him, until he let his bad temper get the better of him. As a dietitian, I couldn't condone his messages. Obviously, he resented someone questioning him, trying to correct his ignorance of the basic principles of food and nutrition." Hannah thought, *Why am I talking on about the guy. I must stop.*

Helen continued to ramble on. "Where did he come from? On the radio he sounded like he came from the boondocks."

Changing the subject, Hannah inquired, "How are the plans going for Aaron's wedding?" She knew that Helen was concerned about the extensive plans being made for her son's wedding.

"You should say how is the money for Aaron's wedding going. Fast. They've taken over a large hotel for three days, and they expect us to pay our share. It's an extremely religious wedding. It has about ten rabbis and a continuous flow of food. We don't know if we're coming or going. Though I must admit, Jeff and myself have had our differences about how to handle this wedding. In fact, we have had some terrible fights. I think enough is enough. Aaron seems to be always going from wedding to wedding, from New York to Los Angeles and Miami. You and Jonathan never argued like we do."

"No, we never argued after the second year of our marriage. There was really nothing I felt worth arguing about after the miserable time we had had when I got pregnant and Jonathan demanded an abortion." It was a time-Hannah found hard to dismiss.

"How is it going with Robert?" When Helen suggested lunch, she might have thought this would come up.

"Your cousin is a wonderful person, with great style. How can one not be attracted to him? Also, he's always so kind and considerate." What Hannah did not say was she'd only seen him a few times. He was always travelling. He also lacked passion and had a bad cough.

"He's no doubt one of the most enticing, eligible bachelors in Montreal, not to mention the wealthiest — a hard combination to beat. I think he's really fond of you," said Helen pensively.

"Well, I'm off to New York the day after tomorrow." Hannah could hardly wait.

As they prepared to leave, she added, focusing on the tall alabaster vases, "*The Île-de-France* was Lady Eaton's favourite ocean liner. This restaurant was designed by architect Jacques Carlu, under her guidance, after its first-class dining room."

"She was lucky to get everything she desired," said Helen. Then she paused and added, "I think Robert would bestow on you anything you desired."

"I don't need or want anything."

"Watch out. You could change your mind. Robert likes diamonds. I think he has a secret source," said Helen with a grin.

"Jonathan thought diamonds were overrated. The price is artificially fixed. Besides, diamonds often have a violent history." Hannah looked down at her wedding band. Though Jonathan had not given her a diamond engagement ring, her parents had. Sadly, it was lost, or rather disappeared right from her bedroom. She could have sworn she had put it in her armoire, but no matter how hard she looked for it, she could never find it. That perplexed her.

"It's true. Jeff got the diamonds for my ring and bracelet through Robert. He said they weren't blood diamonds," proclaimed Helen with pride.

"Where'd Robert get them?" Did he deal in diamonds?

"I don't know." Helen looked uneasy.

Hannah was surprised that inquisitive, perceptive Helen did not know where her diamonds were coming from. It certainly did not sound like her.

"It was good business to build this dining room, which was described at the time as a grand, stylish place to meet and dine. It also was her gift to the people of Canada," continued Helen, as if to avoid the diamond question. "French and English women could bond here. Lady Eaton did so much for women. She was responsible for establishing a minimum wage for women. I believe Eaton's was the first company in Canada to do so. She was a staunch advocate of women in managerial positions. She also established the Eaton's Women's Society, a women's mentoring network. You leave tomorrow for New York. It's going to be torturously hot."

"But it's just for a few days, and it will be air-conditioned everywhere. Do you know the hotel I'm staying at is the Art Deco Waldorf Astoria?"

"That's a luxurious hotel. Robert always stays there."

"It opened eight months after Eaton's, designed by Lloyd Morgan, an architect who had practiced in Paris. He probably knew the architect who designed this restaurant." Hannah had recently read this in *Architectural Digest*.

"I thought Schultze and Weaver designed it?"

"Lloyd Morgan is not often given the credit he deserves. I understand he was the leading architect of the team." Hannah stood up. "It's hard to leave."

They would have been happy to spend the rest of the afternoon chatting, but Helen had to get home to check out the renovations, and Hannah had some last-minute shopping to do. It was a good time to shop, since everything was on sale.

CHAPTER NINETEEN

Closing her suitcase, Hannah was reminded of what her mother had said about unflattering clothes she had purchased: *Never repeat your mistakes by wearing them. Save them and they'll come back to haunt you, burn them and they're gone forever.*

Of course, it would have been wiser to return them to the store or to donate them to some less fortunate souls, but she never liked to admit her mistakes. Hannah wanted to burn her bad yesterdays, as her mother had burned her unsatisfactory clothes.

She realized everyone deals with pain and loss differently, and many of life's misfortunes lessen with time, while others take on a life of their own and grow until they take over one's life. Fertilize pain with constant reflection, and it grows.

*

Next evening, Robert drove Hannah to Dorval Airport for her flight to New York. Jonathan never drove her to the airport, even when her father died. He felt it unnecessary to take time out from his practice. She had always gone to the airport by taxi.

Walking her to the check-in counter, Robert handed her an envelope. "Open it, Hannah."

"It's a plane ticket, first class to New York," she exclaimed.

Hannah, there's no other way to go," he reassured her.

"Thank you so much, I could get used to this." Hannah had never flown first-class.

"You should. I don't know how anyone flies any other way."

"You take care of yourself. Get over your cough and avoid catching the flu again. Stay out of crowds."

"Don't worry, Hannah. You'll see, the cough will be gone when I see you again."

Before Hannah could add another word, Robert said, "Your seat is reserved. Simply give back your economy class ticket. You'd best hurry, or you'll miss your flight. Have a good trip."

CHAPTER TWENTY

Nursing a glass of Champagne, Hannah leaned back in her generous-size seat and stretched her legs on her flight to New York City. She felt indebted to Robert, as she caught glimpses of the congestion on the other side of the long cream curtain separating her from the economy class section.

In addition to her pearl earrings, Hannah wore her engraved octagonal-shaped platinum wedding band, and a gold chain bracelet, from which dangled her cherished compass.

Turning over the small gold compass set in whalebone, she gently rubbed her fingers across the scrimshawed bird in flight carrying a heart in its beak. Thoughts filled her mind of a sailor far out at sea inscribing it for his loved one during a long sea voyage.

At midnight, her taxi arrived at the Waldorf Astoria Hotel on Park Avenue. She was too tired and woozy from her overindulgence of Champagne to appreciate her luxurious Art Deco hotel, the famous hotel which had hosted celebrities such as Winston Churchill, Leonard Bernstein, Marlon Brandon, Albert Einstein, Marilyn Munroe and Marlene Dietrich. The hotel coined the motto, "The guest is always right," and was the home of everyday favourites, Waldorf Salad, Eggs Benedict, and Thousand Island dressing.

Exiting the elevator at the fortieth floor, Hannah felt giddy as the porter unlocked the door and ushered her into her accommodations. The suite had two bedrooms, each with its own marble-clad bathroom. Her head throbbing, she closed the bedroom curtains, stripped off her clothes, and crawled in between the cool white cotton sheets of the king-size bed.

She recalled booking a standard room, but she was not going to complain. It was their mistake. She would worry about it in the morning. She yearned for one peaceful night's sleep, one without nightmares or regrets.

A door closing, then footsteps, woke Hannah. She scrambled into her jeans and T-shirt, thinking it was the porter. Had she forgotten something, or he had come to tell her she was in the wrong room? But she had not heard knocking at the door. After so much Champagne, her head was still spinning. Braless and shoeless, with her hair hanging loosely about her face, Hannah opened the bedroom door to find a tall, pale, fair-haired man putting down his luggage. In her haste to go to sleep, she had forgotten to lock and latch the door.

When he looked up, she immediately recognized his familiar face from the convention pamphlet carrying his glossy likeness.

"I'm sorry to wake you. Very sorry," Kurt said apologetically.

Hannah was speechless.

"Well, what can I say? I thought this was my suite. Obviously, there's a mix-up. It has this suite number on my room card. I'll call down and get this straightened out," Kurt said as he picked up the telephone and started to dial.

On the telephone, all Hannah could hear was, "Yes, yes, yes. I know it's not your fault. Yes, fine."

"They said this is the number of my suite, and there are no more suites available. They can't explain the mix-up." Slumping onto the sofa, he added, "I'm totally exhausted. It's past midnight. I must get some sleep. What do you think we should do? I've been sleeping in a trailer for the past month and been on a plane for the last ten hours. I need a good night's sleep. There are two bedrooms. I'm going to bed. Maybe we can figure it out in the morning."

Weary and hung over after the flight, he picked up his bag and stumbled into the other bedroom, closing the door behind him.

Sitting on the edge of her bed, Hannah sensed a knot in her stomach and a rush of excitement. If she had not been so tired and off-key, she would not have slept.

Rousing to her seven thirty wake-up call, Hannah felt foggy about the previous day's events. Was Kurt Garner really here in her suite, or was she imagining the intruder she had seen so often on the congress program? She tried to focus. Even after a hot shower, her head was throbbing. Sessions began at nine. She pulled on her jeans and T-shirt and took her off-white linen suit and silk beige shell out of her suitcase. They needed pressing.

Leaving her room, Hannah discerned Kurt Garner standing next to the sofa, looking out the window with his hands thrust in the trouser pockets of his wrinkled pale grey suit. It was then it struck her: last night was for real.

"Good morning," he called out, walking toward her. As the sun struck his face, it gave him an eerie, unnatural appearance.

"Good morning," Hannah replied hesitantly with a faint smile.

"Last night you looked drained. How are you today?" said Kurt.

"I don't know yet. My head continues to throb. I'm not used to drinking so much Champagne."

"Maybe a cup of coffee and a good breakfast will help. My name is Kurt, Kurt Garner. I'm sorry, I never got your name last night. I was exhausted."

"It's Hannah."

"Are you the Hannah Epstein Star on the program?" Kurt asked with a wide smile. Then he added, "Your presentation covers ethics and nutrition?"

"Yes, and I believe you're speaking just after me."

"I am. We'll have to get this room thing straightened out after the presentations this morning. We don't have time now." He did not sound too concerned.

"I'm going to iron my jacket. It looks like your suit needs a pressing." Hannah looked at his wrinkled suit.

"It looks that bad?" It appeared he had not noticed or cared.

"It could be helped a little." Hannah thought it looked like he had slept in it the last time he wore it.

"I never iron anything. Whenever I can, I wear casual clothing. I really need some breakfast. I'm starving. If you like, I'll order some breakfast. What do you eat? I believe there's a menu on the table," Kurt said with a sense of urgency.

Hannah found it hard even to think about food. Kurt must have noticed she looked puzzled and added, "Why don't you order anything you like? I'll have orange juice, coffee, oatmeal, and pancakes with maple syrup and berries or whatever they have."

He left the room and came back in jeans. "Where's the iron kept?" he said enthusiastically.

"It's probably in the front closet. You'll find it and the board."

"Would you like to iron first?" Kurt asked, removing the iron and ironing board from the closet.

"No, you go ahead."

Kurt had probably never ironed a thing in his life, but must have figured, how hard can it be to push an iron over some cloth? He had no doubt seen others do it.

Hannah thought surely, he usually rang down and someone took his suit and a few minutes later returned with it pressed. Why did he even attempt to iron — a challenge, perhaps?

As he bent over to pull up the ironing board, it folded up and collapsed on his right foot. He grimaced in pain but said nothing as he struggled to pull the board into an upright position again to lock it into place.

"That always happens to me," Hannah remarked as casually as she could without bursting into laughter.

"Well, I'm in business. Now where do I start? I'll do the pants first, right?"

"You know, suit trousers usually have a crease down the centre you can use as a guide." Hannah showed him the crease then watched Kurt push the iron back and forth over his trousers. Yet the wrinkles remained.

"This is hard labour. There should be a point on each end of the iron. Then you could push it as easily in both directions," Kurt exclaimed as he pushed down more heavily on the iron. In frustration he added, "It's not working."

"Oh! It's not plugged in properly." Hannah noticed.

"Now this isn't bad, but the other side of the pants is getting wrinkled as I iron over it. There must be a way of doing it?"

Hannah went over to the ironing board and straightened out the pant leg. Smiling, he took the iron from her hand.

"Thanks." He began to push the iron over his wrinkled trousers.

She left him merrily ironing and went into her bedroom to put her things in order when she smelled a burning odour and imagined the worst. What if he had scorched his suit? He probably had only one suit with him.

"I was practicing on a towel. I suppose the iron was too hot. I think I've got the knack now," Kurt said contentedly.

He looked at the towel with the dark scorch mark in the middle and remarked, "I'm happy it wasn't my pants. I never realized what potential damage a simple household iron, something housewives use daily, was capable of generating."

Hannah watched attentively as he methodically, slowly, and carefully removed the wrinkles from his suit.

"How do you like it? Would you like me to iron your suit?" Kurt said as a satisfied grin crossed his face.

Then he let out a deep laugh, giving way to a wide grin. Hannah thought at first, *why not let him iron my suit?* Then again, she really needed that suit. His was no doubt beginner's luck.

"I learned something. I can iron a suit," he remarked proudly.

"You know what I do? I put the suit on after breakfast."

"Good idea."

Then he let out another gigantic laugh and added, "Now I've ironed my suit, I really don't want to wrinkle it."

The honesty and momentum of Hannah's movements, doing this timeless task of ironing — silently gliding the gleaming iron rhythmically, back and forth — hypnotized Kurt. After a few moments, he looked up and remarked, "So that's the way you do it. Wouldn't it be wonderful if life was as easy?"

"Yes, if you could just take an iron and straighten everything out."

"Now I see why some women can get so much satisfaction from housework. It's instant gratification. You see results immediately. Wow."

"A short-lived gratification. Clothes and houses get dirty, and then you've got to start all over again. Often no one even notices you've done anything. How many times a husband returns home and says to his wife, what have you been doing all day?"

"I know," said Kurt. "I saw a comic strip once where the man of the house questioned his wife's workday, in spite of the fact she had two small children to care for. The next day she decided not to do any housework. At the end of the day, when her husband returned from work, the house looked like a war zone. Then she said, 'This is what I do all day.'"

There was a knock at the door. "I'll get it," called Kurt.

"Thanks,"

Hannah thought, *It's nice to have someone take care of things, even something as simple as opening a door.* Jonathan would have waited for Hannah to answer the door. It was almost as if he had more important things to do with his time.

Unhesitatingly, Kurt opened the door. No doubt the young porter recognized him. He might have even been told he was at this suite number. With a certain flourish, he set in the centre of the table a low bouquet of deep red roses. Then he put out glistening cut glass bowls of raspberries, blueberries, and blackberries, plates of buckwheat pancakes, golden maple syrup next to folds of sweet butter, yogurt, jam and toast, oatmeal, coffee, and milk.

"Take what you like. I'm so hungry, I'll eat anything that's left," said Kurt. Then a gigantic smile spread over his face. He looked so pleased to see the food.

After five minutes of nonstop eating, he added, "Great berries. You know, I usually eat alone."

"So do I."

"Your husband doesn't eat with you?" Kurt looked up from his pancakes.

"He passed away nearly a year ago." Hannah pictured Jonathan when they first married eating the large buckwheat pancakes she prepared most weekends.

"Oh, I'm sorry."

They said little else. Both seemed to intuitively understand how much each cherished these few minutes of quiet downtime before they started their day. This shared necessity made them feel a close bond and understanding.

"I could sit here forever. It's so peaceful. But it's getting late. We must get ready and go. We're first on today's program; otherwise, I suppose it wouldn't matter when we arrived. Knowing myself, I might not even make it at all." Kurt got up.

"I suppose we should go," added Hannah.

CHAPTER TWENTY-ONE

Hannah and Kurt walked together up to the front of the amphitheatre, where they were directed to their seats. As Kurt sat down beside Hannah, he turned to her with his now familiar grin and said, "Good luck, Hannah," he added as he reached over and squeezed her hand.

After a brief introduction, she walked up the stairs to the stage. Standing at the podium, leaning toward the microphone, she felt her knees tighten up. Focusing for a moment on Kurt and then scanning the room full of mainly male delegates for what some might have found a long pause, she braced herself for an intelligent, tough audience as she reached inside for the right words and flashed a warm, wide smile.

"Thank you for asking me to speak today. I would like to explore with you how, working with the media, acceptance of sound nutrition and food information can become a part of our culture, but we all know that there will always be charlatans and quacks selling quick fixes." Hannah spent the rest of her half hour elaborating on this topic."

Stepping down from the podium after the presentation and the applause, Hannah felt apprehensive as lingering thoughts of the CBSB radio station crossed her mind. How her efforts to tell the truth had been squashed and eventually dismissed. She felt this memory would always stalk her.

Kurt Garner was the next speaker. A hush fell over the audience as all eyes followed him advancing effortlessly to the podium. "I'll get right to the point. Should it be acceptable in the movie industry for self-destructive vices to be portrayed in a glamorous fashion?"

Afterward, a reporter took Kurt aside for an interview. Hannah went on to the buffet luncheon. Here, a middle-aged man, casually dressed in a blue golf shirt stretched across his expansive paunch, eased over to Hannah. He introduced himself as Fred Collier, an American, now living in Rome and working for the Food and Agriculture Organization.

"Your presentation showed an interesting aspect of nutrition information. I'm more interested in food sustainability," he said, balancing his overflowing plate on the edge of the nearby table.

"Thank you," Hannah replied, hoping he would move on so she could have a quiet moment to eat her lunch. Though she recognized his statement was an amiable prelude to his own agenda.

He continued, "There are so many starving people. Overeating seems so trivial, comparatively. The world hunger problem is the true challenge."

"I couldn't agree with you more. Optimum food for everyone is important." Then Hannah held her tongue. She was thinking about the irony of living a luxurious lifestyle in Rome, well-paid to assuage the conscience of First World countries to distribute food and funds to Third World dictatorships, in the hope some of it would trickle down to the victims of famine. Another delegate standing nearby added, "I'm also involved in food security." Hannah left them to talk.

After lunch, Hannah attended a workshop on ethics and the media. Leaving the last session, she felt a hand on her shoulder.

"Hi. Would you join me for dinner? I know this place where they have super sushi. It's not too far from here. I couldn't go to the delegates' dinner. I'm totally wiped out."

"I love sushi."

"I'm starving. I had little time for lunch. I hope you're as hungry as I am."

"I am."

"Let's go before anyone catches up with us."

Hastily walking outside into the warm August rain, Kurt pulled off his tie. "I rarely wear a suit. Never worn one I ironed myself. This is a first," he said with a wide grin and added, "I suppose we should've changed our clothes. The rain is destroying all our work."

"The reason housework, anything to do with cleaning, is not well recognized, is it's so transitory. From clean to dirty, from pressed to wrinkled can be a matter of minutes, at most hours. See all the wrappers collecting on the street? I'll bet this morning the street was spotless."

Just as Hannah and Kurt entered the small Japanese restaurant, the skies darkened, and thunder and lightning echoed across the tops of the tall buildings, followed by giant pellets of pounding rain. Car horns and ambulance sirens joined the loud chorus, adding to the cacophony of the big city.

Once seated on pillows in their own individual booth, they both looked up and laughed with relief.

"It's so good to sit here," said Kurt as he removed his jacket. Hannah undid her own jacket and placed it next to her. She had not intended to go without it, or even undo the numerous small mother-of-pearl buttons parading up the front of her otherwise unadorned garment. At meetings and particularly in television interviews, Hannah found it made life easier to always leave her jacket done up. Under her jacket, she wore a thin silk ivory-coloured camisole, which in the warm, humid air clung to her body like a second skin.

"Take off your shoes. You're really supposed to," said Kurt.

"True. The Japanese are so sensible. They don't wear their shoes in the house. Think of all the dirt and germs we drag in on our shoes."

"Think how much easier cleaning would be if shoes were removed first," added Kurt.

"What do you know about cleaning?" Hannah laughed.

"You'd be surprised."

Kurt's eyes lit up as a young woman placed a colourful tray of sushi on the table. "How fantastic."

"What gorgeous sushi," exclaimed Hannah. Looking out onto towering bamboo plants, azaleas, and waterfalls, she felt like she had escaped to a tropical island with a man who totally entranced her.

"It's good to get away from the conference. I found it so intense." Kurt relaxed as he gazed across at Hannah.

In the limited illumination of the overhanging paper lanterns, the silhouette of her symmetrical face surrounded by a halo of golden hair and her slim, well-toned torso, so lightly clad the lace pattern on her bra was visible, under which glimpses of her breasts could be seen.

"I enjoyed your talk today. You covered a lot of new issues. As you said, there are so many phony nutrition degrees out there." Kurt seemed to understand.

"Anyone who pays can get one." Hannah thought of all the phony nutritionists she had encountered.

"Even a cat. I read recently one applied for a nutrition degree. The fees for the so-called courses were paid, and the cat was granted a degree, with a fancy framed certificate and all. Apparently, in the United States, during the past year, more phony nutrition degrees were granted than legitimate ones. Is this true?" asked Kurt seriously.

"It appears to be true. I read it in the *Medical Post*," said Hannah.

Hannah and Kurt continued to converse like two people thrown together on an isolated island with a lifetime of experiences to exchange. Experiences they were longing to share with a sympathetic listener.

"The Buddhists say to live is to suffer. In retrospect, our suffering today is often so minor compared with people in other times, even in our time."

"So true, Kurt. Many of the generation before us lived through the First World War, the Great Depression, and the Second World War."

"My entire family was killed during the Second World War." It had been a long time since Kurt talked about his war experience.

"How did you escape?"

"At the time, my parents had sent me to England to study. But since I had an Austrian passport, I and others in the same situation were classified as aliens, and we were sent to Quebec and detained in an internment camp," explained Kurt.

"What a terrible experience. Did you understand what was going on?"

"Not as much as I would've liked to. It's only in retrospect we can try to understand the Second, or for that matter the First World War. I had learned in school a higher percentage of German Jews fought in the First World War than any other ethnic, religious, or political group. Some twelve thousand Jews died for their country. My uncle died during the First World War. Ironically, it was a Jewish lieutenant, Hugo Gutmann, who awarded the Iron Cross, First Class, to a twenty-nine-year-old corporal named Adolf Hitler. When Hitler came to power in 1933, Gutmann left Germany and escaped to the United States. For a young man there were so many conflicting viewpoints."

"I didn't know that. After you were released, you were still young?" Hannah felt Kurt's pain.

"When I was released, I was a teenager, and I was placed with the Steinman family to finish high school. Their son, Robert, was my age, seventeen. I will be forever grateful to them. They made me feel so welcome."

"I know the Steinman family."

"If it weren't for the Steinman family, I doubt I would've had a chance to go to medical school. There was a restriction on Jewish applicants. Medical school was to make me independent. Robert studied business and law and went into the family business."

"Where did you go after medical school?"

"To Los Angeles to do my internship. I was always interested in film, like my dear deceased uncle, Teddy. That's where everything was happening. While doing my internship in Los Angeles, I was introduced to a pretty young woman. A whirlwind romance allowed little time together before we were married in a traditional wedding. I discovered on our honeymoon that she was mentally unstable. I was so in love that even as a doctor I over-looked it. I should have recognized the symptoms. Then I thought I could help her. I was wrong. She was a lost soul who didn't want to be a part of reality. After a quiet divorce, she drifted, remarried a few times, and died prematurely. I never practiced medicine. I decided I would pursue my first love, storytelling, filmmaking, like my late uncle."

"Wasn't one of your early films a documentary about the restriction on Jewish students to medical schools?" She recalled seeing the film with Jonathan.

"Yes. The subject was close to me. Restrictive practices limiting the number of Jewish students admitted to medical school began in earnest in the 1930s and extended to the time I went to medical school in the forties and fifties, even into the sixties. In the United States, the number of Jewish physicians who graduated had increased from seven in about 1880 to over 2,000 in the early thirties. By 1934, sixty percent of the 33,000 applications were Jewish, but most, obviously, were rejected."

"Those are amazing statistics."

Kurt continued, "Lawrence Lowell at Harvard University was at the forefront of Ivy League universities imposing anti-Semitic quotas. In 1925, he wrote a well-publicized letter expressing his concern about the extraordinary number of Jewish students at Harvard."

"Why are Jews so attracted to medicine?"

"Jews have had an almost mystical reverence for medicine, going back thousands of years. Traditionally, Jews value learning almost as much as they value life. Christians see their body as no more than a container for their soul. Their earthly existence is a preparation for the next world. Practically, medicine was a stepping-stone to the middle class in a world that denied Jews entry into the civil service. A medical degree is also portable, like diamonds. Jews forced to leave their homelands could bring their medical profession with them."

"I see why many of your mpanyso are about medicine," observed Hannah.

"That's right. I frequently go back to my medical background. It's the reason I'm involved in conferences like this one. A famous survivor of Auschwitz, Viktor Frankl, who happened to be a psychiatrist, reminds us our quest is not for fame or fortune but for meaning. This is what I'm constantly searching for though my work."

"In my writing, I suppose, I'm trying to find some kind of meaning," replied Hannah.

"Frankl also called humour one 'of the soul's weapons in the fight for self-preservation.' That might be how he was able to survive the horrors of the Nazi concentration camp. Did your family escape the war, Hannah?"

"We left England just before the war. I believe we were on the last ocean liner out. But I don't think anyone escaped the war. It truly changed everyone's world. My parents, who were still in their twenties, left behind their families and their fortune. My father went back to Europe in the Canadian army to fight in the war. My mother was left behind, alone with the children. She lived on hopes and dreams and the occasional letter from my father. After the war, they stayed in Canada, but nothing was ever the same for them. I believe the war had left my father with too many scars. He also had too many lost dreams."

"We all do. Do you have lost dreams?"

"Like my parents, I always wanted to be in the arts. When I was on the radio show about nutrition, I felt like I was creating by controlling the topics discussed, whereas when I'm a guest on other's shows, they create and control the show. Now my writing helps fill that need."

"I see what you mean." Then he paused and added, "What about your marriage?"

"It's too painful to recall and equally painful to forget. My husband was an internist. He died in Waskaganish, where he worked in a medical clinic a few times a year. As I said, it was about a year ago. He was found dead in long grass near the roadside, shot. It was hunting season. We had no children. We lived for our work."

"I remember the Steinman family had a house in Waskaganish. I've been there and will be returning to do some filming."

CHAPTER TWENTY-TWO

Kurt had memories of Robert's violent behaviour. All these years later, he could still recall Robert, with the aid of friends, locking a classmate up in the trunk of his car after his date at the school dance had paid too much attention to the fellow. At the time, it seemed like a foolish prank.

It was one of those cruel late December nights, which found the streets of Montreal desolate and deserted. As the temperature dropped to close to minus thirty degrees Celsius, the wind howled, the snow piled up into huge drifts reaching six feet high, visibility was reduced, and driving was dangerous. Everyone was drinking too much. They were sensible enough to leave the car parked and take a taxi home. They forgot about the boy in the trunk. A patrolling police car found him and took him to hospital. The next day, the Steinman family left for their home in Palm Beach. No one ever mentioned the incident.

Presently, Kurt was awaiting word from Robert on the financing of his latest proposal, a film set in Northern Quebec, Cree country, using Waskaganish as the headquarters. Not since his youth had Kurt spent time in the area.

*

Hannah wanted to forget all that bound her to the past. She wanted to wrap her thoughts around the present. She wanted to share Kurt's laughter and see the wrinkles form around his clear blue eyes when he smiled and be mesmerized by the sound of his articulate voice. She wanted to watch the light catch each of the long, fair hairs on his arms and feel their silky texture.

"Would you like more sake?"

"If I eat or drink any more, you'll have to carry me."

"You'd be easy to carry."

It was still raining as they walked back to the hotel, hand in hand. At the door to their suite, they both laughed as they removed their wet shoes.

"I couldn't wait to get those heels off."

For about five minutes they stood beside each other, looking out the window overlooking the city, transfixed by the lights gleaming in the rain. Slowly, Kurt turned toward Hannah, took her in his arms, and kissed her.

She placed her head on his shoulder and her arms around his neck. Effortlessly, he picked her up, carried her into the bedroom, and gently laid her on the turned down bed. After removing her clinging camisole and bra, he unwound her damp hair, which fell into golden clumps around her naked shoulders. The pupils of her eyes dilated into two vast, dark, bottomless pools.

Then she watched him unbutton his damp shirt and trousers. Though his face conveyed his years, his buffed body defied them.

Time stood at bay as Kurt moved gracefully toward her, kissing and embracing the warm contours of her body in ways she had never experienced. For Hannah, a feeling of bliss and ecstasy, brimming with expectations, turned to excitement as Kurt's silken hairs pressed against her body and she moved to his rhythm.

Next day, as Hannah gathered her things together, she turned to Kurt, hesitant to ask, "Now what about the suite?"

"I phoned down. Apparently, it has all been taken care of."

Hannah knew it must be Robert who reserved the suite for her and paid for it. By mistake, the reservation clerk had double booked the room. Kurt no doubt thought one of the conference organizers had paid for it. He was used to such perks.

"I must leave on a noon flight. I really want to stay," said Kurt, looking tenderly at Hannah.

"I wish I didn't have a morning flight," said Hannah.

"I'll be in Montreal in about six weeks to speak at a benefit. We'll be able to meet then."

"It seems so long."

"I know. I'll phone you every day. Would you like some breakfast?"

"Yes."

As they kissed goodbye, Kurt said, "I'll see you in Montreal soon. I want to etch these last few days in my mind forever and ever."

"So do I."

At the door, Kurt took her in his arms once more. Hannah looked back to see her gold bracelet, with her treasured charm, the small compass set in whalebone ivory, sitting next to Kurt's watch on the table. She left it. She felt she had to leave something tangible of herself behind.

CHAPTER TWENTY-THREE

A ringing telephone greeted Hannah as she entered her house. Dropping her luggage, she answered it. "Hi, Helen. My trip to New York was great. How are you?"

"We'll speak when you return from your trip to Europe."

Helen and Jeff planned to rent a car and explore southern England and Wales.

Hannah relished her nightly calls from Kurt. She had never known anyone with whom she could converse so freely.

Usually after Kurt's much anticipated nightly—phone calls, Hannah slept well, but for the past few days she had felt off-key, waking in the morning nauseated. It was a nausea that lasted all day and one she recalled from ten years ago. She was also very tired and couldn't concentrate. At the pharmacy she picked up a pregnancy test, which verified what she had suspected.

Four weeks later, Helen was on the phone to Hannah. "We just got back. The flight from London was late. When can I come over? Actually, I'll be downtown shopping at Holt's. I'll come directly after."

"Wonderful. See you soon." Hannah put water on for tea. As the kettle whistled, she heard the doorbell.

"You're just in time for tea. Let's sit down so you can tell me everything about your trip." Hannah set the table with tea and muffins. She wasn't hungry but hoped Helen was.

"We had a really good time. Saw places we'd never seen before. We visited Bournemouth, your birthplace. Went to synagogue at Wootton Gardens. Jeff took rolls of photos. They're being developed," said Helen as she sipped her tea.

"I can't wait to see them." It had been a few years since Hannah visited her place of birth. She was exciting about hearing the latest.

"You'll come over for dinner, and Jeff will do his slide show." Jeff, like Jonathan, was known for his photography and slide shows. "How was New York? Hannah, did you meet the fellow on the program, the one you talked about before you left?"

"I did meet Kurt Garner."

"I met him years ago, when he was a young man. He lived for a short time with the Steinman's. He's in the film business. He's good-looking."

"He's also intelligent. He's coming in a few weeks to address a benefit. You'll get to meet him."

"You look tired. Are you okay?" said Helen with concern.

"Probably simply need to get to bed earlier."

"You know, Hannah, I must be on my way. I promised to pick up Ruth for a fitting. See you."

The next day, Helen was on the telephone to Hannah. She sensed something was bothering her. She looked so exhausted and anxious.

"Okay, Hannah, what's the matter? I'm coming over right now."

"You don't have to."

"Then what is it?"

Hannah thought it might be easier to tell her on the telephone. She blurted out, "I think I'm pregnant."

"You think. Either you are or aren't. No one is just a little pregnant. Did you take a pregnancy test?" inquired Helen anxiously.

"Yes. It was positive," said Hannah, trying to remain calm.

"I'm on my way." It seemed like a minute before Helen was at the door.

"Hi. It's good to see you. You really didn't have to come."

"I wanted to."

"Come in. Would you like something to drink?" Hannah asked as they walked into the dining room and sat at the table.

"No. Don't bother, unless you want something? How do you feel?"

"Miserable. Nauseated," Hannah replied as she rubbed her hands across the satin-smooth oak tabletop and leaned back in her chair.

"That's good. It means something's going on. Get lots of rest and try to relax. Does Robert know?"

"No. He's not the father."

After a moment Helen replied, "Are you sure? He'd be delighted."

"Yes, I'm sure."

"Then who is?" inquired Helen.

"Kurt."

"Have you told him?"

"I thought I'd wait until I see him in Montreal in a week. I can't tell him on the phone."

"Has Robert asked how you are? You must admit, you look a little green."

"Robert's away. He won't be back for a week. I don't think he's been feeling too well himself. I don't know why."

"What can it be? Probably wheeling and dealing too much. He always looks like he's up to something." Helen laughed.

"Very funny."

"Nothing's funny. Your pregnancy has to be dealt with. Take care of yourself. Rest. Sleep. Don't take medications, coffee, or alcohol. You know, I don't have to tell you. Have you told anyone else?" Helen pretty well knew the answer, but she wanted to hear it from Hannah.

"Of course not, only you. I've decided to go to the country this weekend."

"Unfortunately, we can't join you there. We have a charity dinner on Saturday."

"We'll speak later."

*

With little traffic on the Champlain Bridge, Hannah arrived at her country house in Austin on Lake Memphremagog just before eleven, hoping to relax and look clearly to the future.

Gazing out over the meadow, her thoughts drifted back to the long, hot summer days, when the sun beat down on the fields, rendering the grass a pale beige, infused with a tapestry of buttercups, snow-white daisies, pink clover, and drooping sneezeworts. Towering over the perimeter of the meadow were sturdy oaks, maples, and pines displaying their coats of varying shades of green. Streams dried up, ponds were low, and wells struggled to provide adequate water.

Rain had fallen continuously the night before Hannah arrived. A chill permeated the air as she donned her woollen jacket and high rubber boots before making her way through the meadow grass. Between the tall blades of grass and fallen red and yellow leaves, she sought out the scant remaining flowers. Even yellow dandelions, which in summer would have been considered intruders, weeds, were welcome. Now she picked them to place in small glass vases on the wooden windowsills, cherishing them as one of the last reminders of summer.

Every year, Hannah witnessed the survival of the fittest flowers, and the demise of the others, without a trace of their existence. One year, the road leading up to the knoll where the house stood was lined with black-eyed Susans. The next year, to Hannah's dismay, there were none. For a number of years, there were milkweeds with bunches of drooping deep pink flowers covered in colourful monarch butterflies. In recent years, barely one could be seen in the meadow.

All of nature renews itself or dies, thought Hannah. What would she leave? What had Jonathan left?

Now she wondered whether he had left his genetic code in any number of offspring. Before the police report on Jonathan's death, Hannah had never imagined Jonathan might have fathered children from other sexual encounters.

Jonathan never wanted his own children. An unplanned pregnancy early in their marriage had sent him into a rage. Day and night, he argued it was best for her to have an abortion. It didn't matter how handful Hannah tried to reason with him that she wanted the child. He would not back down. Her obstetrician, with Jonathan's prodding, sent her to a psychiatrist who concurred with Jonathan. He said, "If your husband doesn't want a child, you shouldn't go against his wishes." He explained a child should be brought into the world cherished and wanted by both parents.

Thus, Hannah recalled her memories of ten years ago. In her eighth week of pregnancy, early one morning, frightened and alone, exhausted from days of Jonathan's badgering, even threatening to "break every antique in the house," Hannah went to the abortion clinic and confirmed her presence with the attending nurse. She noted all the young women waiting had their partners with them. Feeling an urge to leave, she started out the door. A nurse stopped her. She expressed her apprehension to the nurse, who abruptly said, "Dr. Tetley is waiting. We can't keep him waiting, can we? He has a busy schedule. You are his first patient. Come, pull yourself together." Hannah signed her name on the dotted line to legally allow the abortion.

Jonathan returned in the evening and ate his supper as though nothing of consequence had happened that day. Hannah ate little and went to bed early. The next day, she returned the blue and white floral-patterned Laura Ashley dress she had purchased to wear for her pregnancy. She was beside herself but could not show it, since she had work to complete and people to see.

In her grief, Hannah consulted a female psychologist, Dr. Margaret Halley. She implied the abortion was a two-way decision, and she should have been strong enough to do what she felt best, not what someone else wanted her to do. Sadly, Hannah blamed herself for lack of willpower and control. The abortion was boldly recorded in her hospital chart for all future consultations with doctors to see and to presume it was she who had desired the pregnancy be terminated. From her reading and conversations with other women, Hannah knew she was not alone. Many women had abortions because there were men who did not want to father a child.

Divorce had crossed Hannah's mind. But she was in so much pain, she could not even think rationally. If she were to leave, where would she go? Unlike in the movies, there was no one for her to run to. She knew millions of women had left their husbands and found a new destination and happiness. Not being able to entertain this option made her feel hopelessly inadequate and weak.

She thought of her mother, who was so proud of her daughter's marriage to "the doctor." She wanted to share her pain with her but thought it was unfair when there was nothing she could do to change the outcome.

It was the future, tomorrow, just as when she was a child, which helped Hannah accept the situation. Jonathan was a physician; he had a bright future, one promising security and prestige, which she would share. At thirty-three years of age, she still had plenty of time to have children.

Then she thought of Jonathan, and something inside her cried out, no. She felt sorry for him. Though there were plenty of other women for him, if she left him, she knew he would be scarred once again. As a young boy, his birth mother had abandoned him. At three years old, he was adopted. That, she reasoned, accounted for his aloofness.

Hannah was never pregnant again. Nor did she forget the agony and despair the abortion had caused her, nor did she ever drink Tetley tea again. Jonathan acted as though he had forgotten the whole event, and all was well.

Now she realized a man who truly loved a woman would never let her suffer. He would want her children. Jonathan had never loved her.

In the quiet of the country, and with nothing pressing to do, Hannah found herself questioning everything. She was still mulling over what Kurt had asked. Who killed Jonathan and why? Could it be proven a hunter shot him by mistake?

*

Sunday morning, Hannah returned to Montreal to attend Stanley Nowak's funeral. On the previous Wednesday at 11:00 a.m. she had visited him in his hospital bed. One thirty in the afternoon, he took his last breath.

Dr. Stanley Nowak, a renowned researcher, had been Jonathan's mentor when he was a medical student. In the nine years it took for the cancer to take him away, he was awarded some of the most prestigious honours, including the Order of Canada. Distinguished physicians were flown in to advise on his treatment, but nothing stopped the cancer's progress. Researchers joined at his bedside to pray for him and mine his fertile mind, which continued to astonish and enlighten them until he took his final breath. When he died, he was putting the finishing touches on a research paper on lung disease. It was his lungs, the space for which was taken over by the enormous growth, robbing him of his breath and life.

At the front of the altar, Stanley Nowak's dark mahogany casket, covered with a mammoth wreath of yellow roses and chrysanthemums, appeared small and alone in the ornate Catholic cathedral. Hannah understood, from what had been said, that the embalmers had done a remarkable job. He had the appearance of a man resting contentedly. During the service, the priest reminded everyone his funeral was the celebration of a great life, a life encompassing all that was good and righteous.

Images of Jonathan's funeral appeared. She was grateful for its simplicity. Jewish law forbids embalming, since it is considered a desecration of the deceased person. To allow the body to decay, thus permitting the soul to ascend to heaven, it is washed and clothed in traditional burial shrouds, Tachrichim, simple white garments. Regardless of status, only a simple plain wooden coffin is allowed, because before God all are created equal.

What about women in the Jewish faith — were they always treated equal? Hannah recalled the graveside funeral of Joseph Cantor, an elderly art dealer she had befriended.

It was a sad, black day. A steady stream of freezing rain fell as the twelve women and nine men, which included the rabbi, waited and waited on Mount Royal for the arrival of the tenth male. He never came. The Kaddish, the traditional prayer, cannot be recited without the presence of ten males over the age of thirteen years, which is called a minyan. The Kaddish was not said for the elderly man. Everyone wept for him. There was nothing they could do.

The rabbi refused to say the blessings unless there was a minyan. Thankfully, his wife of sixty years did not have to experience the humiliation. She had died the year before, and they had no children. Hannah had heard of this happening before, but she had never experienced the severe pain it caused.

After the ceremony, Hannah found herself at the reception in the midst of the sandwich-munching masses. The well-dressed crowd devoured the small, crustless, snow-white salmon and egg salad sandwiches like they had just returned from a twenty-mile hike.

Once home, Hannah watched from her window workmen across the street repairing the road. They looked content. She thought of the words of the noted Quebecois architect, Ernest Cormier: "It's not work that kills a man, it's worry."

CHAPTER TWENTY-FOUR

"**H**i, what time do you expect Kurt?" asked Helen on the telephone.

"Any time before the presentation. He said he hoped to get in this afternoon so we could spend some time together."

"Have you seen Robert?"

"No, he's still out of town, He'll be back in time for tonight."

"We'll pick you up at seven. I'll phone first," said Helen.

"I must get off the line in case Kurt calls." Hannah was anxiously waiting to hear from him. She was afraid to leave the house in case she missed his call.

Instinctively, she went into the kitchen. From the drawer she removed a long, white butcher's apron and wrapped it snugly around her body, tying it in the front like protective armour. Hannah could never understand how anyone could prepare food and stay clean without an apron.

In the electric flourmill she placed superior hard, red Saskatchewan wheat kernels and watched them grind to a fine flour before adding them to her warm water, yeast, and salt mixture. For her, like the French who define their daily bread by these basic ingredients, there was no need to add fats and sugars. It robbed the bread of its robust flavour. When Jonathan was alive, a few times a week she would get up early in the morning to make golden loaves of sourdough bread. Today she made basic whole wheat bread.

Methodically, Hannah rubbed flour into the smooth surface of the white Carrara marble countertop once used by nuns in a nearby convent. Rhythmically kneading the warm, elastic dough, her arm muscles contracted and relaxed as the gluten developed a feeling of serenity replaced her anxiety and nausea. Hannah formed the dough into a round, satiny ball, covered it with a damp cloth, and left it to rise to double in size before punching it down and shaping it into two identical loaves.

When baked to a golden brown, their seductive aroma filled the house.

Recently, for lunch Hannah had satisfied her fickle taste with two slices of her freshly baked, moist, dark bread with a thick slice of cheddar cheese melted between them, a salad, and a cup of organic Assam Banaspaty tea.

When the doorbell rang, Hannah ran to get it. Without looking out, she flung the door open.

"Hi, I tried to call. The phone was busy. I hope you don't mind. It was faster to just come over."

"Kurt, it's so good to see you." He enclosed her in his arms. She could feel his heart pounding. Then he stepped back and looked around.

"I knew you would live in an old house with book-lined walls." Before she could answer, he added, "I really wanted to spend some time with you before the presentation. I'd hoped to get here earlier."

"Would you like something to drink? Eat?"

"I'll have something cold; water would be great. Smells good. Like bread baking." He followed her into the kitchen.

"It's warm in the house," Kurt remarked. "The bread is a work of art."

"Would you like to try it?"

"A little later. I'd love to."

"What kind of water would you like?"

"Regular tap water. Montreal is supposed to have some of the best water in the world. I know it's safe. Bottled, well, who knows?"

113

"You're right."

On a similar warm autumn evening about ten years ago, Hannah recalled a dinner party in their small flat in lower Outremont. Jonathan had invited Jacob, a fellow physician, and his fiancée to dinner. Jacob had recently become an observant Jew. His fiancée, Frances, a Catholic, French-Canadian laboratory technician, a convert to his faith, had finicky eating habits. Jacob mentioned she enjoyed turkey.

Much to Hannah's dismay, the kosher turkey the butcher delivered was so mammoth that Jonathan had joked it must be some kind of supersized mutant. With one wing and a half a leg missing, this cosmetically challenged turkey looked like it had died in a knife fight and took hours to cook.

They arrived late due to an emergency at the hospital, and the house was swelteringly hot because the oven had been on for hours. At the end of the meal, Jacob and his fiancée, dressed in warm woollen autumn outfits dripping with sweat and the lingering aroma of roast turkey, departed. Shortly after the catastrophic dinner party, they broke off their engagement. Six months later, Jacob married the daughter of a wealthy industrialist. Two years earlier, with his wife he had died in a freak accident aboard their yacht. Hannah and Jonathan had attended their summer wedding on Long Island.

After a few moments, Kurt added, "It's great to be here. I love the heat."

"It's not usually this hot. I had this urge to bake bread. Not a good idea on a hot day. Let's go sit in the sunroom." For the moment, the sun had hidden behind a hovering cloud.

"It's wonderful here. You can feel the pulse of the city." Kurt stood looking out on the panorama.

To Hannah, it was amusing how differently everyone viewed the traffic and pedestrians passing by. Some saw it as an annoyance to be avoided, others the soundtrack to a celebration of life, a life to be viewed and shared. Visiting her friend Karin high on Mount Royal, it was as quiet as a tomb. Hannah was happy to return home.

A former landlord's response to a tenant who complained about the street commotion made Hannah smile. Instead of refuting her statement, he opened the door and took her out on to the balcony. He asked her if she could hear the noise. "Yes, definitely yes," she said. He replied, "You're lucky you can hear." She never said another word about the noise.

"I can see you love your house. It's decorated with such passion." Kurt eyed her collection of Petersen silver displayed in an antique oak cabinet and the eclectic array of plants — avocados and chamomiles, along with African violets and orchids — housed in ornate Victorian planters, from a time when it was the vogue for gentlewomen to cultivate plants as a pleasant pastime.

"I never thought I'd ever have my own house."

"Why?"

"Well, Jonathan never wanted a city house. He said we have the country house, no children, and he wasn't home all day. So why do we need a house?"

What Kurt was seeing was Hannah did not live the conventional life he had first visualized. He sat silent as Hannah continued.

"I wanted a house. I didn't want to live in a rented apartment. I was so determined," she paused, and then with a laugh added, "I saved the money for the down payment. It was before the last Quebec referendum in the seventies. Everyone was nervous, and house prices plunged. I bought this house at a bargain price. Fortunately, Quebec voted to stay in Canada."

"What did your husband say?"

"I think he was happy. Actually, I had my eye on another house. He wanted this one because it was near the hospital he worked at."

"So the deal was sealed."

"Yes."

"He got a good deal."

"I think he was too smart for me. He always ended up getting what he wanted."

"What about you?"

"I tried," said Hannah in a reflective voice. "Maybe all men do what they want. That's nature."

Then she almost immediately looked pained. She thought of the child she had lost.

With the sun catching Hannah's golden hair and face, she continued, "Recently, I had the small-paned windows replaced. They leaked. The new large-paned windows let in more light and have a better seal. The room is so much brighter."

When Hannah looked at Kurt he seemed totally enraptured.

"I don't think I've ever seen your face before in daylight, sunshine. You have astonishing amber eyes. I feel I've seen them before, but where? Have you ever lived in Bournemouth?"

"Yes, as a child."

"I sold Mr. Epstein, the jeweller, a blue diamond on a necklace just before the Second World War. It was over forty years ago. There was little girl there with amber eyes."

"It was me! My parents gave me the blue diamond necklace as a wedding gift," said an astonished Hannah.

"I can't believe it," he said with tears in his eyes. "I can't believe I didn't recognize you when we first met. I think I've always tried burying dark times, with all the bad memories. The good ones also got lost."

"I cherish the blue diamond necklace."

Hannah continued, "I also cherish my father's story of the day he purchased the blue diamond necklace. It had snowed. This was unusual for Bournemouth. Just when he was about to close, a bright young man with a shock of blond hair and eyes as blue as the diamond he held came to the shop."

They both sat for some time in disbelief.

"I brought your gold bracelet you left behind in New York. It's in the hotel suite. I'll bring it later. Where did you get that remarkable whalebone compass?"

"When I was sixteen years old, I received it as a gift from a friend of my father, Mr. Levy. It was during my summer vacation from school. I was often with my father in his shop. Mr. Levy, a fellow antique dealer, visited often. He shared with my father a particular interest in gemstones. People came from all over the world to see my father's collection. Like Mr. Levy, they had their tales of triumph and failure, but Mr. Levy's stories were the best. This day I remember vividly. He told my father he would shortly be going on a journey to a place where there were more precious stones, emeralds, diamonds, rubies, and sapphires than either of them had ever seen. My father anxiously asked where."

"Where was this place?" inquired Kurt.

"He never said."

"How mysterious."

"Mr. Levy's tales were the best because at the end of each visit he'd reach deep into his big trouser pocket and bring out a surprise. He seemed to know what pleased me. This day was no exception. He brought out the small gold compass set in whalebone. He said it was from a place close to my heart, Nantucket, an island off Massachusetts. Then he hesitated. I knew his wife had died a month earlier, shortly after their trip to Nantucket, and he was deeply hurt. There was no long tale related about Nantucket. He simply added as we said our goodbyes, 'Try to visit Nantucket. Once you get there, Hannah, you'll understand how unique it is.'"

"Did you get there?"

"Yes, many times."

"I've also visited the Little Grey Lady of the Sea many times, and I keep going back. Recently, I bought a cottage there,"

"That's amazing. The greatest flattery I can ever recall was when someone asked me if I was an islander."

"I can see you there. I hope one day you will come with me to Nantucket."

"I'd love to."

"Hopefully, there will still be some of the island to enjoy. The last time I visited, there was a raging storm shaking loose two feet of shore on Surfside. I watched clump after clump of red earth and grass drop a full twenty feet into the violent sea. It looked like the sea was bleeding," said Kurt.

"It must have been frightening."

"It was. I feared for the island, which as you might well know is a pile of sand left by retreating glaciers. Some say it could eventually disappear. I'd like to make a documentary about Nantucket. About how the sea, which year after year draws thousands back to the island and in the 1800s made it one of the world's leading whaling ports, and inspired *Moby Dick*, is the sea that's destroying it," replied Kurt.

"When one reads about Nantucket, it's not something generally mentioned."

"The unpredictability of the sea is generally the stuff of legends, not travel brochures. The monsters and gigantic eruptions sailors report seeing at sea were probably rogue waves," explained Kurt.

"Having lived near the sea, I can never imagine why anyone would believe the sea and places bordering the seas are always paradise."

"Travel posters often portray the serenity and beauty of the sea," said Kurt.

"True. In *Moby Dick*, Herman Melville caught the essence of the island and its whaling history. Strangely, he wrote his epic journey before he had ever set foot on the island. It was based on his readings." Hannah had reread *Moby Dick* recently. It was fresh in her mind.

"The majestic sea captains' houses remain to remind us of the prosperous whaling industry. Did you ever compare notes about your visits to the island with Mr. Levy?"

"No. After he gave me the whalebone compass, neither my father nor I saw him again. It wasn't until years later I learned he'd died, or as my father said, 'He joined his wife.' Some say he died of a heart attack, others of a broken heart. I always wondered if he ever travelled to the city of precious gems he spoke of the last time I saw him."

"He probably did," said Kurt in a reflective voice. "Perhaps one day we all travel there."

"I will show you my paradise. Come. It's on the roof."

To reach the rooftop from the first floor, they took two flights of wide oak stairs up to the third floor. Then it was necessary to climb a narrow winding staircase up to the rooftop.

"We built the greenhouse about four years ago."

"This is fabulous. What an array of plants. What a view. It's even better than from the sunroom. Those poplar trees, the river, and the church steeples. Everywhere you look in Montreal you see a church steeple. You feel like you can reach out and touch them."

"Many are rather modern, from the forties and fifties, when Catholic families attended mass together. After the Quiet Revolution in the sixties, church attendance declined," added Hannah.

"When I arrived in Montreal, nuns still wore habits. It seemed like nuns were everywhere. That was in the 1940s."

"I also remember in the early seventies, when they abandoned their habits for civilian clothes. Many came to see me for diet advice. Previously, their robes had disguised their expansive girths."

Kurt thought for a moment and replied, "Uniforms in general seemed to be abandoned in the seventies. Making movies, you're aware of these changes."

"At the time, I recall dietitians gave up their standard hospital uniforms, as did nurses. There were all sorts of reasons given, from the cost of laundering to the social implications."

"I must say, a nurse in a white starched uniform is much more attractive than in a multi-.

coloured polyester pant outfit. The nuns in their habits were mysterious figures," said Kurt with a grin.

"How things have changed in our lifetime." Hannah was trying to imagine what other surprises would be in store for her in the coming years.

"I wonder if uniforms will ever come back. Things seem to go in cycles. Many of the old Victorian homes had sunrooms and greenhouses. Now I notice more people are adding them," observed Kurt. "It's like being in the tropics. What a wonderful smell." He took a deep breath.

"This is my paradise. I feel at peace here. Even late at night when I can't sleep, I come up here." Hannah looked toward the orange blossoms.

They stood in silence for some time before going back down the narrow, winding stairs to the third floor, then the stairway to the second floor.

As the late afternoon light filtered through the French doors, the bedroom filled with passion, which said more of desire than any spoken words. Kurt drew Hannah in his arms and made love to her.

The telephone rang. By the time Hannah answered, the caller had hung up.

"I must get back to the hotel to change for tonight. I really need to shower."

Hannah did not want him to leave. Every minute seemed so precious. She submerged her nausea and her intent to tell him of her pregnancy. She wanted to continue on the magical journey of passionate pleasure for a little longer. Reality could destroy the spell.

"Why not take one here?"

As the lather of Hannah's favourite grapefruit scented soap fell from Kurt's lean, muscular back, her thoughts turned to the newfound joy lying within her, which in a little over seven months would be hers. She wanted to share the source of her profound pleasure and nausea with Kurt. One she was determined this time would not escape her. But the moment was not to be.

"Can I grab a cab?"

"Just outside the door."

"I'll see you at the Ritz Carlton."

Dressing for the evening, Hannah thought it was strange that Kurt, in spite of his medical training and observational skills, failed to notice the changes in her body, the engorgement of her breasts, and the buttery soft skin of her inner thighs, due to the increase in hormones brought on by her pregnancy, when he embraced her.

CHAPTER TWENTY-FIVE

Kurt was deep in thought when the front desk called. "Send him up."

"Hi. I hope you had a good trip?" asked Robert Steinman.

"I did."

"I came early. I wanted to make sure you got to the lecture in good time. I understand you arrived this afternoon?"

"This afternoon, yes. It was nice to have a little time in Montreal."

As Robert's eyes scanned the room, they settled on Hannah's gold bracelet with the small compass set in whalebone sitting on the table.

"The movie's a go. I just heard this morning. All the finances are lined up," said Robert quickly, trying to keep on track and not be distracted.

"What's the schedule?" asked Kurt.

"That's the hitch. Your lead, Max Milford, can only swing it if we start immediately. We're on a really tight schedule. Shooting in Waskaganish and other northern scenes has to be done before the cold weather sets in."

"You mean like yesterday?" replied Kurt.

"Right. We'll discuss it later. Let's go."

"Just a minute." Robert watched Kurt carefully take up the gold bracelet and place it in his breast pocket.

Once in the elevator, a familiar scent caught Robert's attention, the fresh fragrance of sweet grapefruit. He felt the blood rush to his head. Few would have noticed the subtle scent. But Robert, who since childhood had prided himself, and astonished his parents, on his acute sense of smell, did notice. Over the years, he had used this gift to his advantage. Recently, he was particularly sensitive to the stench of cigarette smoke.

*

When Hannah, Jeff, and Helen entered the Ritz-Carlton ballroom, Robert came forward to greet them. He was delighted she was wearing his favourite Wedgwood blue dress. Kissing Hannah on each cheek, he no doubt detected the scent of grapefruit. What he failed to see was her necklace with the sparkling blue diamond.

Eager fans already surrounded Kurt. He could scarcely manage a quick smile to Hannah before Robert whisked him off to meet various patrons. Then it was time for his presentation.

Hannah turned to Helen and said, "I don't think I'll ever see him again."

Helen laughed. "The crowd really likes him, particularly the women, young and old. He's a handful one to catch."

"What's he got, every woman wants," Jeff observed.

After Kurt's presentation, while Hannah was in the ladies' room, Jeff said to Helen, "I feel pained for Hannah. Kurt looks like the constant philanderer, counting his conquests as he travels from city to city and woman to woman. I'm not concerned about her shattered heart. It will heal. I'm disturbed by the escalation of that new, baffling, sexually transmitted disease confronting doctors. I hate to see Hannah's life ruined by one false move."

A few moments later, Hannah returned.

"You look tired, Hannah. I think we should take you home," said Helen with concern.

As they were leaving, Kurt caught up with them. "Hi. Sorry I couldn't get away."

"I'm Helen, Robert's cousin. We met years ago. This is my husband, Jeff Bloom. Your talk was fabulous. I very much enjoyed it. Hannah has told us about you. About your work."

"Hannah has also mentioned you. It's good to meet you again."

"We were just on our way. It's been a long day," added Helen hastily.

"Hannah, I have to stay. I'll call you," Kurt said apologetically.

*

Once home, Hannah barely had the strength to undress. She threw her clothes on the chair. Before she crawled under the covers, she tested the telephone to see if it was functioning, not off the hook. She often checked when she was expecting an important call. It never rang.

In the morning, Hannah picked up the telephone. It was dead. The repairman first assumed an old wire had deteriorated and snapped. When he was leaving, he added, "It's an old telephone line, but it looks like it could have been deliberately cut."

As he was leaving, a courier arrived with an envelope for Hannah.

Dearest Hannah,

I was caught up at a meeting all night. The movie is a go. We start shortly.

I tried to call numerous times. The phone was dead. I couldn't get over. I already miss you. I'm off to location. Until we speak,

I love you.

Love,

Kurt

Now she understood why she never heard from Kurt. What she did not understand was who cut the telephone wires and why.

On her way upstairs, the doorbell rang. Could Kurt be returning? Her heart began to pound.

It was a delivery. On opening the familiar florist's box, Hannah removed the small white envelope nestled between the long-stemmed red roses. She took it over to her favourite chair and sat down. Her heart continued to pound in anticipation.

Dear Hannah,

Sorry I couldn't spend more time with you last night. Saturday night I'll pick you up at seven for the museum dinner dance.

See you then,

Kisses,

Robert

Hannah's heart ached. If they had been from Kurt, how different the world would have looked. Lost in thought, she placed the bouquet of perfect red roses in a clear crystal Daum vase and filled it with water. All Hannah could see was a carefully composed still life. She did not want to perceive them as the symbol of love roses are known to represent.

CHAPTER TWENTY-SIX

Weeks ago, before his business trip and before Hannah had met Kurt, Robert had asked Hannah to join him for the museum's annual dinner dance. She had promised and felt obligated to go.-Would she buy a new dress? She did not have the desire, or strength, to shop. All she craved was more sleep. She would wear her long black silk dress. It would have to do.

At exactly seven o'clock on Saturday night, from the window Hannah watched Robert's Mercedes pull into the driveway. This was the first time she had seen Robert in a tuxedo. Its form-fitting tailored lines imparted to his slender frame an elegance that beguiled her. Slowly, she walked to the door.

"Hannah, it's so good to see you. You look beautiful." Robert bent forward and kissed her. "I have something for you." He handed her a long blue box and silently watched her open it.

"A diamond necklace. They're just for tonight?" exclaimed Hannah.

"They're yours forever and ever." He looked directly into her soulful amber eyes.

"They're exquisite. I can't take them," insisted Hannah.

"You'll be doing me a great honour by accepting them. It's I who will be enjoying them. When I look up, I'll see them reflecting the sparkle in your eyes."

Hannah felt the sparkle in her eyes had dimmed when Kurt left. There was nothing left but two big black empty holes.

"Let me put them on you." He carefully fastened the clasp.

"They're perfect. How did you know?" exclaimed Hannah with delight.

"I think I know you, Hannah. Shall we go?"

"I'll get my purse."

Inside the museum, at the top of the grand red-carpeted staircase, Hannah and Robert were greeted by a reception committee and lavish decorations, which transformed the opulent marble hall into a medieval English castle. Surrounded by this surreal setting, Hannah and Robert took their seats at one of the festively decorated round tables Robert had reserved. Ritzy ball attendees stopped by the table, engaging in polite exchanges and eyeing Hannah. Was she simply another of Robert's numerous escorts or the next Mrs. Steinman?

Hannah reflected on how different this event was from the sombre medical association dinners she had attended with Jonathan. It was a whole new world.

Even though the price of a ball ticket was three hundred dollars or more, it barely covered the cost of the lavish gourmet dinner, live band, and extravagant decoration. Tax-deductible donations from sponsors made these fundraisers successful. Robert was one of the sponsors.

Hannah had been observing the hundreds of gowns by such noted designers as Armani, Chanel, Yves Saint Laurent, Oscar de la Renta and others — too many to count. How much money could be raised if all the money spent on these luxurious gowns, jewellery, shoes, handbags, hairdressing, manicures, and cosmetics was donated to the benefit? But Hannah appreciated this fashion parade was a part of the allure.

She knew her dress was no match for the luxurious one-of-a-kind creations worn by the socialites who usually accompanied Robert to such functions. But she had convinced herself even a simple, well-cut black silk dress on her well-toned, willowy figure had elegance and style. In spite of her nausea, she maintained her radiant smile, the one she had cultivated over many years of practice.

Nauseated, sitting back in her deep, plush chair Hannah's feet felt like they were in a vice; her stylish-high-heeled black satin Ferragamo shoes were crushing her toes. Adding to her discomfort were her pantyhose, which were tight at the crotch and waist. Like an overstretched elastic band, they felt ready to snap.

Shifting her focus to Robert's highly polished black leather shoes, Hannah remarked, "What comfortable-looking shoes you're wearing." Then she thought, *What a mundane statement to make in the midst of all the festivities.* Yet it was understandable; when your feet hurt, you become obsessed with shoes.

"I have these shoes custom-made by an Italian shoemaker. They fit like a glove. Until I found this shoemaker, I never knew what it was like to have truly comfortable shoes. One thing I did discover along the way was I could make a pair of shoes more comfortable by changing the inner soles. Before I had my shoes made for me, I had inner soles crafted for me. I say if your feet don't feel right, nothing feels right."

"That's true."

"Tonight, I find the cigarettes most irritating, more than usual," Robert said with disdain.

"So do I." Hannah ran her fingers over the cool surface of her newly acquired diamond necklace, which made her feel special and cherished.

In the ladies' lounge, with chubby cherubs looking down from the top of an enormous ornate, antique gilt-framed mirror, she bent over, removed her pantyhose, and stuffed them in her small purse.

Returning to her seat next to Robert, hidden under the folds of her silk dress, her bare feet and legs felt free. But her feet still hurt, particularly when she stood up.

At times like this, she wished she could emulate the young bride she saw at an orthodox wedding a few years ago. For the services, under her magnificent billowing white satin gown, she wore ballet slippers. Later, to take part in the array of traditional dances, she changed into rhinestone-covered white satin sneakers.

Hannah appreciated that heels can impart to a woman an air of elegance and confidence no low-heeled shoe can match. She loved the height and even the shape they gave to her body. Wearing heels placed her body weight on the balls of her feet, arching her back, which pressed her chest forward and gave her a more curved body, with the illusion of a smaller waist.

"Would you like to dance?" asked Robert.

As she danced the foxtrot, Hannah pictured her parents attending a ball in Bournemouth before the Second World War. She could see her mother wearing a long bias-cut gown, swaying in her father's arms to the popular pre-war music of Sid Phillips and his big band.

Her mother stored her silk gowns, along with purses and shoes made of soft calf leather, in the same Louis Vuitton wardrobe trunk in which they had crossed the Atlantic. Occasionally, as if to relive the happy early years of her marriage, her mother would open the trunk and try on a gown. Hannah marvelled at how these custom-made garments followed the curves of her mother's small-framed, five-foot figure.

Her parents would foxtrot around the living room as her father hummed songs such as "Can't Help Lovin' Dat Man" To Hannah, who had rarely danced, they looked wonderfully graceful together. Her mother often mentioned the ballroom dancing competitions they had won, although Hannah saw no trophies. It might not have been true. Her father never corrected or criticized her mother, even when she said the most outrageous things. He truly loved her. Hannah longed for the same unconditional love.

"Dancing is unimportant. Concentrate on your studies," Hannah's mother had repeatedly told her. Hannah wished she could dance as gracefully as her parents.

Thankfully, for most of the evening Hannah and Robert had merely exchanged small talk with a number of acquaintances from the cultural charity community. Now, at the end of the evening, dancing to a slow waltz, Hannah felt more and more nauseated. Just when she envisioned collapsing in the middle of the dance floor, a polka began to play, and Robert led her off the floor. After a limited number of farewells, they left.

"I'll call you tomorrow," Robert said as she unlocked the front door and stepped into the vestibule.

"Yes, that would be good. I'm so tired."

"I know, Hannah. Get a good night's sleep."

*

Returning home, in spite of feeling off-key, Robert immediately dialled his answering service. There was a call from Avrum Wood: "Things are going well. I'll be flying to New York early tomorrow morning."

Robert could no longer socialize into the early morning hours. His chronic cough and flu-like symptoms were annoying and tiring. On his family physician's advice, he had visited a medical expert in San Francisco familiar with patients with similar symptoms. He could not find the cause of his problems or a solution. Robert was understandably frustrated.

*

The next day, Robert asked Hannah if she would join him at the upcoming Stars Dance Gala, where leading classical dancers were invited to perform for a children's charity event. The dancers donated their talents. Though Hannah loved to watch dance, she had never attended the annual Stars Dance Gala, since she believed it was another scam using the drawing power of suffering children.

Hannah knew Henry Lobchuk, the organizer of the Dance Gala. She had met him a number of years ago when she was on the Children's Hospital Charity Dance committee. Being well known for her newspaper column, television work, and organizing skills, she was frequently asked to volunteer to chair and organize charity events. For the Children's Hospital Charity Dance, leading dancers were invited to perform. It was a big success.

Shortly after, Lobchuk spoke to her about how it had been organized. The next year, he christened the Stars Dance Gala. Advertisements gave the impression the profits supported research into childhood diseases. In reality, Hannah knew, only a portion of the profit from the cocktail party prior to the performance went to childhood diseases. That was written in small print on the promotional material, which she doubted anyone read. Organizers would line up a few prominent people to attend the gala, provide them with free tickets, and list them as the guests of honour. It was handful for them to refuse, since they believed the galas truly benefited the cause.

Although Hannah felt she was acting against her principles, she decided to see what the fuss over the Dance Gala was about.

Early in the afternoon of the gala, as Hannah said goodbye to her last patient, Mr. Roseman, called. He sounded distressed and upset. Without giving any specific reason, he said he wanted to see her today, if possible. He said he lived close by. Hannah told him to come right over.

The month before, he had been doing fine. With the help of his wife, he was adhering to Hannah's advice. His chest pain had entirely disappeared. He was happy. In fact, he said he felt like a new man.

Hannah wondered why he had to see her so urgently. He even arrived early. She was free and asked him to come in.

Slumping in the chair opposite her he said, "Something terrible has happened. I have lost my dear wife. She died suddenly of a heart attack." Then he paused and added, "I had to talk to someone. She died at home, in her favourite armchair, right in front of the television. I watched it happen. I couldn't help her; neither could the emergency team when they arrived. The cardiac surgeons had said she was cured when she had her bypass a year ago."

Hannah had never seen a man so downhearted and forlorn, like his whole world had collapsed. As they spoke, she realized what a priceless love he and his wife had shared for over forty years. They had survived the concentration camps, the death of a son, and a number of other devastating experiences, but their love remained intact. When he left nearly an hour later, she was exhausted and saddened — but inspired by the possibility of the existence of such a love.

It was four months ago that this small man, who had chest pain on exertion, proudly introduced his rotund wife to Hannah. Apart from his wife's girth and a magnificent diamond ring worn on her arthritic finger, Hannah noted her contented countenance.

Mr. Roseman assured Hannah the diet and lifestyle advice were for him alone, not his wife. With great satisfaction, he proudly announced his dear wife had recently had a quadruple heart bypass operation and was thus cured. She did not need a diet.

"Yes," he said, "Luckily, I arranged for my wife to go to the best heart clinic and get the operation. I can assure you it was well worth the sixty thousand dollars for my beloved wife. It was my anniversary present to her. I could afford it. Why not the best for the best? Her blocked arteries were discovered on a routine medical check-up. But thank goodness, we got it in time. She had had no pain. The doctors in Montreal wanted her to wait. For what, I said. Yes, she still has knee and back problems, arthritis, but her heart has been given the best, the very best."

Hannah tried to explain to them they both should take her advice. If his wife did not follow the advice, her other arteries could clog up. There was nothing Hannah could say to change their mindset. His wife was cured, and she could eat as she wished. Mr. Roseman inferred one of the reasons for the operation was to allow his beloved wife to eat whatever she liked.

CHAPTER TWENTY-SEVEN

Waiting for Robert, Hannah wrapped a long, flowered silk scarf over the same fine wool slim-fitting blue dress she had worn the night of Kurt's talk. It covered her expanding waistline.

Robert was unusually late. Hannah questioned how she was going to have the patience to sit through an evening of dance. When the doorbell chimed, she ran to get it.

"I'm sorry I'm late. I had some last-minute business. It couldn't wait."

Hannah noticed his voice was hoarse. He also seemed unsettled. Business never usually fazed him. It must be something else.

"I'm happy you came a little later. I had a few things to finish up." Then she added, looking at the red roses, now in full bloom, "They are magnificent. On Sunday they arrived a few minutes after the telephone repair man was leaving. They said the wire was cut. I was so upset. They cheered me up. Thank you so much."

He put his arms around Hannah and gently kissed her. "I have something to go with the diamond necklace you're wearing." He presented Hannah with the same style of blue box the necklace had come in.

Hannah felt overwhelmed as she graciously thanked him for the matching bracelet.

"Let me put it on you."

Robert understood the power of presents as tangible reminders of generosity, care, and concern. He had witnessed them open the door to impossible opportunities. Now they also helped Hannah forget about the cut telephone wire and Kurt.

When wearing the diamond necklace, Hannah could only observe its reflection. Now, looking down at her wrist, the sparkling bracelet did not escape her admiration. It held her attention at the lengthy gala, which seemed endless. She wondered if the diamonds were from his secret source.

After seeing at least a dozen local and international dancers pirouette and leap through the air, what started out as thrilling and unique became tedious. A lavish supper buffet served at midnight had little appeal to Hannah. Sleep seemed more enticing. When they arrived at Hannah's house at nearly two in the morning, both were weary.

*

The next day, tired and impatient with herself, Hannah tried to make sense of recent events. She even questioned if she really loved Kurt. Last night, Hannah felt happy and content with Robert's arms around her.

She got up and walked around the house, noting the different views from each window. Her attention settled on a gigantic oak tree, its light brown dead leaves clinging to its outstretched branches waiting patiently for a fierce nor'easter to blow them away. Beyond to the north, Mount Royal, part of an ancient volcanic chain eroded to a fraction of its original size, reminded her once again of the transitory nature of all things. Now clothed in subdued tones of brown and purple, it would soon be blanketed in snow, by day glistening in the low winter sun, by night shimmering under the ever-present, illuminated ninety-eight-foot-high Christian cross, erected at the top of Mount Royal in 1924 by the Saint-Jean-Baptiste Society.

A reminder of Montreal's founding fathers, the cross marks the January day in 1643 when Paul de Chomedey, Sieur de Maisonneuve, the founder of Montreal, kept his pledge to erect a wooden cross on Mount Royal if the colony survived the threat of flooding.

In May of the previous year, 1980, the cross was draped with a sign saying "OUI" for the yes side in Quebec's sovereignty referendum. Six out of ten Quebecers voted against independence from the rest of Canada.

Since the election in November 1976 of a separatist political party, the Parti Québécois, political uncertainty was endemic in Quebec.

Thirteen years earlier, when the 1967 International and Universal Exposition, Expo 67, took place in Montreal, Quebec was basking in the glory of hosting the most successful world's fair of the twentieth century. Montreal was the most populous city in Canada. After years of political unrest in Quebec, Toronto supplanted Montreal as Canada's largest metropolis.

Hannah reflected on how Quebec was no stranger to controversy. In the thirties, it was a hotbed of fascism. Montreal's mayor, Camillien Houde, spent five years in an internment camp for his fascist sympathies and for urging people to resist conscription into the Second World War. Released after the war, he was re-elected.

One of the few people who had found a positive aspect to the exit of Montrealers from Quebec due to the volatile political situation was Jonathan. He had said, "Good riddance. Now there is more space for me and everyone who stays."

Trying to reason why she stayed, Hannah thought of the romantic feeling evoked by a city built on a mountain, surrounded by a mighty river, punctuated by a multitude of sky-piercing steeples bearing witness to the former power of the church, which after the Quiet Revolution of the 1960s was supplanted by the Quebec state.

Churches, icons of a former era when families with their numerous children prayed together, were built with opulence and grandeur to impress the worshippers with the power of the church, unlike many of the gigantic glass-and-concrete rectangular boxes, cathedrals of commerce conceived to satisfy the architect or developer.

Hannah recalled the beauty and mystery of midnight mass on Christmas Eve at a small church in the Laurentian Mountains where she used to ski, when the temperature had dipped to minus thirty Celsius and her Italian friend of long ago, Giuseppe, wrapped his long, warm woollen scarf around her. It reminded her of slipping away to confession with Catherine, her best friend from grade school. Though satisfying her curiosity, she felt guilty simply being in a place of

Christian worship. She never told her mother, who would have reprimanded her.

Distracting thoughts could not indefinitely submerge Hannah's feelings for Kurt. She felt guilty and questioned why she did not fly to Waskaganish and seek him, if she was so determined and in love with him. What if she was humiliated? She hungered to tell him she was carrying his child; but she did not want him to pity her and to commit to a relationship and marriage due to her pregnancy. She valued a love-inspired bond.

On the other hand, she reasoned, why would she travel thousands of kilometres to Waskaganish feeling exhausted and nauseated, when he could not even call or write her?

*

A week, then two weeks passed. Hannah never heard from Kurt. She knew he was directing a film set far up north, but she could not understand why he never contacted her.

A whirlwind of social events with Robert and a busy practice afforded her little time to contemplate her future. She was content to get through her days.

Two weeks and two days since Kurt's visit to Montreal, after a quiet dinner, Robert presented Hannah with a square blue box.

"I understand this might appear sudden to you. But I have thought about it for some time. I love you. I can make you happy. I hope you will marry me."

Hannah cautiously opened the box containing a glittery Tiffany-style emerald cut diamond ring. "It's beautiful."

"You don't have to answer now. We'll talk tomorrow."

After he said goodnight, Hannah telephoned Helen. "Helen, I hope this isn't too late."

"Not at all. What's new?"

"It happened. He asked me to marry him. Robert."

"Why are you surprised? I knew he would. Listen, I'm coming over," said Helen without hesitating for a moment.

"Right now?"

"Yes. Right now."

*

"Helen, it's good of you to come, but it could wait. We could talk tomorrow or the next day," said Hannah, opening the door.

"Hannah, you don't seem to realize you can't wait. You must make up your mind. Have you heard from Kurt?" Helen said with concern as she followed Hannah into the living room.

"No, but it's just a little over two weeks." To Hannah the two weeks felt a world away.

"You obviously have feelings for Robert," insisted Helen.

"But not the same as for Kurt. It's his baby."

"Then where the hell is he? Why isn't he on the phone? Why isn't he here?" It seemed Helen wouldn't rest until she had convinced Hannah she had to make up her mind.

"He's no doubt shooting far up north, past Waskaganish. It's stormy up there, bad weather. Often the lines can be down, and no doubt he's busy night and day shooting." Hannah too was trying to figure out why he had not called.

"At the grocery store, I saw a photo of him on the cover of the latest movie magazine. Obviously, he's still very much alive and kicking. Do you really want a guy who's here today, gone tomorrow? If he was the slightest bit interested in you, he would have gotten in touch. He has been single, alone, all these years. Obviously, he doesn't want to settle down with one person."

"You're tough." Hannah did not feel up to arguing. She knew the magazine cover was shot months ago.

"I have to be. You're a softy. What do you want? Robert has a great track record. He was married for twenty years. Also, he's well established. I find him much more charming and sophisticated than that blue-eyed, self-serving Kurt. You're merely infatuated by a roaming star."

"I really don't know what I want. Maybe I don't want anyone."

"That's great for you, maybe, but what about the future?" Helen pressed.

"Jonathan left me little security. His death was so unexpected. He was young and healthy. There was no insurance. He didn't think it was important, as we had no children, and I suppose he thought I could always work."

"I'm old-fashioned. I feel a child needs security and a father. What are your options? Struggle as a single parent or live in luxury with a great guy who's crazy about you? Don't tell me you don't care for him! I remember, even when Jonathan was alive, you had something for him, didn't you?"

"I suppose I've always gravitated toward him. He's kind and attentive to me, and he makes me feel special. But I'm worried about his cough and hoarse throat and fatigue."

"I'm sure he's simply working too handful. He needs a vacation," Helen assured her.

"He's been busy shopping and showering me with gifts."

"A diamond ring would be nice."

Hannah said nothing. She rightly knew that if she showed Helen the ring, it would have compelled her to be even more assertive. Hannah had never mentioned to Helen the recent gifts of diamonds.

"Think seriously. Don't wait too long. He might not wait. I must say goodnight."

They never discussed the necessity of telling Robert she was pregnant. A miscarriage was a possibility. Helen obviously assumed Hannah and Robert were sexually involved.

*

No doubt her pregnancy and Helen's advice coloured Hannah's decision. Though nauseated, a veil of tranquillity fell over her as she put aside her reservations and accepted Robert's marriage proposal. She assured herself that sex would come. He was from a different generation; he wanted to wait.

Removing from the bookshelf a photograph of her mother and father on their wedding day, she wiped off the dust covering its elaborate Victorian silver frame. For a winter wedding, her mother had explained to her, she had chosen an off-white silk velvet dress cut on the bias, as was the style in the thirties. Hannah was perplexed as to why her mother would choose to marry in February. She knew of no other parents who were married in winter. When she asked her mother, all she repeatedly said was that it was an elaborate wedding.

*

Four days later, on her wedding day, Hannah, dressed in an exquisitely designed gown of layered pale ivory silk, smiled as she scrutinized her refection in her armoire mirror.

Early in the afternoon, a small group of friends and Robert's close relatives-gathered for the wedding of Hannah and Robert in the small chapel of the orthodox synagogue where Robert had married his first wife more than thirty years earlier in an opulent ceremony.

Helen and Jeff's joy was palpable. Whenever Hannah looked their way, they were beaming. Avrum sent his best wishes. He was abroad on business. With such short notice, he could not make arrangements to return to Montreal in time for the wedding.

Hannah's brother did not attend. He seemed annoyed at the suggestion of coming to Quebec. But since Hannah gave him such short notice, he conveniently said he had other plans.

CHAPTER TWENTY-EIGHT

After a Champagne and caviar reception, followed by a sumptuous luncheon at a private room in the Mount Stephen Club, Hannah and Robert made the hour-and-a-half drive from Montreal to Robert's lakeside country house in the Eastern Townships of Quebec. There they were greeted by a dazzling view of Lake Memphremagog.

Mercifully, the lake was not overrun by deafening motorboats as it was at the height of summer when owners of high-powered yachts raced the thirty-two kilometres from Magog to the Landing Restaurant in Newport.

Robert and Hannah both agreed that the familiar surroundings of his country house was the ideal destination to start a life together. Hannah's modest country abode was just a few minutes' drive from Robert's, so one might have assumed they would have frequently run into each other, but they never did. In the city, it was common to live even a block or two from someone but year after year not to even catch a glimpse of them. It was the same in the country.

Strolling together along the shoreline, Hannah had the urge to abandon her warm fall clothes and throw herself into the cool, clear water of Lake Memphremagog. As a child walking along the Pacific coast, at Semiahmoo Bay, she frequently had the same impulse. Today, she was not as willing to pay the numbing price of freedom.

Close by, the bells of Abbey Saint-Benoît-du-Lac peeled, reminding her of the resident Benedictine monks, who were convinced some greater being determines our destiny. She thought, *They're lucky, they're not free — or are they?* Is anyone really free? If she was free to do as she pleased, she would have married Kurt, but desires and circumstances dictated the extent of her freedom. The monks had made the ultimate free choice to deny themselves freedom.

Looking beyond the shoreline toward the towering abbey, which sat in marked contrast to the rolling green hills sloping down to the lake, Hannah felt indebted to the French Benedictine architect Dom Paul Bellot.

In the late thirties, he had been invited to lecture in Canada. Due to the Second World War, he was unable to return to Europe. Amongst other projects, including Saint Joseph's Oratory, he was involved in the abbey's design.

His dramatically composed work, with brick cloisters featuring parabolic arches now known as the "Dom Bellot Style," left Hannah in awe and appreciation for his work and sacrifice. Originally trained as an architect, he sought the monastic life in 1902, at the age of twenty-six, after his fiancée had abandoned him to become a Carmelite nun.

Yet if Bellot had not entered the monastic life, the world would have been deprived of some of its most exceptional ecclesiastical architecture. It was an architecture Hannah felt was propelled by his great romance.

Today, she felt his pain and sense of loss woven into every brick, and she fantasized that the architect continued his relationship with his former betrothed. The truth was buried with him at Abbey Saint Benoît-du-Lac, where he was placed to rest in 1944 in a small cemetery enclosed by a white picket fence. It was a serene place Hannah often visited. She found it a humble setting for a man who left so much of himself behind.

Detouring through the woods on the way back to the house, with the old spruce trees bending and creaking in the wind, Hannah continued her introspection. Gazing at squirrels' mushrooms drying on the tree branches, she was reminded that man was not alone in preparing for the long, cold winter to come. She had read that all summer from early morning until dusk, and also on moonlit nights, red squirrels, which do not hibernate like other squirrels, busily collected and stored conifer seeds, mushrooms, and truffles. This genetically determined pattern of living helped their survival. In contrast, man's technological capability lead to destruction of the environment and chronic lifestyle diseases.

As Robert and Hannah left the forest and crossed the meadow, the sun was setting, and a chilling breeze rolled over the knoll. The few remaining pansies had hung their heads, more resigned to winter than Hannah, who wished that summer would last forever.

Curls of smoke from the massive fieldstone chimney of Robert's rambling house signalled welcome warmth within.

Indoors, they warmed up in front of the fireplace while drinking hot chocolate. Hannah was impressed with Robert's collection of Canadian art. Paintings by Louise Scott, Jean Paul Lemieux, Frederick Simpson Coburn, Cornelius Krieghoff, and Alfred Pellan lined the walls. Hannah speculated, outside of museums, that his collection might be one of the finest in Canada.

For Hannah, the silence in the country seemed to make everything more intense and meaningful.

"Do you like the paintings, Hannah?"

"They're unbelievably wonderful."

He led her to a locked cabinet in the dining room. When he opened it, Hannah was amazed at what she saw. "I know you collect Petersen silver. So did my mother."

Here in front of her was an extensive collection, one dwarfing hers.

"Did you know that in 1958 Petersen redesigned the Stanley Cup? It's the oldest sports trophy in North America."

"I did. But I'm surprised you know." Hannah was delighted that he shared her interest.

"As a child, I can remember my mother taking me with her to his workshop on Mackay Street. It saddened my mother when the elevated price of silver, coupled with increasing wages, forced him to close his studio after thirty-five years of making silver for a clientele that supported local craftsmen. At the time, my mother acquired much of her collection."

"I'm intrigued by how Petersen integrated into his designs the ideals and even some of the motifs of William Morris. You can see it in his plant forms. Like Georg Jensen." What made Petersen extra attractive for Hannah was that it was made in Montreal; also, it was no longer being produced.

"Petersen apprenticed with Jensen in Denmark prior to coming to Canada. He was also Jensen's son-in-law. You know, my wife and I had no children. Though we always wanted them. We considered our art collections our adopted children. I'm so happy I can share them with you."

Dominating the bedroom was a canvas of a solitary figure against a background of snow, with a mountain in the distance rising against a grey sky. Hannah knew it could be none other than that of the remarkable Quebecois artist Jean Paul Lemieux, whose paintings she had seen in books and magazines and the National Gallery of Canada. His stark, haunting images that captured humanity's anxiety and solitude in the face of destiny were hard to forget.

Standing in front of the large window, Robert appeared to mirror the painting's subject. Unlike the solitary figure in the painting, whose face could not be seen, Robert's visage was clearly visible, revealing a pale, exhausted man.

"Don't look so worried, Hannah. I think it was the rich meal we had," said Robert as he slowly sat down in one of the wing chairs looking out across the lake.

"Yes, it could be. I don't feel so great myself. Let's get a good night's sleep. We've had so many late nights. You know I'm not much of a socialite. I can't stay up late."

Since her pregnancy, it had taken all of Hannah's fortitude to deal with her queasy stomach. Throughout the night, Robert's coughing and restlessness disturbed her sleep.

Much to Hannah's distress, her marriage was not consummated on her wedding night, or on the following week in the country. Robert's health became her major concern.

*

Returning to Montreal downhearted and perplexed by her unconsummated marriage, Hannah turned to a distraction, as she had done in the past. Within days of returning from the country, she began to plan renovations of Robert's cut-stone, Georgian-style house at the top of Mount Royal.

Most immediate was the dark, dilapidated kitchen. This turn-of-the-century building had ample space for the kitchen, unlike many houses built in the fifties and sixties. After the Second World War, architects and planners allotted small areas for kitchens in the belief that popular processed, packaged foods, "foods of the future," required limited space to prepare.

Hannah fancied a warm, inviting room evoking the feeling of a carefully crafted English kitchen. No uniform rows of cabinets as seen in the popular fitted kitchen, but an unfitted kitchen of precisely designed furniture groupings constructed of Canadian maple, with its pleasing light colour and superior strength. Adjoining the kitchen would be a family room, with informal dining.

During a February visit to Copenhagen, she recalled the luxury of standing on the hotel's heated, tiled bathroom floor. She planned heated floors in the kitchen and bathrooms by installing hot-water pipes under the stone floors.

Through French doors from the kitchen to a patio, Hannah planned a kitchen garden for her table and medicinal herbs, and a variety of vegetables. In the colder months, a small greenhouse would provide fresh produce year-round.

Renovation exposed three safes hidden behind wall hangings, one in his office, another in the living room, and another in the entrance hallway. What could he have to hide in these safes?

Hannah's projects were not only a necessity but also an escape.

Unfortunately, she soon realized no renovation project could displace her concern for Robert's health, her unconsummated marriage, and her undisclosed pregnancy. Finding the best way to approach Robert haunted her every moment.

*

One morning, about two weeks after they had returned from the country, Robert glanced up from his breakfast coffee and asked, "Is there something you want to tell me, Hannah? Has something happened I should know about?"

"Why do you ask?" replied Hannah.

She felt she needed more time to plan how she was going to disclose her secret.

"Just have a feeling. Can I help you?"

Hannah was surprised Robert would notice anything, apart from the disarray around him, and the hammering and sawing of the carpenters and plumbers. She had no idea he had deciphered any changes in her body or behaviour, though he could very well have.

For a pregnant woman daily cares and concerns often seem far removed, as she copes with the transformations taking place in her body. Possibly he had observed the distant look in her eyes, her lack of interest in her meals, her fatigue, or her fluctuating moods. Also, if he looked closely, he would have noticed the increase in her waistline.

She blurted out, "Someone, for the millionth time, reminded me of how they used to listen regularly to my radio show. I was thinking about how miserably it all ended."

This was a remark she might have made months ago. Today, it was far removed from her thoughts. Like a method actor, she reached inside to recall this event as a source of aggravation and distress, knowing it would distract Robert and buy her time.

"It's funny, if it's bothering you so much, that you've never mentioned it to me before. Tell me what happened."

"I just didn't want to get started on it. But you know what I realized today?"

"What?"

"He really did hate me."

"Who really hated you? I'm sorry, you'll have to fill me in. Was this an old lover?"

"You know I was a part of a radio show on CBSB?"

"Yes, I'd heard."

"Well, it seemed so petty and rather stupid, but on the last show we were on together, the so-called exercise expert, Mike Manson, screamed out now he hated me more than ever."

"If anyone had said that to me, I would have feared for my life. Did you? I also would have assumed he was mentally unstable."

"Until now, I dismissed Manson's behaviour as merely a bad temper combined with a bad day. Recently, however, I've read so much about violence. People acting on their basic impulses."

Hannah was now thinking of the day Manson could barely open his swollen black eyes as he limped into the radio station on crutches. He said, "You should have seen the other guy." There was a disagreement, and Manson gave it to him. Hannah thought, I should be thankful he didn't beat the pulp out of me. *He could have, if things hadn't gone his way.* She recalled the look on his face the day she sat in the chair he called "his chair." She wondered, maybe rightly so, whether she should be frightened. This reaction was no doubt evoked by her natural protective instincts due to her pregnancy.

"You look frightened. Please don't be. You're safe here. I'll take care of you and this problem."

"How?"

"There are proven ways," said Robert rather quietly. "Do you know anything about this guy, Mike Manson?"

"Nothing, really. Every time I asked, I never got an answer. People called in and asked for his credentials. He'd get angry and say he had years of experience."

"What kind of experience?" asked Robert with a mischievous grin.

"That's what everyone asked."

"Well, it's bloody easy to find out."

Robert knew about the radio show. He once had an unsavoury encounter with its producer in a San Francisco bar. It was an encounter he would rather forget.

Over the next few days, Hannah, surrounded by a maze of paint and fabric samples, was so engrossed in decorating that she hardly noticed Robert was away.

In refurbishing her previous abodes, limited funds had compromised her creativity. With ample resources, it should have been easy. But it was not. The number of choices and decisions was more extensive and mind-boggling.

When the telephone rang, she welcomed the distraction. It was Helen. "Hi, have you heard the latest? Muscleman Manson and his partner are out, dead meat. The station is reorganizing and dropping them. Jeff told me; a patient told him."

"Who's taking their place?" Hannah was hoping it would be someone with credibility.

"I haven't heard. How about lunch tomorrow? Noon at the Abacus?"

"Good. See you tomorrow." Hannah was looking forward to seeing Helen and visiting the Abacus, one of her favourite restaurants.

CHAPTER TWENTY-NINE

Hannah's last patient before lunch was Marsha Jacks, a forty-five-year-old women's wear designer with one perplexing feature: her eyebrows, or rather, the lack of them. These she pencilled in. Their thickness, length, and place on her forehead varied with each visit, just like her clothes.

"Your waistline has come down six inches. That's a remarkable amount of fat to lose in three months." Hannah appreciated that abdominal fat is not only unattractive, but also a major health hazard. It made one more prone to various diseases such as diabetes and heart disease.

"Just where I wanted to lose it. This time I'm going to keep it off. To think I'm eating more food. Regular meals. All those fruits and vegetables are filling. I have a lot more energy. I'm even beginning to move and walk more like the models I work with," said Marsha with determination and pride as she scanned her food diary before looking up with a radiant smile.

Hannah had noticed that with her weight loss, her face even had more pleasing proportions, reminding her of a quote by Jean Anthelme Brillat-Savarin, author of *The Physiology of Taste*: "Nothing is so common as to see faces, once very interesting, made commonplace by obesity." Hannah kept this masterpiece, many believed the most famous book ever written about food, in the bookcase directly behind her office desk. First published in 1825, she frequently referenced her 1971 edition.

On this chilly fall day, Hannah was pleased as she put on her woollen coat and new raspberry suede gloves before leaving the office to meet Helen for lunch.

The Abacus restaurant, with its delicate shades of mauve and pink, was a relaxing setting. The Szechuan food was well flavoured and the flowers always fresh. They were seated at their favourite table near a window overlooking Mackay Street.

"You look well. You must be relieved now Robert knows." Helen, contented, settled back in her chair.

"Knows what?" said a startled Hannah.

"I thought you told him you were pregnant," Helen said warily as she placed her napkin on her lap.

"What gave you that idea?" Hannah leaned forward, almost knocking over the small vase of pink azaleas on the table.

"I just thought you had," replied Helen ineptly.

"No." Hannah was wondering how she got that idea. But she was far more concerned about Robert. He had not mentioned a word to her about her pregnancy, though he looked like he had something on his mind he wanted to say.

"Let's enjoy our lunch. It certainly is well presented." Helen was no doubt trying to refocus Hannah's thoughts away from Robert, sensing something was not right. Visibly uneasy, she started to eat her salad. After a few silent moments she added, "How do you feel?"

"My stomach is still off-key. I hate the feeling."

"Well, grin and bear it. It will pass, and you'll forget about it after you hold your baby. You know, being over forty, you'll have to have an amniocentesis."

"I know." Hannah knew it was important. But she didn't look forward to being prodded with a needle. She had also heard there was a slight possibility of losing her baby. That was a concern, but her major worry was Robert.

"Hannah, are you sure about your dates?"

"Yes, why do you ask?" Helen was probably trying to infer that based on the dates, it could not be Kurt's baby, but rather Robert's.

"You seem so much bigger than I remember being early in my pregnancies."

After a few minutes, Helen took up the conversation again. "It's little wonder the nutrition and fitness show you were on has been cancelled. Have you heard their latest?" Helen never missed a beat in the ongoing drama.

"Yes, from a patient." Hannah wanted to forget about the radio show and everything that connected her to it. No one else seemed to want to.

"Then you must know why they're off the air. It's now general knowledge the diet advice they gave made absolutely no sense."

"I feel so angry. People like Manson and Mace give any diet and nutrition advice they please and get away with it since they are not regulated like dietitians."

Looking out the window on the quiet street scene, Hannah remarked, "How Montreal has changed."

"I know."

"Remember Expo 67 and the 1976 Olympics? Montreal was Canada's economic and cultural centre."

"But Hannah, Montreal will come back, and we'll be here to enjoy it."

"I feel sorry for all those who've left. Who fled in fear." Hannah recalled all those who left behind their friends and families and businesses and homes that were sold for a fraction of their worth.

"You're right. I'll never leave. My family has lived here for three generations," Helen replied passionately.

A pause in their conversation provided Hannah time to simply relax and observe her surroundings. Seated at a table next to a wall covered with exquisite Asian fans was a group of stocky ladies, all wearing long jackets with exaggerated shoulder pads. They reminded her of the ladies she saw in her office. Like them, their shoulder pads expanded, as did their girths, while their jackets grew longer.

The night before, Hannah had dreamed she was the guest speaker at a luncheon. There she saw obese women bedecked in heavy gold chains and glittering diamond rings, mini-length skirts slit up the back, met by tall, tight-fitting boots, some of shiny patent leather, others plain or patterned leather, gulping down party sandwiches and oversized puffed pastry apple turnovers.

After her presentation, a lady of enormous girth approached her, wearing a striking pair of leopard-patterned glasses with a matching scarf and tall boots, crying for her to save her from her fat. Eyeing Hannah, she proclaimed, "You're too thin, too thin. Life is not fair. You can eat everything and not gain weight like me." Then she continued to fill her plate with copious amounts of pastry.

"Who said life was fair," Hannah heard herself screaming. Then she clenched her teeth to refrain from saying at the top of her lungs, "Who says you can eat everything in sight?" It was so painful. She woke up exhausted.

This was the type of individual Hannah knew she could never help by counselling. She would say she knew everything about food. She might very well have but never applied it. She would cite the most bizarre diet schemes and the most logical. Some would say she was addicted to food. This might well be, but most of all she was part of a permissive society full of people who believed they could do and eat anything they desired. No one or nothing could stop them. They hung their hopes on a magic pill, potion, or operation to banish their extra fat.

"I must get back to the house, and you'll be late for your next appointment if we don't hurry. Let's go." Helen looked at her watch. It was just past one thirty.

At the top of the Guy Street, Hannah said, "Drop me off here. I'll talk to you later."

Waiting to cross the street branching off in front of the First Church of Christ, Scientist, Hannah thought of the huge revenue the police could make if a ticket was given to everyone who went through the red light. The week before, a child coming home from school had been hit and injured. Even if the light was green, Hannah watched and waited for the cars to stop before crossing.

Just as she prepared to cross on the green light, a bright red sports car zipped through the red light. She questioned if her eyes, or mind, were playing tricks with her. It looked like Dr. Mace going through the light: the small frame, the mop of black hair, the chiselled-out nose she had observed closely when he was on during her last radio show. After lunch, he could have been speeding up the hill to return to work at the hospital.

"I just saw another car go through the light," Hannah remarked to Dr. Fred Marble, who was walking by.

"They always go through the light," he said with a twinge of annoyance. Then he added, "I wish they'd do something about it. It's dangerous. With the schools close by, there're so many children in the area."

Then he ran across on the red light.

Hannah watched the light turn green and started to cross. Looking up toward the oncoming traffic, she saw the same red car as before coming directly toward her. She quickly jumped to the side. It was the last thing she could remember before she woke up in the hospital emergency ward, where Dr. Allen Cape was standing beside her bed.

"No, no, no. I'm pregnant," she was screaming as he bent over trying to calm her down.

"You're lucky. You and your baby are fine," said Dr. Cape.

Robert had just arrived and was in the corridor outside her curtained-off area when Dr. Cape came out.

"She has some bad bruises and lacerations and a possible fractured wrist. In her condition, it's important for us to keep a close eye on everything. We'll keep her overnight. You'll have to excuse me. I have an emergency."

Dr. Cape was gone before Robert could thank him. He straightened his tie and entered the small cubicle.

"I came as soon as I heard. We'll have plenty of time to talk later. For now, you must rest," Robert insisted as he bent over to kiss her.

Hannah had no idea if Robert knew she was pregnant, or time to find out, before an orderly arrived.

"Madam Epstein, we're going to do an X-ray of your wrist now. You'll need to cover your abdomen with a lead sheet," he announced.

As Quebecers are required, Hannah had her maiden name on her Medicare card and all her official documents. This rule was instated after the passing of the 1976 Quebec Charter of Rights.

Robert accompanied her across the hall to radiology and waited in an adjoining room while they took her into a stark white room full of X-ray equipment. A few minutes later, they wheeled Hannah out.

A tall, lanky resident, all dressed in white, who reminded Hannah of Jonathan, met them in the corridor. "Hello, I'm Dr. Steven Stern. Her right wrist is fractured. We'll bring Madam Epstein to the plaster room and have a cast put on."

Hannah, with Robert at her side, watched as the white plaster cast was carefully molded around her right arm to just below her elbow, then dried. The brightly lit plaster room accentuated the network of deep lines on Robert's face, the dark grey circles under his eyes, even the wrinkles on his neck, making him appear older than his fifty-six years. Hannah felt concerned for his well-being, as she had been since their marriage.

"We're moving you into a private room now. You'll be more comfortable," said Dr. Stern.

"Robert, I'll be fine. You go home and get some rest. I'll see you tomorrow."

He did not resist her suggestion.

CHAPTER THIRTY

With her belongings piled next to her on the narrow gurney, an orderly wheeled Hannah down the dimly lit corridor to the elevator. Here, healthy young people elbowed their way into the crammed elevator in front of the patients. She could never understand why these active people did not take the stairs, as she always did. The elongated window on each level of the stair rewarded one with a view of the ever-changing mountain flora.

From the elevator they proceeded along another extended corridor to her room, where she was deposited on a high hospital bed with a grey metal frame. Her clothes and purse were placed in a tall grey metal locker like the ones she remembered lined the corridors of her high school – the ones with the combination locks that never seemed to want to open, especially when she was late for class. Today, she was in no hurry to go anywhere. Since the locker closure and lock were broken, and no one had bothered to have them repaired, the door remained ajar when the orderly placed her belongings inside.

"It will be okay. If you need anything, simply ring the bell," he said and left.

Over the bed was one fluorescent light tube, which flickered on when Hannah pulled the makeshift frayed white bandage pull replacing the original metal chain. The colour scheme of the small, square room, from the painted walls, to the metal locker, to the one metal chair with the vinyl plastic seat, to the commode with the patterned Arborite top, was various shades of grey.

The windowsills were also grey metal, as were the window frames and the radiator-covers. Hannah decided that everything in the room, even the grey linoleum on the floor, dated back to 1952, the year the structure was built, except for one wooden chair with an orange vinyl plastic seat sitting in the corner. When the hospital was furnished, metal, vinyl, plastic and linoleum were the modern materials considered appropriate for a health facility because of their presumed sanitary properties.

Signs of decline and neglect were everywhere, in the threadbare white polyester and cotton sheets, too short for the mattresses they struggled to cover; in the heavy white china teacups with their hairline cracks; and in the small stainless-steel teapots with broken lids, served on scratched and chipped orange plastic food trays covered with unappealing pale green paper mats.

Even the nurses, attired in pale pink or mint green polyester uniforms evoking memories of waitresses in greasy spoon cafeterias, often located in run-down hotels on the wrong side of town, seemed immune to their environment and their sense of propriety. Hannah felt like an uneasy guest in a sleazy hotel that had seen better times.

In stark contrast to the deteriorating interior was the solid brick exterior. A continuous band of south-facing windows provided Hannah with a view of the city and the Saint Lawrence River beyond. This spectacular vista made her feel alive and a part of the city, not someone confined to the sombre inner workings of a run-down hospital.

The hospital, which was located on very valuable real estate high on the mountain, signified the high esteem medicine was held in at the time it was built.

Now there were rumblings of change. According to appointed hospital consultants, the hospital needed more space for high-tech equipment. Renovation would be too expensive. A new location to build a totally new health care facility was recommended. They were calling for an outside, independent evaluation.

Hungry developers were already conferring with hospital boards, as they anxiously awaited word on the take-over the old hospital and the valuable land it occupied, on the pretence they were helping the city rid itself of an outdated facility.

According to inside information from hospital board members connected to the railway, the word was there soon would be extensive tracts of land available when the rail yards closed. Mind you, it would be highly polluted and away from the medical school and the downtown population concentration. Besides decontamination, it would require a new road structure to access before a stone was laid. On speculation, developers were quickly buying up real estate in the vicinity of the old railroads. They were waiting and ready. As one businessman said, "If the hospital moves, the opportunities are mind-boggling." The city board of trade had already given its support.

Removed from her familiar surroundings, Hannah recalled when she had first met Jonathan in the corridors of this very building. Then, it was a hospital graced with nurses dressed in spotless, starched white uniforms and caps, constantly making rounds to assure their patients were well attended.

It was a time when dreams were within reach. Hannah and Jonathan had found a ground-floor apartment with a small front yard near Saint Lawrence Boulevard in Montreal's immigrant area. When frost was no longer a threat, they planted vegetables and flowers on their small plot of land, giving them a sense of independence and place.

Hannah closed her eyes and remembered the small red-brick neighbourhood synagogue built in the late 1800s, with its enchanting arched windows and entrance. The Bagg Street Shul located at the intersection of Clark Street and Bagg Street in the Plateau region of the city resembled structures in the pictures of synagogues in the old country, Poland.

In the shul, the men sat praying downstairs on the first floor, while the women climbed a steep flight of shaky wooden stairs to the upper balcony, where they occupied long wooden benches covered with deep red velvet pillows. From high up, they looked down on the worn wooden walls painted an eggshell blue, and the colourful stained-glass windows enclosed the men as they prayed. Like Hannah, they must have often pondered the fate of the women who came before them to share this space. On cool fall and winter days, dressed in unpretentious woollen dresses, or on the occasional warm day, cotton frocks, the small group of women sat together praying to the same God, all with different dreams and expectations. The Plateau area attracted a diverse cross section of Jews. For Hannah, life was full of promise. Her thoughts were soon disrupted by a knock on the door.

"May I come in?" a voice called out.

"Yes," said Hannah.

"How are you doing, Madam Epstein?" asked the young man with a stethoscope around his neck, wearing the outfit of a medical resident: white pants and jacket.

"Fine."

He looked down at her chart and then up at her. "We'll probably be letting you go home tomorrow. We just want to keep an eye on you overnight."

CHAPTER THIRTY-ONE

Robert had not disclosed to Hannah an innocent remark by Helen congratulating him on the impending new addition to his family. It was made a few days before the accident had revealed her pregnancy. It sent him into a rage. Mad thoughts ran through his mind. What would an orthodox rabbi advise — a divorce?

Now, on reflection, he appreciated there was a bright side to Hannah's pregnancy and was ashamed of his initial reaction. He realized that in spite of the child being fathered by another man, he would have all the pride of fatherhood to treasure. What better way to camouflage his health concerns and to appear young and vigorous?

Many other things became clear to him. If Hannah had not been pregnant, she might not have married so expediently, or for that matter, at all.

Robert's major preoccupation and fear was his own health. Even his long-time physician, Dr. Joseph Meyers, could not explain his numerous infections. He recommended Robert seek the advice of another specialist in the San Francisco area who had treated a number of similar cases. He expressed the high possibility it was contagious, spread in the semen. This petrified Robert. He was willing to pay any price to find a cure.

*

Arriving home from the hospital in time for dinner, Hannah was famished. All she relished was pizza with anchovies. Since the kitchen was under renovation, they had little choice but to order in.

Once seated at the table, Hannah could no longer contain herself. She burst out, "I was hoping to tell you about the pregnancy before we were married, but it just never happened."

She paused, looking directly at him. "I suppose just like you didn't discuss your health problems, I didn't discuss my pregnancy. You know what it's like. You somehow think the right moment will come, and with time things will resolve themselves."

"I see," he replied, reflecting on what she said. Then, after a moment, looking over at Hannah, he must have realized how pregnant she was and how he had been so preoccupied with himself he had never even noticed. "All being well, our child will be born and give us much pleasure. Hannah, I wish I could be as hopeful about my health. Things seem to be getting more and more complicated."

He looked so downhearted, Hannah wished she had not been so outspoken, or at least had waited until after they had eaten to discuss their problems. Then she would have been more relaxed.

She reached over and took his hand. "Please, tell me what you have found out about what bothers you. Is there anything new?"

"Nothing encouraging." He explained the best he could what the doctor had told him.

"I'm sure they will get to the bottom of this. We just have to be patient. We have many, many years ahead of us together to enjoy our relationship. Waiting for me is no problem," Hannah assured him and herself.

Twelve years had passed since the death of his wife. Ultimately, entering into a marriage with a compatible, fruitful woman was something expected of him, a successful businessman and philanthropist. He wanted to quash any rumours that he was bisexual. He was beginning to suspect his lifestyle could have contributed to his health problem.

Hannah was increasingly distracted by the pain radiating up her entire right arm, particularly at night when she tried to sleep. At times, the cast became so tight, it felt like it was cutting off the entire circulation to her hand. She feared losing her fingers. To relieve the pressure, she had to elevate her arm. Doing everything with her left arm was cumbersome, though as the days passed, she was becoming more proficient at using it.

A week after returning home, Hannah was still waiting for a call from the police station. Her anxiety did not go unnoticed by Robert. He looked up over his morning newspaper and asked, "Hannah, is something bothering you?"

"I still haven't heard from the police station about my accident. What should I do?"

"Hannah, don't worry. We'll have to wait to hear from them."

The telephone rang.

"It's for you, Hannah," said Robert.

Hannah took the call in the next room. It was the producer from the CWQR TV Station.

"I almost forgot," Hannah said to Robert after she hung up the receiver. "I have a CWQR TV interview for tomorrow. I must look up the figures."

"How much are they paying you for the interview?"

"Nothing."

"You mean they asked you to do research, look up figures, and do a show for nothing?"

"The figures were my idea." She was conscientious. She never knew what she could be asked and wanted to be prepared.

"That's ridiculous. Tell them to get someone else. Some other sucker. You don't need to work for nothing." Robert was unusually irate. No doubt he was fed up with anything to do with the media.

Of course, Robert was right, to a degree. Why should she work for nothing? On the other hand, she enjoyed doing the shows. She also felt an obligation to share her knowledge. Who would do the show if she didn't? There certainly were plenty of quacks waiting to spew their verbal venom.

At one time, Hannah was flattered when asked to comment on radio or television. That was until she found out the stations invited many dietitians to participate in their programs, but most refused. No doubt they refused because there was no remuneration and hardly a thank-you.

Labour day weekend she recalled being asked to be available Sunday morning, between six and seven, to comment on the recent increase in olive oil consumption. She got up early, read over her notes, and waited for their call. They never rang until later in the day. They simply said there was breaking news, and they had run out of time.

*

A day after Robert left for San Francisco, Helen telephoned and said she was on her way over. She had some news.

"Hey, you look good," said Helen as Hannah greeted her at the door.

Once seated over tea, Helen proclaimed, "Have you heard the latest news about the characters on that nutty radio show you were on?" Before Hannah could answer, Helen continued, "Jeff saw Dr. Mace in the hospital. He was walking around on crutches and was all bruised up." She added in a in sarcastic tone, "Do you think Manson beat him up? Blamed him for the radio show cancellation because of his nutty ideas?" Helen relished her role as the informer.

"I don't know," replied Hannah, half-suspecting Robert had a hand in it. After she told him how they had treated her on the show, he probably had one of his goons do the job.

Even the brief time they had been together, she realized he took care of things his way. He could very well have had both of them beaten up.

"When you're dealing with such a bunch of lowlifes, anything is possible. It's just like those old gangster movies. Each gangster has to watch his back."

"True."

"I must be on my way. We'll see you in the country."

Hannah had not shared with Helen her concern for Robert's health or his impotence. Though she knew, with Helen's acute perception of human frailties, like sickness and love, it would merely be a matter of time before she found out.

When Robert returned, Hannah was surprised to see he had the start of a beard. "Do you like it?"

"It's a nice change. Any news from the doctors?"

"It's wait-and-see. As I've said before, don't get discouraged. Are we still going to the country on Friday? I have some work to finish up."

"Yes, we'll leave early to avoid the traffic."

Robert left the room. Hannah could see him placing some manila envelopes in the front hall safe. Each time he did, her curiosity spiked.

*

After lunch on Friday, Robert and Hannah left for the country. On arrival, an exhilarating nip in the air greeted them. Following a restful day, on Saturday evening Helen and Jeff joined them for dinner.

Hannah had prepared and frozen tomato sauce slowly cooked in her favourite heavy iron pot, which leeched extra iron. To the sauce, she added dried chanterelle mushrooms from their old growth forest, oregano, parsley, sweet basil, and stevia from her garden. Since stevia is a hundred times sweeter than sugar, a few crumbled leaves were adequate to add a touch of sweetness. Although it grows easily in northern Canada, she wondered why it was not used as a non-caloric sugar substitute. The sauce she served over multigrain spaghetti.

A dark green salad, crusty Italian bread, cheeses from the nearby Abbey Saint-Benoît-du-Lac, fresh fruit, and her famously satisfying chocolate fudge pudding cake completed the late fall meal.

During his last bout of flu, Robert had lost his sense of smell. Apart from sweet, salty, sour, bitter, and umami (the taste elicited by glutamate), he could not perceive food flavours. The doctor told him his loss of smell could be temporary, and in a month or two it might return. Preparing satisfying meals for Robert was now a challenge. Texture, temperature, colour, and appearance were major considerations. Hannah was aware that people who lose their smell also lose a significant amount of their ability to enjoy eating.

As they relaxed over dessert, the doorbell chimed.

"We're not expecting anyone," Robert said as he got up to answer the door. A minute later, he returned. "It was a neighbour warning us that there have been a number of robberies in the neighbourhood."

"Have you ever had a break-in?" asked Jeff.

"No, never," Robert assured him.

"You're lucky, since you have a lot of valuables," responded Jeff, who had always been amazed to see such an impressive art collection in the country house.

"I'm not lucky. Everyone knows not to bother me." Robert continued, "Well, there was one incident. About twenty years ago, in the dead of winter, I hear my dogs howling. I ran down to find an intruder. I shot over his head with a rifle. I lined him up against the wall and made him strip naked. Then I told him to get walking. About an hour later, I found him outside and gave him back his clothes. I phoned the police and told them there was a naked man on my property. For two years, I never heard a word about the intruder. Then, one day on Main Street in Magog, I ran into one of the local police. He said, 'You know, Robert, that fellow you called about. The one who was naked? Well, we found him. He was trying to tell us some foolish story that you'd stripped him. He was delirious. We took him to the Providence Hospital. He had severe frostbite. They had to amputate three of his fingers and four of his toes. Poor fellow.'"

Robert looked up and added, "None of the local hoods ever come near my place."

"Well," Jeff muttered, "I see why no one comes near here. That's quite a story."

Helen looked mesmerized. Then after a few silent moments, she said, "So everyone still remembers."

"I hope so," replied Robert as he got up and straightened one of his larger paintings.

"I'm surprised you reacted so quickly." Jeff was wrestling with his words. He could not believe what he had heard. For him, a man who had devoted his life to helping people avoid any bodily harm, it was difficult to picture such an inhuman act. But of course, he did not know the details. The intruder may have had a gun and was threatening Robert, or have tried to rob him before, or tried to cause destruction to his property.

"I felt I had to. I had my wife to consider as well. At times, she came out here alone. I had to send a message; I wouldn't tolerate deviant behaviour on my property. It wasn't the material possessions. There's lots where they came from."

"Would you do it again?" Jeff curiosity had been piqued.

"I wouldn't. Now I'd have one of my men take care of the problem. I'm not as young or naïve now. I was really bluffing it. I could have been in big trouble. He could have had a gun and taken me down. He also could have had accomplices with him."

After a few moments of thought, Jeff added, "These situations are always more complex than you imagine."

All night, Robert's story resonated through Hannah's mind. Robert seemed to be capable of anything. Could he possibly have had a hand in Jonathan's death? He had enough goons to call on to do any job. That Jonathan was shot with more than one bullet was suspicious. A hunter, she believed, would have used only one. She could not dismiss his demeanour at Jonathan's funeral or his unwillingness to discuss Jonathan's death. But why Jonathan? She had never shown any affection for Robert. It had to be something else, something she had no idea of.

The next day, they packed up and left for Montreal. The city was grey with low-hanging clouds. Hannah was anxious to have her cast removed.

Six weeks to the day since the cast was applied, it was sawed off. Her fingers and wrist were stiff and painful. She was amazed at the muscle wasting that occurred with a lack of movement. Her right hand was thin and delicate, like that of a lady of leisure; it also had long, hard, attractive nails, unlike her well-used left hand.

It would take weeks of physiotherapy to bring her arm and hand back to normal.

CHAPTER THIRTY-TWO

Hannah's obstetrician confirmed her suspicions. The ultrasound revealed she was expecting twins. He explained to her the difficulties she could encounter giving birth after age forty, particularly to twins. Hannah was ecstatic and would have liked to dance down the street and shout her joy out to every passerby. Arriving home, reality set in. She felt frightened and apprehensive.

As always, Robert's worsening health problems overshadowed her other concerns. Recently, much of his travelling was devoted to seeking medical advice. Now there was another shadow surfacing, one even more stressful than his vanishing health – his tendency to brutality. Hannah knew it was not good for her or her babies to dwell on these problems. She had to keep calm and focused on the positive things in her life: the beauty of the moment, happy memories, which often included Kurt, and above all, the anticipation of the new additions to her family.

In the evenings, when the carpenters had left, Hannah's thoughts often turned to Kurt. She pondered whether her children would inherit his deep blue eyes and flaxen hair, his quick, creative mind, and his charismatic presence. Answering the telephone, she hoped to hear his voice, but it never happened. Then she would wonder, what she would say to him?

Tabloid headlines furtively scanned at the supermarket checkout counter were her main confirmation of his existence.

*

In early March, Hannah and Robert flew to New York to attend Aaron's much-anticipated wedding. Robert was pleased Hannah had chosen to complement her flowing, Wedgwood-blue silk dress with the diamond necklace he had given her — a magnificent, eye-catching necklace Hannah was hoping would distract from her growing girth.

When they arrived at the opulent, newly completed hotel, already bustling with guests and caterers, a circus-like air prevailed. Jeff and Helen greeted them with open arms. "It's wonderful to see you."

Standing next to them was Avrum. "It's certainly a bustling wedding. I've been to many. This is one of the liveliest."

A tall, dark-haired woman nursing a colourful drink came over and joined the conversation. "So you're his Montreal friends?"

"We are," responded Helen, "And you're Avrum's New York friend?"

Before she could answer, Aaron appeared with his bride. "Robert, we appreciated your help in obtaining the extraordinary diamond for the engagement ring."

"You can also thank Avrum. He chose it. That's his expertise, choosing diamonds," declared Robert as he and everyone else demanded a close look at the ring.

On the wedding day, the continuous flow of food and drinks, starting with mammoth platters of hors d'oeuvres, was mind-boggling. After the official wedding ceremony, there was a sit-down dinner, followed by an abundant sweets table and dancing. Over four hundred people attended, including rabbis from New York and beyond.

If Helen and Jeff were disturbed by the ostentatious nature of their son's wedding, they hid it well. They were glowing with pride.

Hannah kept thinking about diamonds. Where were all these diamonds coming from? She wanted to get to the root of this. Yet she knew that for now she had more immediate concerns: her pregnancy and Robert's illness.

In the early hours of the morning on May 24, 1982, Hannah, with Robert's insistence, left the comfort of her home for the maternity ward of the hospital.

Hannah would have preferred to give birth at home, instead of the unfamiliar hospital environment. But at forty-five years of age, she was well aware of the complications she could encounter, as had one of her heroines, Émilie du Châtelet, the most famous female physicist of the seventeenth century, who six days after giving birth died of an embolism at the age of forty-three.

In spite of all the medical advances, Hannah was dismayed by obstetricians' attitudes toward the pregnancies of older women. She sensed that her own obstetrician did not greet her pregnancy with enthusiasm. She recalled that at a symposium four years ago a physician voiced his opposition to pregnancy after forty years of age. Another group of male physicians at the symposium were opposed to abortions.

These were the random thoughts filling Hannah's mind as she lay in the delivery room on a high, flat, narrow bed surrounded by bright lights and a full array of instruments. This obstetrical equivalent of the surgical operating room Hannah found intimidating. She pondered why-she could not be in a comfortable room.

Now the pain was becoming more intense. She was fortunate to have stayed home through the first part of her labour. Because of her age, her obstetrician suggested a caesarean section, which Hannah resisted, much to his displeasure. She told herself she could do it. She was prepared for the wait. Reluctantly, she consented to an epidural to ease the pain.

As the sun began to set, the cries of her firstborn, a son, filled the room. Hannah had never felt so much love. Six minutes later, her daughter was born.

In Hannah's eyes, they were the most beautiful babies she had ever seen. Quietly, she said the names, David and Sarah, the names Hannah and Robert had decided upon long before their birth. David was the name of Hannah's father, Sarah the name of Robert and Hannah's mothers. Within minutes of their arrival, they were placed at her breasts to benefit from her first milk, colostrum.

Robert was anxiously waiting in the adjacent room. Years ago, his father had told him the delivery room was no place for a husband. Dressed in a dark blue Italian-cut suit seen more frequently in a boardroom than in a hospital, he stood in awe as he watched the newborn twins feeding at Hannah's swollen breasts. Hannah smiled and tried to put him at ease.

After the nurse had taken the children, Hannah reached forward and took Robert's hands in hers. "You're cold. Are you tired?"

"It's you who must be tired. You need your rest. I'll be back later. Try to get some sleep."

*

Shortly after supper, Robert returned clutching a gigantic bouquet of deep red roses wrapped in layers of cellophane. Without saying a word, he placed them in Hannah's outstretched arms. Carefully unwrapping the magnificent blossoms, a wave of sadness overtook her, just as when she had received roses from Robert before they were married and had wished they were from Kurt.

"They're such a wonderful colour. I'll have them put in water."

After the nurse left, from his briefcase Robert handed Hannah a long silver box. "I hope you like them. They were specially chosen for you. The salesman was a great help. He even asked me your colouring."

Placing the long, opera-length pearl necklace around Hannah's neck, he fastened the clasp. As her fingers moved over their smooth, satiny surface, for an instant Hannah thought once again of the young salesman who many years ago had slipped a similar expensive string of pearls around her neck.

"They're perfect on you. The proprietor was right. They're your colour." Robert looked pleased as he sat down. "It is one of a kind. The clasp was designed for you. Turn it over."

"I love pearls. The clasp is exquisite." Hannah noticed on the other side of the diamond clasp was a heart-shaped red gem set in white gold. "It's so unusual."

"It's a garnet. Did you know garnets and diamonds are often found in diamond mines together? The clasp can also to be worn at the front, whether you wear the necklace as a single or double strand."

"I will treasure them. As much as I'd like to wear them, you must take them home for safekeeping." Robert carefully unfastened the diamond and garnet clasp and placed the pearls in Hannah's hand.

After holding the pearls for a moment, she returned them to their silver box.

Robert put the box back in his briefcase and gently kissed Hannah. "I'll see you tomorrow. Sleep well."

When he left, Hannah could still register his exhausted appearance.

It occurred to her that pearls were like-life; they were not perfect, though they might appear so. Each pearl had its imperfections. Hannah could love imperfections, but not lies and brutality.

*

Once at home with the twins, Hannah became restless and distressed about Kurt. How could she keep the news of the birth of his children from him? She confided her uneasy feelings to Helen. "I feel so badly. Kurt should be here. He should know."

"Hannah, you're making yourself miserable for nothing. If Kurt cared about you, he'd have gotten in touch with you after he left you in Montreal."

"Maybe he couldn't."

"That I doubt. It's not good for you, or the babies, for you to torture yourself."

"I know you're right, but..."

"But what? You hate to be happy."

"It eats at me."

"Forget it. At least for now, give yourself a break. By the way, I made your chocolate pudding cake, the one you served in the country last fall. It was fabulous. I made it for some visiting cardiologists. No one could believe it had such nutritious ingredients, and no added fat, and it seemed so rich and moist. And it's so simple to make."

"I've been thinking of coming out with a line of food products. I've always wanted to."

"Sounds like a good idea. That'll keep you busy."

"And out of trouble, right? That's when I have the time. I'm simply thinking about it."

"A good thing to think about."

"Hi, Helen." Robert walked in with a pile of manila envelopes.

"I didn't even hear you come in. When did you get home?" asked Hannah.

"A few moments ago."

"What kind of strict diet do you have Robert on? I need it." Helen was eyeing Robert, who looked unusually slender in his dapper grey suit.

"I don't."

"Maybe you're too busy to eat?"

"I'll leave you two to chat. I've got some work to finish." Robert left them to talk.

"I hope he didn't hear us talking about the twins."

*

On the eighth day after the twins' birth, before the traditional Brit Milah, or bris, linking a child to his Jewish brothers throughout the world, Hannah watched Robert fondly cradling his son. With his newly grown beard, he reminded her of the statue of Saint Joseph holding the infant Jesus on the Sulpician grounds.

Hannah turned around to see Helen and Jeff.

"You look like you're in another world. We came early."

"Thank you for coming early. I really need you." Like all first-time mothers, Hannah was apprehensive.

"David will do fine. He's healthy and strong. Relax. Rabbi Moshe Fineman is the best mohel one can find. He circumcised our son. A fabulous fellow, and so skilled."

"Well, all went well," said Helen after the circumcision was completed. "Now I see how the decorating has come together. It's a wonderful job you've done on the house. It's like a different house."

"Yes, I'm pleased, particularly since we finished before the twins arrived. Let's have something to eat." Hannah led the way to the food-laden table where everyone was gathered.

"Congratulations, they're gorgeous children," said Avrum, who had been quietly observing the room.

"Thank you, Avrum, and thank you for your lovely gift." Hannah was happy to see him. "How are you? I don't see you as much as I used to."

"I'm pretty busy, travelling a lot. I'm the youngest son of a family of five. There's always events to attend." Avrum seemed more relaxed than Hannah had ever seen him. She pondered if something had changed in is life.

"Where does your family live?" Hannah knew he was American.

"Most live in Queens, New York. I'm the black sheep. The only one who left the U.S., also the only one not married." Just as Hannah thought how wonderful it was to have the time to converse with Avrum, Robert came over to introduce him to a fellow guest.

Helen, joining Hannah, said, looking toward Avrum, "Avrum is an attractive man."

"He is. Rather a mystery. I'm still trying to get to know him." Hannah was always perplexed by how little she knew about him.

"He's American, as you might know. He attended Columbia for undergrad and Harvard for business."

"Hardly the black sheep, as he said. But how did Robert meet up with him?" To Hannah, Avrum and Robert together in business always seemed strange. They were so different.

"He apparently graduated in business, was looking for a job, ended up here. I've heard pieces of his story. I'm sure one day he'll tell you about his adventures and why he came here."

"He and Robert get along well. They always seem to be conferring about something. I wish I knew what." She thought it might help explain his frequent travels.

CHAPTER THIRTY-THREE

Over the next four years, apart from the twins, Hannah was occupied with the house, the cultivation of rare plants and herbs, the development of new recipes, and, as always, her writing. But it was not those tasks that exhausted her, causing her to fall into bed in despair at the end of the day. It was her continuous worry over Robert's health, his weight loss, fatigue, and frequent bouts of flu. Lately he had developed strange-looking purple bumps on his arms and legs.

As Robert withered away, Hannah noted the appearance of every man she met. She analyzed their skin tone, carriage, and walk for signs of affliction and compared them to Robert. It was like when her feet ached; she would become transfixed by others' feet, wondering how they managed to find properly fitting shoes. She longed for a solution to his condition so she could forget about illness and concentrate on living.

One frigid day in December, winter showed its more forgiving face. Bright sunshine streamed through the sunroom windows, bouncing off the ornate, shiny silver teapot, accentuating the deepening lines on Robert's face. Outside, the chirping and pecking sparrows continued to fight for a place on the bird feeder. A plump sparrow dominated the feeder, threatening any approaching birds, a reminder to Hannah that nature's bounty was not always equally shared.

"Hannah, I'm happy to see you using my grandmother's Birks tea set," said Robert, sitting back on the plush, down-filled pillows covering the wicker sofa.

"I love it. With its heavily embossed pattern, I don't have to worry about scratching it."

"My grandmother always served from it. She received it as a wedding gift."

"As much as I appreciate the lines of my Petersen teapot, I fear marring its unadorned surface." Hannah knew her Petersen teapot was much more valuable than the Birks – a shame to keep it in the cabinet. She thought next time she entertained she would use it.

Hannah had recently taken a particular fondness to the grandiose, elaborately decorated Victorian tea set. The Canadian-made Birks set of copper, heavily plated with silver, had a pleasing swirling pattern.

Pensively watching Hannah pouring tea into willow-patterned china teacups, Robert looked up at David, who was happily playing with Sarah, and observed, "He seems to strut just like Kurt."

"And Sarah?"

"Oh, she's just like you." A smile spread across his face as he continued to sip his tea with a homemade scone still warm from the oven loaded with clotted cream and strawberry jam.

"I miss you terribly." Hannah squeezed his hand and kissed him.

"I do have business. Also, I hope to find a solution to my health problems. I love you, Hannah."

"It's hard for you." Hannah could not think of anything worse than not being well, and not knowing why.

"You're the brave one. Tomorrow I leave again. I understand you have many questions."

"I do. I question everything, but your health is the most important thing to me. I wish I knew more about your business. Maybe I could help you?"

"It would be good if you did know more about it. Avrum has been very much involved in my latest ventures. It's been exciting, going in different directions. We'll talk when I return."

Leaving Robert to answer his messages, Hannah went to the dining room. Carefully removing her Petersen teapot from the cabinet, her mind drifted back to the day she answered the Gazette advertisement.

"I'm selling the tea set for my mother, who received it as a wedding present in the forties." The woman hesitated a minute and added, "I hate cleaning silver. I think she also is tired of cleaning it."

"I can see how the decorations of entwining bunches of grapes at the top would be difficult to clean," said Hannah, running her hand over the smooth surface of the rotund teapot as she carefully examined it. One after the other, she picked up the remaining pieces of the tea set, the tall coffeepot, the globular cream and sugar, and the sizeable square tray, and checked for imperfections. There were none, not even a scratch. It had been packed away all these years and never used.

A reasonable price was asked. There was no need to negotiate further. Hannah had learned, if the price is right, do not quibble. You could ruin the deal.

With the tea set wrapped in layers of newspaper and placed back in the old Steinberg's grocery shopping bag it had been stored in for years, Hannah was about to say goodbye when the lady remarked, "You're so fit. I've been trying to get into good shape, seeing a nutritionist."

"Good, I'm a dietitian-nutritionist."

"You ought to do something about your colleagues. The one I saw needs disciplining. Whom should I report her to?"

This sudden outburst was totally unexpected. At first Hannah hesitated, then she asked, "Who was the nutritionist?"

"It was Robin Beachwood. You know, I wasn't going to pay her because what she said was so ridiculous. I was to stop eating all wheat products. I'd never had trouble with wheat. She grabbed my arm and threatened me if I didn't pay her. She's mad."

"Robin Beachwood is no nutritionist. Why don't you complain to the Better Business Bureau?"

"You might have heard, she's left town. Rather, was run out of town."

"You're not alone. Many people were enraged and hurt by her, particularly by the advice she had for children."

*

It's well known that a parent's love for their child is so strong, they will go to extraordinary lengths to help them. Thus, hefty sums of money can easily be extracted. Obviously, Robin Beachwood understood that well.

From her first encounter with Robin Beachwood a number of years ago, Hannah realized she had no legitimate credentials or even common sense or conscience. Mike Manson, the CBSB radio station's self-styled, so-called exercise expert, was of the same ilk.

Hannah recalled when he announced on the air that in order to lose body fat, one must eat lots of fatty foods. He did not understand their initial rapid weight loss was water due to an extremely low carbohydrate intake. She tried to explain to him the only way to lose body fat is to eat less calories than your body uses. Since he persevered with his strange fat-loss theory, she suggested they consult an expert in the area. "Why, a Ph.D. is worthless," he remarked. Hannah laughed at the time, thinking he must have met a lot of people with fake doctorates, even Robin Beachwood, who paid fifteen thousand dollars for a Ph.D. in nutrition from Donsbach University, a nonaccredited correspondence school in California with a shady reputation.

The Beachwoods and Mansons made desperate people their victims. Preying on the frailties and hopelessness of the obese, sick, and lonely was a more lucrative way to make a living than selling encyclopedias or shirts. Since they were members of no recognized professional nutrition or dietetic association, they had no one to answer to, no professional license to protect, and nothing to lose, as long as they were not exposed, and people did not register complaints with the Better Business Bureau.

Hannah suspected Clara Green was the driving force behind Robin Beachwood's departure. Clara had once said she owed nothing to anyone. Her sole aim in life was to make herself happy. Robin must have ceased giving her any pleasure or satisfaction. In all likelihood, her advice caused her much confusion and unnecessary aggravation.

*

Nine years ago, on a stormy winter afternoon that had closed down the entire city, Clara had miraculously appeared in Hannah's nutrition office for advice on how to shed fifteen pounds recently acquired on a trip to Mexico. She declared, "It was the endless flow of tequila."

Hannah could still picture her in a long, loose white T-shirt, black tights, and black aerobic shoes, over which was draped a full-length black female mink coat that brushed the floor as she walked. No doubt, the coat length had been measured when she was wearing heels.

This day, as on all subsequent visits, she wore an identical outfit, including a medium-length, double string of perfectly matched Tiffany pearls, a gold bracelet watch — the kind you see advertised in *Architectural Digest* — and a ring with an oval ruby in the centre surrounded by brilliant diamonds. She never removed her jewellery when she was weighed, or, for that matter, when she exercised at the gym. Her jewellery, she explained, was a part of her. All she ever carried was a small, black, woven-leather Bottega Veneta purse about three inches square. From it dangled a chain with a remote control that opened the doors to her black Jaguar.

Within a few weeks, Hannah found herself frequently in Clara's company. They even took trips together, an unusual gesture for Hannah, who rarely struck up friendships with her clients.

Brazenly declaring herself a nonpracticing Orthodox Jew, Clara shopped when other Jews were praying on Yom Kippur, the most sacred of Jewish holidays, and justified it by saying, "It's not where you carry your feet or what you carry in your hands that counts. It's what you carry in your heart and soul." She also added, laughing, "None of the observant Jews will see me shopping. They are busy praying for their souls. A good time to shop."

Everyday habits she took for granted, Clara made Hannah question. Clara never read the daily newspaper, proclaiming with pride, "If it's something I must know, I'll find out. Why waste my time?"

In spite of, or perchance because of their differences, Clara and Hannah became close friends, until Hannah questioned the advice given her by Robin Beachwood. Clara had rewarded Robin with generous sums of money for her unorthodox advice on everything from marriage to diet.

After many years of being an important part of her life, Hannah missed the time she had spent with Clara.

*

On one of her frequent visits, Helen surprised Hannah with the latest on the continued saga of the CBSB radio station cast, which Hannah thought was history.

"Jeff tells me Dr. Mace has found a big drug company to back his clinic. He'll be trying out a new drug to reduce cholesterol levels. Mace tells his patients they can eat anything they like."

"I doubt it's that simple. The pills simply give one license to eat anything."

"He has this hypothesis: clogged arteries have little to do with diet. So, to cure it, all that's needed is exercise plus this cholesterol-lowering drug."

Hannah did not feel in the mood, or have the energy to debate his theory.

She reflected a minute and said, "No one wants to hear about curbing their appetite when there's an alternate quick fix. The drugs might become a problem, rather than a cure. We'll have to wait and see."

Then Helen added, "Do you know exercise man Mike Manson is back again?"

"Another reincarnation? What's he up to now? I hate to ask." Hannah did not even want to imagine how crazy he could get.

"He's opened a liquid vitamin supplement store. He's trying to convince everyone they need this stuff to gain muscle. He's doing infomercials on it." Helen didn't add that some of her best friends were sold on his liquid vitamin supplements. They thought the supplements would help them lose weight.

"What a racket. It's a lucrative business. Anything for a buck. You can sell infinite amounts of pills and potions. It's such a waste of time talking about it. Let's have tea." Hannah had heard this approach so often; it was tiring to discuss again.

"I see Robert continues to travel a lot. I thought he'd stay home more with the children, now that they're older." Helen sounded concerned.

"This is his lifestyle. He has a lot of business to attend to."

"Aren't you afraid to let him roam alone, far from home? He could be enticed by a fair-haired damsel," said Helen, half-joking.

"I suppose I'll have to take my chances." *Obviously,* Hannah thought, *Helen does not understand how sick Robert is.*

"I heard that widowed women of a certain age, and there appear to be more every day, are so desperate for men that they're checking obituary columns for deceased wives."

"Should I ask why?"

"If it sounds interesting, they follow through by going to the funeral and giving the bereaved husband their condolences. Do you know how Betsy Brown met her new mega-millionaire husband Jacob Turnbrow?" Helen sat back and waited for Hannah's answer,

"No." Hannah had no idea how Betsy Brown met Jacob Turnbrow.

"At the hospital, coming out of the elevator, she noticed a devastated-looking man. She also noticed his chauffeur and limousine waiting for him. So, she goes over to him and asks him if she can be of any help. He tells her his wife has just passed away." Helen paused and looked up at Hannah, and seeing she still had her attention, continued, "Betsy tells him she can't leave him alone like this. She stays with him. Five months later, they're married."

"That's quite a story."

"You know, you're awfully quiet today. Where's the gab I used to know? You can be open with me."

"I'm concerned about Robert's health," said Hannah.

"I thought he was feeling better."

"He's not."

"I'm sad to hear. I'm sure it's nothing a little rest won't help. He should spend more time at home. Let me know how it goes. I must be on my way. It's supposed to rain later. I wonder when it's going to snow. It was so crazy to have no snow on Christmas Day."

"I know."

Helen had noticed Robert did not look himself. Jeff had even commented on his weight loss. Did he know something he was not sharing? Robert was constantly teased that his energetic wife was wearing him out. Others felt Hannah had him on a caloric-restricted diet, even a strict vegetarian regime.

Hannah did not have it in her to tell Helen about the health problems Robert was encountering, because it all seemed too difficult to comprehend.

CHAPTER THIRTY-FOUR

Immediately after Helen said goodbye, Hannah donned her wool-lined trench coat and boots, took her umbrella, purse and gloves, and left the house. She knew if she pondered a moment, she would not go. Once in the car, she sped down the mountainside.

Robert had said he would be home in time for dinner tonight. She wanted to shop for fresh, unusual fruits and vegetables and specialty bakery breads and cheeses he would enjoy.

Now, sadly, it seemed his sense of smell would never return. Consequently, all flavours tasted the same. Hannah went to great lengths to prepare a variety of dishes that had an appealing appearance and colour. She also concentrated on varying the texture, mouth feel, and temperature. It was a challenge.

As the rain fell, Hannah was having second thoughts about leaving the house. She could have simply telephoned in her food order and had it delivered.

It was December 27, yet there was still no snow. Over the holiday period, the children had looked forward to using their new red and white sleighs in the country. It was not to be.

Without snow to reflect the light and make everything appear warmer and brighter, Montreal streets were desolate and cold. Freezing rain fell continuously as Hannah went from vendor to vendor. When the wind changed its course, her umbrella did not always protect her from the downpour. Rain rolled down her face and under her coat collar to dampen the back of her neck where her scarf separated. It formed streams and ponds and crept into pavement cracks and froze. Where normally there were clean cement sidewalks or fluffy snow to dig her heels into and cushion her falls, Hannah repeatedly slid on dark patches of ice. Overhead, tall buildings, laced with icicles glistening like merciless jewels, formed tunnels through which the wind whistled and howled.

At the entrance to the supermarket, a bright orange sign screamed out its message, *Home-style, coconut cream pies, only three dollars.* They were the largest pies Hannah had ever seen. A short young man with an athletic build bent over and placed two of the fifteen-inch pies in his cart. Hannah unconsciously said, "Wow."

"What is it?" asked the startled man.

"Are you really going to eat those pies?"

"Why, yes, what's the matter?" Then he paused and added, obviously trying to defend his choice, "I'm very athletic. I run, play squash. I can eat anything I like."

Hannah hesitated for a moment, then said, "Maybe you can occasionally, but…"

Before Hannah could complete her sentence, he added, "So it's true. I'm a junk food addict, but I run. I run three times a week. My kids also love sweets, like me. I know it's bad for them to eat sweet foods so often. But what can I do?"

As Hannah walked away, she noticed he had put the pies back on the table.

Her next stop was Atwater Market. In the 1970s, when the market, built at the height of the Depression in the prevailing Art Deco style, saw its business shift to the supermarkets, Hannah retained her loyalty. She feared for its future and was filled with sadness. It was like seeing a valued friend die from a lack of love and compassion. High up in its lofty skyscraper-like brick tower, even the enormous black hands of the illuminated clock, framed in elaborate ironwork, that once moved across its white face sat still and no longer chimed.

Selecting cheeses from imported and regional specialties, as well as a variety of fruits and vegetables, she marvelled at the imposing geometric patterns of the white and pale green-tiled walls and the gleaming stainless steel, glass-encased showcases, decorative elements no longer appreciated. Hannah imagined her growing collection of artefacts of the early nineteenth century, many of which she purchased nearby at the antiques shops on Notre Dame Street, would feel at home here.

After shopping, she was happy to return safely home to the sound of crackling logs in the open fireplace and the laugher of David and Sarah. Walking through the foyer, an oil painting of Montreal bound in snow comforted her for a fleeting moment. This was the way she remembered the city in winter. She craved the familiar. It reassured her all was right with her world.

She recalled the Canadian landscape painter Maurice Cullen, famous for his technique for painting snow, not blank white, but as he saw it change from cream to rose and blue and violet, saying one of the main things he asked from life was snow.

Then, as if out of nowhere, the children ran forward to greet her. Behind them was the butler.

"I have a message for you from Mr. Steinman. He had to leave on an urgent matter. I believe he said he had to fly to Waskaganish," he said. Looking up, he added, "It seemed sudden."

"Are you sure he said he was going to Waskaganish?"

"Yes, I believe so."

Hannah tried to hide her anxiety from the twins. She thought there was maybe a mistake. Why would Robert unexpectedly go to Waskaganish?

After lunch, she would deal with the problem. Happily, the twins enjoyed their vegetable soup and hot chicken sandwiches with gravy. Baked apples stuffed with plump raisins, brown sugar, honey, and cinnamon to enhance their sweetness were forgotten in the refrigerator. Hannah only took a bowl of soup. She had little appetite.

She reasoned there could be a clue in his room. Under a pile of papers in his desk drawer, a copy of an invoice caught her attention. Written on a Steinman and Company stationary invoice was a numbered company with coded names for items totalling about two million dollars. What items were being referred to?

Hannah was still waiting for Robert to discuss his business with her, as he had promised. She was frustrated she knew so little.

By supper, she still had not heard from Robert. She decided to telephone Avrum; he would know where to find him. The answering machine went off. Was he on vacation? As the hours went by, she grew more and more concerned.

There was no answer when she telephoned Robert's house in Waskaganish. Then she thought Rebecca Stone could fill her in on Robert's whereabouts. There was no answer at her number. All seemed so strange. Someone had to be home.

She waited another hour. Now, when she called Robert's number, the telephone lines were dead, a common occurrence during a storm. The operator confirmed the lines were down. She told herself she should not panic; if anything was wrong, she would hear soon enough, one way or the other.

Her mother always used to say, "No news is good news." Hannah was not convinced. The family knew her mother hated bad news, particularly about sickness, and never informed her of distressing events, except when it was absolutely necessary. When anyone in the family died, it was the greatest shock to her. She would always say, "Why, they weren't even sick." In reality, they could have been ailing for months, even years, before they passed away.

Hannah found not to get all the facts was to invite disaster. Yet often she found herself adopting her mother's attitude.

In spite of telling herself there was nothing she could do but wait, in all probability Robert would be contacting her right now if the telephones were working, she tossed all night. By six, when she got up, she was exhausted.

At ten, she telephoned Helen and voiced her concern. Her friend tried to reassure her not to worry. But she could tell that a few words on the telephone were not enough to calm her.

"I'll be right over."

"Be careful on the road."

"I will be. It's just around the corner."

They were nearly neighbours, but they both knew of accidents happening within a block of one's house.

*

"It's funny to be in town over the holiday period. But with no snow, what would we do in the country?" said Helen, embracing Hannah.

"It feels like it will never snow again. Nothing seems right," said Hannah with a heavy heart.

"It will. It always does, and all will be well," Helen assured her.

"Don't be so sure. Robert never goes to Waskaganish during the holiday period either," said Hannah emphatically.

"But nature is more predictable than man."

"It is? I wonder."

"Where are the twins? How are they?"

"They're fine. They're busy assembling their new train set. It's sophisticated. Robert got it for them in San Francisco. They're used to him being away. Though I had told them he would be home early for dinner."

"So what did you say?"

"He had to go to Waskaganish for something important." She wished she knew what. Then maybe she could relax.

"I know you're worried. Since we're in town, why don't we go shopping? They're having their big sales at Holt's, big markdowns on everything." That Helen loved to shop was evident in her remarkable wardrobe.

"How can I think of anything else until I hear from Robert?"

"Well, sitting here worrying isn't helping. It's making matters worse. When Robert returns, you're going to be a wreck. You're all tense and nervous. Shopping always makes you feel better." Looking at Hannah's forlorn face, she added, "By the way, what kind of business was Robert doing in San Francisco?"

"He wasn't there on business. He was consulting with a specialist Dr. Meyer referred him to regarding his frequent flu episodes and fatigue."

183

"Why a doctor in San Francisco? There must be a doctor closer to home he could consult?" Everyone appreciated that Montreal's medical system was first-class, and all its services were under Medicare.

"Apparently, doctors in San Francisco have seen similar cases. They're the experts."

"What did they find?"

Hannah tried to explain. "It seems to be some kind of syndrome, something to do with the immune system."

Helen had discussed Robert's symptoms with Jeff. He said it sounded like an immune problem seen amongst gay men in Los Angeles and San Francisco; a new syndrome scientists initially named GRID, for Gay-Related Immune Deficiency. It was recently renamed AIDS or Acquired Immune Deficiency Syndrome, since they found it didn't just affect gay men. The word "acquired" was used because, unlike other immune deficiency illnesses, it was a sexually transmitted disease.

About three months before, in October 1985, the headlines of every newspaper announced the death of actor Rock Hudson at age fifty-nine from AIDS. Helen had seen photographs showing the ravages of his illness, his once-brawny frame now gaunt, his face haggard.

Helen was quiet. She did not even want to imagine this was the health problem Robert was harbouring.

"I suppose you know about immune system problems," Hannah continued.

"Yes," replied Helen quietly. She wished she didn't. As she supposed everyone wished. But now it was here, what did you say or do? "How are you?"

"I'm worried."

"I can see why. I think you should take care of yourself and get some rest before Robert returns. I'd like to stay, but everyone is at home waiting for me. We're expecting one of Jeff's aunts and her family. I can come back later. Call me, promise."

"I will. Thanks for coming. You're the best."

Helen felt terrible as she closed the front door. She also felt guilty. Was the marriage a bad idea? By supporting her marrying Robert, Helen thought she was protecting Hannah from the likes of playboy Kurt Garner or the fate of a struggling single mother. Many unanswered questions ran through Helen's mind. *What kind of sex life does Robert's condition allow? What if Hannah has been infected?* If Hannah was infected, the twins could also be.

CHAPTER THIRTY-FIVE

After Helen left, Hannah walked back through the foyer, again pausing at a painting of a winter scene. It depicted a typical French-Canadian house heavily laden with snow, in front of which stood horse-drawn sleighs and family members warmly dressed in long woollen coats and scarfs and head-hugging hats. The scene by Cornelius Krieghoff, like so many Canadian paintings, reflected Canadians' preoccupation with winter, with ice and snow, with how they see their land and themselves.

Montreal still had no snow. Without it, Hannah felt lost in an alien land, a land where nothing seemed right, including a husband who left suddenly in the middle of winter to travel hundreds of kilometres to a distant, freezing land where he never ventured in the winter. In addition, he left in his drawer a copy of an invoice to a numbered company for about two million dollars.

Seeing Hannah in the kitchen, the twins came running over to help make what they nicknamed their "party plate." With cookie cutters, they cut various shapes, trees, animals, moons, and suns from sliced cheese, which, along with cut-up fruit and vegetables, they arranged on a platter into familiar patterns and figures.

Hannah jumped from her chair to answer the telephone, leaving the children to relish their snack. "Hello."

"Hi, Hannah. The phone lines have been down," said Robert over the interference on the line.

"I've been so worried."

"I know. I had to leave immediately. I'll tell you everything when I return."

"When?"

Hannah was so anxious, she hardly allowed Robert to finish his sentences.

"All being well tomorrow, weather permitting. Is everything okay?"

"It is now," replied Hannah.

"See you tomorrow. Please don't worry."

"I won't." Then the line went dead. She slowly placed the phone back on the receiver and turned to the twins and said, "Daddy will be home tomorrow, if the weather is good."

She didn't want to disappoint them if he didn't come home. They were eager to show him their assembled train.

Hannah immediately phoned Helen to tell her she had heard from Robert. Then she walked into the kitchen and removed her shoes. She basked in the warmth of the heated floor before taking down a jar of dried golden chanterelle mushrooms. This reminder of summertime pleasures would add its magic to her winter stew. Not only the enchanting flavour and aroma, but also the outstanding nutrient content, made these mushrooms a wonderful addition to all kinds of dishes.

Chanterelle mushrooms, along with a few other mushroom species, are the only plant food that can replace the sun's rays to serve as a source of vitamin D. For up to six years, dried mushrooms had been shown to store the vitamin D they synthesize from the sun. Next to cod liver oil, chanterelles are one of the most concentrated sources of vitamin D. It was no wonder they are so cherished in the low sunlight northern reaches of Europe.

Hippocrates, the "Father of Medicine" who lived from 460 BC to 377 BCE, prescribed mushrooms for healing. Ancient Egyptians believed they would make you live forever.

Sitting alone, when the twins were in bed, Hannah once again wondered what urgent matter could compel Robert to go to Waskaganish in the winter, something he'd not done in their five years of marriage. All she could decipher, from the melancholy tone in his voice, was it must have been something urgent, even tragic. Lying in bed, peaceful sleep eluded her. Nightmares and sleeplessness prevailed.

While eating lunch the next day, Hannah heard a car pull up. From the window, through sheets of icy rain, she saw Robert in the back seat of a black limousine with a small boy at his side.

Hannah rushed to open the door for Robert and the small boy. At the door, Robert reached forward and took Hannah in his arms. Then he kissed the twins.

First looking to Hannah, then the twins, he said, "I have brought you someone very special. I have brought him with me from Waskaganish. His name is Jonah."

"Welcome," said Hannah with a warm smile. "May I take your parka, Jonah? You may leave your boots right here."

The twins smiled. They loved company, particularly, of other children. Hannah had never seen the boy before, though his name sounded familiar.

Indicating the young boy, Jonah, who appeared to be a year or two older than the twins, was going to stay for some time was the number of suitcases the driver deposited in the entrance.

"I bet you're both hungry. We're just having lunch. Come on," said Hannah, ushering everyone to follow her.

At the ample-sized maple kitchen table, Hannah poured two more bowls of hot chicken soup thick with chunks of chicken, onions, celery, carrots, peas, and pasta. Robert handed Jonah a napkin and a slice of dark bread. While Jonah quietly drank his soup, every so often he turned toward Robert. He appeared at home with him, like they had often spent time together. It was clear they certainly were not strangers.

Hannah found it hard to eat anything with Robert looking so drawn, distraught, and sad. Jonah's eyes were bloodshot and his voice barely audible; Robert's face was drawn and sad. After lunch they slept, as did the twins. All the excitement had exhausted them.

Restless and confused, with so many questions her head was ready to explode, Hannah turned on the highly polished chrome taps sitting above the deep, oval bathtub. Relishing the warmth of the heated porcelain floor beneath her clammy, cold feet, she reached forward to set the dial for the Jacuzzi and closed the bathroom door to eliminate any cool air from the adjoining bedroom.

Replicating an ancient ritual, she sprinkled rose oil over the water's surface. As the flowing water released the oil's volatile scents, she lowered her body into the perfumed bath. Relaxing in the tub, her arms floating on the surface of the water.

Jets of water shot through the calm water onto her limbs. The continuous motion of the water massaged and relaxed her weary body. Stepping out of the bath onto the warm tiles, she wrapped herself in a huge white towel. Around her dripping hair she wound a small white towel before settling down amongst the white linen-covered pillows on the wicker lounge.

*

By the time Robert and Jonah awoke, it was dark outside. With the staff off for the holiday period, and unable to concentrate on making anything requiring a lot of preparation, Hannah readied a simple meal of broiled salmon steaks with brown rice with peas and carrots and fruit with sponge cake.

At dinner, Robert and Jonah still looked weary. Again, Robert sat next to Jonah, attentive to his every need. Hannah, sitting across from them, found something familiar in the boy's grey-blue eyes.

Huge, icy drops of rain continued to fall as if the skies were weeping, while the radio played "White Christmas."

Hannah pondered how strange life was. No one would have imagined the biggest-selling Christmas single of all time was written by a Jew, Irving Berlin, born Israel Baline in Mogilev, Russia, while living in Florida when he wrote the holiday classic.

Like the words to the song, Hannah craved contentment and the familiar snow.

With the children asleep, Hannah and Robert knew it was time to talk.

Before a glowing fireplace, giving warmth and life to the quiet room, Hannah placed on the coffee table a Victorian black lacquer and mother-of-pearl papier-mâché tray holding a pot of steeping cranberry tisane and a plate of her own holiday rum-soaked fruitcake made weeks before from a mixture of dried fruits and nuts, which included apricots, cranberries, cherries, mangos, figs, dates, prunes, pecans, slivered almonds, and pine nuts, all held together by a sweet dough. This was Hannah's ode to the season to be jolly.

Tonight, the carefully arranged slices of jewelled cake and crystal glasses filled with colourful tisane served to comfort and remind Robert and Hannah of the joys and pleasures of the holiday season.

"Hannah, I know you've a million questions. You've been so patient," said Robert, turning toward her as he sat down beside her on the soft down-filled sofa.

"Yes," replied Hannah, waiting attentively.

"Everything is more difficult than you could imagine, Hannah," said Robert with downcast eyes.

"Why did you suddenly go up north to Waskaganish?" she burst out.

"There was a death. Rebecca Stone died," Robert said with tear-filled eyes.

Hannah felt at a loss. She took Robert's hands in hers, sitting silently while waiting for an explanation. There certainly was no rush.

"She was the doctor at the clinic up north where Jonathan practiced. She and Jonathan were colleagues and friends. They went to medical school together," said Hannah quietly. She felt no need, nor was it the time, to elaborate on their relationship.

"Yes, and Jonah is her son."

Hannah wondered why he would be the caretaker.

He continued, "He's my godchild. I'm also his grandfather. It's complicated. Until now, I never knew Rebecca was my daughter.

Being a friend of Rebecca's as well as Jonah's godfather, I was contacted."

"You had no idea you were her father?" Hannah was shocked.

"When she first came to Waskaganish, I suspected she might be my daughter. But she told me her father was killed while serving in the armed forces overseas."

"Why did you suspect she might be your daughter?"

"I had a teenage summer romance with her mother, Yvonne Stone, when I was about seventeen years old. It was in 1942. The world was in a state of disarray. I didn't return to Waskaganish until after the war. I never knew what had happened to the young Cree girl I'd fallen in love with that summer. I never heard from her again, though I tried contacting her. By the time I returned to Waskaganish, I was married. All I heard was she had died."

"How did you find out you were Rebecca's father?"

"I went to Rebecca's house to retrieve some of Jonah's clothing to bring back with us. As the executor of Rebecca's estate, I looked around. In her bedroom, hanging from the edge of her dressing table mirror, was a necklace with a small silver heart. I immediately recognized it as the necklace I had given Rebecca's mother. I put it in my pocket and left. Then I wondered if she might have bought it, acquired it. In the car, it fell out of my pocket. Jonah picked it up and said it was his grandmother's necklace. He also said, 'She died when my mother was born.' I had to tell him the truth. He'd been told his grandfather was killed during the war."

"It must have been difficult to tell him."

"I said there was a mistake."

"Did he believe you?"

"I think he did. He wanted to believe there was still someone there for him. Rebecca and I were good friends. I felt an alliance of spirit with her," added Robert.

"I remember Rebecca at Jonathan's funeral. She had flown down with you, I believe."

"I can't believe she's gone. She loved living in Waskaganish. She said it was the only place she felt at home."

"What we want is not always what is best for us. But most important, was she happy?"

"Yes, she was happy, particularly since Jonah was born. After his birth, she tried to work less, but she really never slowed down enough." Then he paused. He looked pained, like he was reliving a nightmare. "She was brutally beaten and left to die, like a dog."

"Who would do such a vicious act? Was there a robbery?" Hannah had heard brutal things happened up north, but then again, they could happen anywhere.

"The police are investigating. They say there were no witnesses. Whatever I do, nothing will bring her back. By the time I arrived up north, she was gone. She was buried in the Anglican graveyard beside her mother and her aunt."

Hannah realized that to lose a child is the cruellest of tragedies. Years ago, on a train from Toronto, a Chinese woman said to her, "To lose a child upsets the natural order of life." *How true it is,* thought Hannah.

"As you know, my first wife and I had no children. I wanted children. Oh, how I wish I'd known. It's been said a daughter has a particular place in a father's heart."

"I understand how hard this is for you." Hannah felt and saw the depth of his pain. His hands were cold and his body frail, and even his step was unsure.

"I wish I could take a magic wand and wish it all away. Life is not always fair. As you know, my husband died in Waskaganish."

"I remember." Robert was now focusing on the glowing fire.

"I felt cheated. I had little of him to hold on to, not even a child, after ten years of marriage. Now I have David and Sarah. Sometimes I think there is a reason for many things, however sad the reason." That was what her mother would have believed.

Robert remained silent for about a minute, but to Hannah it seemed eons.

Then he got up, walked over to the window, and looked out into the darkness before asking, "How do you feel about Jonah living with us?"

"He seems like a wonderful boy. It would be a blessing to have him. It would make the twins and myself happy. But what about his father?"

Robert hesitantly said, "Apparently, he's dead."

"Are you sure? It would be good to know who he was."

"True. It would be good," said Robert with some thought. Then, leaning on the fireplace, as if he were cold, he continued, "I'd like to adopt Jonah."

"Yes," was all Hannah could muster. It had been a long day. Instinctively, she felt there was something missing in Robert's story that would surface in time.

Robert had the habit of rationalizing his actions, however devious or dishonest. He reasoned that to divulge Jonathan as Jonah's father would unduly upset Hannah and undoubtedly colour her relationship with the young boy. As ever, his perspective was time would take care of it. The years would pass, and events and details that at the time appeared important would long be forgotten.

Before going to bed, Hannah made a quick call to Helen. Her friend was relieved to hear Robert was safely home but saddened by the circumstances surrounding his trip.

Hannah thought, *We often wish things that are not so.* The necklace with a small silver heart could have been given her by anyone. It was a popular gift in the forties and fifties.

CHAPTER THIRTY-SIX

Next day after breakfast, they packed up and left for the country.

Although it was an easy hour-and-a-half drive to Austin, it felt like a world away. There they could attempt to escape life's disturbing realities.

As the car made its way along the Eastern Townships autoroute, looking beyond toward the purple peaks of Mount Orford, Hannah felt the full impact of the unusual winter. With no snow or leaves to cover its towering curves and hidden scars, it stood like a naked lady shivering in the bitter wind.

Arriving at noon, she immediately prepared a simple lunch of vegetable soup, grilled spicy turkey hot dogs, specially made for Hannah by the butcher, served on homemade multigrain buns, fruit compote, and oatmeal cookies. After eating, Robert excused himself and retired to his office to make some phone calls.

While the sun was at its peak, Hannah was determined to take the children for an outing. Dressed in her long, hooded sheepskin coat, with the children in tow bundled up in their colourful snowsuits, warm hats, scarves, and gloves, they ventured out on foot through the windy, desolate meadow. In the absence of snow, missing were the friendly, familiar footprints of rabbits, deer, dogs, or fellow pedestrians one usually encountered etched in the snow. These tracks would have assured them they were not alone.

They retreated back to the meadow. Beyond, the forest beckoned.

Nestled amid the creaking balsams, pines, and maples was a frozen pond. With delight, the children slid across its glistening surface to the other side, where they were spellbound by the sight of what looked like a gigantic amoeba frozen in its tracks. Under the massive heap of ice formed from the artesian spring, water could still be heard gurgling as it ascended from the earth.

The children, led by Jonah, immediately took hold of the opportunity to experience its slippery undulations. For the rest of the afternoon, they slid over its inviting surface, registering every ripple as they bounced in great jubilation down its vertical drop. No snow-covered hill could compare with this rolling mountain of ice.

As the sun slid west over the disrobed forest, causing the tall trees to cast a long, dark shadow across the fields, the children reluctantly started back to the house. Hannah promised them that tomorrow they would continue their adventures. She pointed to a smaller frozen pond with the silhouette of a huge weeping willow presiding over it and said, "That's where we'll go tomorrow. You may swing on the low branches. It's great fun. Now let's go back to the house and make those roasted chestnuts."

Although it was just past four in the afternoon as they happily ran across the meadow to the house, it was already getting dark. Robert was pacing back and forth.

"I just can't concentrate." He looked at odds with the world.

"That's understandable. It's been a difficult time. The most difficult one will ever have to endure." Hannah felt helpless. She wanted to ease his pain.

"I really should be in Waskaganish. I just can't sit here and let the lunatic who took Rebecca's life roam around."

"You need rest. You need time."

"I don't have time."

He went back to his room. Hannah could hear him on the telephone. "How could this happen? I thought she had guards and took every safety precaution."

After supper, for the first time since Robert had left for Waskaganish, Hannah tried to relax and gather her thoughts. It occurred to her that Jonah must have been fathered by Jonathan. She had little doubt. They had the same grey-blue eyes. The timing was right.

She immediately got up and went to Robert's office.

"Is Jonathan Jonah's father?" Hannah demanded, looking directly at Robert.

"I believe so."

"Why didn't you tell me yesterday?"

"I was going to. I just didn't want to upset you yesterday. There was so much to tell you." Robert was uneasily. He could barely look up at her.

"I'm trying to understand," Hannah confessed.

"I know. It's hard for you. Do you know anything about Jonathan's relatives?"

"His adoptive parents both passed away. He never knew his biological parents. He was an only child. He never mentioned any relatives." As Hannah answered, she realized how strange her reply sounded.

"What was Jonathan like? I'd met him, but he seemed so reserved. I remember he wasn't very sociable." Jonathan rarely attended social events, so he had little contact with Robert.

"I was married to him for ten years. There was a lot I didn't know about him."

CHAPTER THIRTY-SEVEN

Over the next few days playing with the children, Robert seemed to put aside his despair. It was as if he had lost everything and now for this brief period had found peace in simple, everyday pleasures. He appeared at ease for the first time since returning from Waskaganish.

Hannah did not have the heart to ask him the million questions on her mind. Why did Rebecca require protection? What kind of business was he up to that he left copies of receipts for two million dollars in his drawer? What was the business dealing with Avrum he wanted to talk about?

As was her habit, she put her questions aside, deeming they could wait.

Back in Montreal, still the winds brought no snow. Grass was brown and soggy. Some areas were covered with inordinate amounts of dog waste. This unusual turn of events had everyone confused. Day after day, weather forecasters announced the latest snowstorm had missed the area. Even usually balmy British Columbia was besieged by snow.

Hannah kept the children busy with a variety of excursions.

"Guess who we're going to visit? Aunt Helen," she said. "We'd better get ready. We're going over to her house to see her new puppies."

"How many are there?" asked Jonah, who was beginning to feel like a part of the busy household.

"I believe two," replied Hannah.

Helen was waiting with hot chocolate.

Hannah and Helen chatted while the children played with the main attraction, the puppies. Jonah's grey-blue eyes and determined nature did not escape Helen's attention. She immediately realized their connection. According to her calculations, Jonah was conceived on Jonathan's last trip to Waskaganish. She remembered the date distinctly. She and Jeff were visiting Israel at the time they received the telephone call telling them of his death. She felt now was not the time to discuss this with Hannah. Though she was concerned what Hannah's reaction would be when she did make the connection. Did Hannah already know and wanted to keep it her secret?

"You're awfully quiet today." Hannah had barely said a word since arriving at the house.

"Oh, I didn't notice. I was so fascinated by the puppies."

"They're a handful. But how are you managing? How does it feel to have another child to care for?" Helen inquired as they walked into the kitchen, leaving the children playing with the puppies.

"Oh, fine. It's a pleasure to have Jonah."

"He appears bright."

"He is. Thank goodness you gave them a snack. Before they were getting grumpy."

"You were the one who always reminded me of how important snacks were. Nutritious snacks."

"Never get hungry, if you want to stay fit and happy. Even overweight people fare better with healthy snacks."

"I have so many friends who won't feed their children or themselves snacks, because they believe it will ruin their supper."

"Then they wonder why they're hard to get along with."

"Talking about fat," Helen said with a grin, "well, it sounds like that exercise fellow, Manson, has gone bankrupt. His business flogging sports drinks went under." She hoped this would distract Hannah from her concerns.

"Oh?"

"Fred Brown told Jeff that a gentleman of means was looking for a trainer to travel with him on his yacht. Manson seemed a good match. Now he's out at sea." Helen snickered.

"A good place for him, far from mankind. But mark my word, he'll be back before you know it. As long as there are gullible people, he'll be back with another scheme to sell. He's first and foremost a salesman, a hustler."

*

It was not until the first week of January that a light snow began to fall and cover the icy ground. The sun reflected on the white flakes, and the world seemed a little brighter. Day by day, Jonah's pain and sense of loss lessened. Before Hannah's eyes, his young heart was healing. His grey-blue eyes gained their sparkle as he assumed the outgoing nature he had possessed before the death of his mother. *Children's resilience is nature's miracle,* thought Hannah.

When there was sufficient snow Hannah drove Jonah, David, and Sarah with their brightly coloured sleighs to the eastern slope of Mount Royal. For hours, they ran up and down the gentle mountain slopes. Jonah was particularly focused and determined, unbending when he had his mind made up, at times frightening Hannah. He was so much like his father.

Neither Robert's immaculately tailored Savile Row suits nor his handmade Italian shoes could camouflage his pain. He found all his power and money were no match for the brutality, passions, and diseases that had destroyed his health and his life. His last bout of flu-like symptoms left him tired and depressed. He was angry, determined to find out who was responsible for Rebecca's death and to bring them to justice.

*

In spite of a forecast of continuous storms and below-average temperatures in the northern regions of Quebec, Robert was bent on flying to Waskaganish. It was a little over a week since Rebecca's death. He had a mission to find the person who had brutally beaten his daughter to death.

"I must go."

Embracing her as he said his farewells, his frailness struck her. A deep sadness engulfed her.

Lionel Gross, a loyal employee and friend, accompanied Robert. Hannah had considered going with him, but Robert convinced her it was best she stay home with the children. She reasoned he wanted to deal with the situation his way.

Next day, a heavy snow began to fall. Any minute, Hannah expected the children to run in from the park for their snack when the telephone rang. It was Avrum.

"Hi, Hannah, I'm on my way over."

It was not unusual for Avrum to drop by with little notice. What was odd was the tone of his voice. It was not as upbeat as usual, but rather slow and well-modulated.

As Avrum entered the house, he looked bewildered and strangely quiet.

"What is it?"

"Bad news," he burst out. "It's Robert. Lionel just phoned from Waskaganish." He took Hannah's hands. She noted his hands were cold and clammy. "I came over as soon as I could. Lionel found Robert on the floor. He'd been beaten up. He was eating his supper alone. According to Lionel, Robert had wanted some down time. He was tired; as you know, he has been tired for some time, though he hated to admit it, even to himself. He simply kept going. By the time Lionel returned, he was dead."

Hannah and Avrum embraced. He was shivering. His face was ashen.

"This is terrible, so terrible. Please sit down. I'll get some tea."

Hannah could have had it brought in, but she needed a moment alone to compose herself. As she filled her familiar Windsor stainless steel English kettle with water and placed it on the gas flames, she could not help but think back to five years before, when Avrum brought the news of Jonathan's death. He was totally composed, though compassionate. Today, he looked distraught. She slowly poured the steaming hot water over the loose black leaves and watched the tea steep before pouring it into tall bone china mugs.

"Hot tea is good for the soul." Hannah was trying to keep calm. She placed the hot beverages on the low table before she sat down. Her hand was shaking.

"I haven't spent much time with Robert in the past four years. I don't even venture to Waskaganish anymore," explained Avrum.

"I know. Robert travelled a lot," Hannah said quietly.

"My business keeps me abroad, and I visit my family in Queens often." Avrum continued, "Apparently, Robert was eating his supper when it happened. He must have been grabbed and beaten up and left."

"It sounds similar to what happened to Rebecca. What is going on? Is there a connection?" Hannah was getting tired of getting no answers.

"There is so much to think about. For now, as hard as it is, we must get through the next few days." Avrum tried to help her concentrate on the moment.

"I know. You're right. I think the official announcement should be he died suddenly while on a business trip. Let everyone assume what they please. I suppose ultimately the truth will prevail, put for now it's no use alarming everyone. Thankfully, Robert made his funeral arrangements some time ago. He was always concerned about his health, and death."

"I know. If there is anything I can do, let me know."

They embraced again and said their goodbyes.

*

Two days later, Hannah sorrowfully took on the widow's role once again, but now it was more complicated. There were her children and Robert's family, and friends and associates, and the numerous people all touched by his death. Condolences came in from many people, some familiar, others foreign to Hannah, as she contemplated how to honour the life of an icon in business, philanthropy, and art collecting.

With Sarah's small hand tightly entwined in hers, and David and Jonah hovering beside her, Hannah and the children were seated. Next to them were other family members, including Helen and Jeff. Close by was Avrum, who was carefully scrutinizing the room. As Hannah silently waited for the service to begin, her right hand constantly settled on the cool, comforting surface of her diamond bracelet. It was a reminder of her husband's generosity.

Her eyes scanned the crowd. Hidden from view, far to the right at the back of the room, was Kurt Garner, trying to remain inconspicuous. His well-known face did not go unnoticed amongst the steady stream of executives with their exquisitely dressed wives, nor did his presence escape Avrum.

Kurt had flown in from location for the funeral. Hannah never noticed him come or go.

CHAPTER THIRTY -EIGHT

Eight days had passed since Robert's funeral and the Shiva period. Hannah was trying to relax in her room when the doorbell rang.

A few moments later. the deep, well-articulated voice of Kurt Garner echoed through the house. It was the first time Hannah had heard his voice since their last encounter in Montreal five years ago. She had always imagined he would appear one day, because Robert was a producer of Kurt's films; but he never did. Newspapers, magazines, and the occasional television clip were her sole clues to his whereabouts.

"I'm sorry, we're taking no visitors," the butler informed him.

"I meant to come earlier, but I couldn't get away. Please, I would really like to give Hannah my personal condolences."

"Mrs. Steinman gave me explicit instructions," insisted the butler. "Your name, sir."

"Kurt Garner. I'm an old friend. I've come a long way. I won't keep her long."

"Come in."

He ushered Kurt into the drawing room.

"Do sit down."

Hannah was in her bedroom. Her long hair hung wet around her shoulders. Washing it usually refreshed and revitalized her, but not today. She felt drawn and tired, in need of time alone. Then, as ever, her prime concern was the children, particularly Jonah. With Robert's death, another close bond with young Jonah's past was broken.

Since Robert's death, Maria, the nanny, had taken care of the children for nine days straight. Hannah had given her the morning off. David and Sarah were running up and down everywhere. Jonah had stayed up late and was taking a nap. The twins, hearing a visitor arrive, ran downstairs. To fetch them, Hannah would have had to run after them. She let them go.

Peeking in the drawing room, Kurt caught two pairs of bright blue eyes staring at him. They started to giggle. "Is your mother upstairs?"

"Yes," they replied in unison.

"Do you think she's coming down?"

"No," said David.

"Her hair is wet," added Sarah. "It takes a long time."

"Wait. What are your names?"

"I'm Sarah. He's David."

"How old are you?"

"Four," they replied together.

"Both of you?"

"We're twins," said Sarah.

"I once had twin cousins." Kurt paused and added, "What month were you born?"

"May," said Sarah.

"Victoria Day," added David.

"That's a nice day."

"We always have a big party for our birthday. Why don't you come? There's a big cake," said Sarah.

"That sounds like fun."

"Do come," said Sarah.

"I will try."

"It's May twenty-fourth," said David.

"I'll try to come to your party."

The twins smiled at each other. Then they looked serious.

"Our father just left us. He's not coming back. Ever," said Sarah.

"Never," echoed David.

"I should go now. Your mother sounds very tired," said Kurt.

"No, stay. We like you," said David.

"She would like you," said Sarah.

"Tell me, how do you know?"

"You have the same colour hair as us. She loves us. She says our hair looks like spun gold," said Sarah.

Kurt patted Sarah's hair and said, "Spun gold, like the gold Rumpelstiltskin spun."

"Mommy has read us that story," said David.

*

Hannah quickly dried her hair and slipped into her blue jeans and cornflower-blue cashmere cardigan. Quietly, she walked downstairs into the drawing room.

"Kurt is here," Sarah announced.

As Hannah entered the room, Marie was there. "When did you return, Maria?"

"Just now. I just came in. Would you like me to give the children a snack?" she asked.

"Yes, that would be nice."

"Do you have a minute, Hannah?"

"Yes, Kurt."

"I'm so sorry to barge in like this. I wanted to give you my condolences."

"I understand," said Hannah. "It's been hectic here."

"I wish we could talk for a moment."

"That would be good."

"It's so long. I don't really know where to begin. No one answered the day I left Montreal. I tried to reach you," Kurt tried to explain.

"My phone was down the day you left. The phone wire cut. But what about after you left? You never phoned."

"I was in northern Quebec shooting a film. I wanted to call, but there were storms and the lines were down for much of the time. I figured I'd call you and see you as soon as I returned. Next thing I heard was you'd married Robert. Later, I was told you were pregnant."

Seating herself on the sofa, with her head in her hands, Hannah wept.

"Have I said something to disturb you? Please tell me. Is this a bad time to talk?" said Kurt as he sat down beside her.

"No."

"Then what's the matter? Do you want me to leave? I really shouldn't stay much longer. I've a plane to catch."

"I tried to reach you many times after you left me in Montreal. I could never reach you. Then I saw pictures of you with various stars, and I thought I meant nothing to you," said Hannah, wiping the tears from her face.

"Today it was difficult to get a hold of you. I phoned the house, and I was told you weren't taking calls or seeing anyone. That's why I didn't call first. I thought I'd take a chance."

"Excuse me one minute," said Hannah.

*

The laughter of the children, including Jonah, who had just joined them, echoed down the hall. They burst into the room with Maria chasing them.

"I was out of the room only a moment," said Maria.

"Hello again," said Kurt. Then he added, "Jonah!"

"Hello, Uncle Kurt," said Jonah.

"Jonah, how long are you visiting? Is your mother with you?"

"I now live here. My mother's dead," replied Jonah.

"Dead," said Kurt in disbelief. He had been secluded while doing the final cuts on his latest film.

"Come, children," said Maria.

The children said their goodbyes to Kurt and left with Maria.

*

As Hannah approached the drawing room, she was taken aback by the scene. Kurt was sitting with his arms folded across his chest. He looked frightfully forlorn. She hesitated to enter.

Spotting Hannah, he slowly rose and walked toward her.

"Hannah, I must go."

"Don't go. Please stay a little longer. Please. Let's talk a little longer."

"Hannah, you're lonely. I know what that's like. I'll be in touch soon. I promise you. Now I must go. It's best."

They walked in silence to the front door, where he took her hands in his, kissed her on both cheeks, said goodbye, and without another word left in his waiting car.

Just as the car drove away, Avrum arrived.

"Kurt dropped by to give me his condolences. Come in. Would you like some tea? We'll sit in the sunroom." She felt the sun would be comforting.

"I came by to see how you were doing and pick up some envelopes that are in the safe, before I go home for the day."

Avrum had no explanation. It was as if Hannah knew what was in the envelopes.

"Try to get some rest. We'll have plenty of time to talk," said Avrum.

After they said their goodbyes, Hannah wondered what was in the manila envelopes. Next time she would ask. Today she was too tired to inquire. There must be something valuable, since they were kept in the safe.

CHAPTER THIRTY-NINE

Leaning back on the cushioned window seat, huddled in a bulky woollen sweater, Hannah looked out over the snow-covered garden. A chill crept through her tired body as she thought of how confusing life can become when lines of communication are disrupted. She also could not dismiss how distraught Kurt was on hearing of Rebecca's death.

Pain caused by a breakdown in communication is not uncommon. Hannah recalled the emotional tale related in a television interview by former Canadian Prime Minister John Diefenbaker.

With tears streaming down his face, and with a heavy heart, he told how a lost letter had altered his entire life. He had mailed a letter proposing marriage to "his beloved Olive," whom he had met as a university student. He never received a reply and consequently married another, as did Olive. Some years later, after both of their mates had died, they met again and joyously married. It was then that Olive told her new husband that she received his letter of proposal two years after it was mailed. By then she had already married another suitor.

Memories of a young man Hannah had madly loved years before her marriage to Jonathan surfaced. She had placed his letters in the back of her closet in an old shoebox sealed with masking tape. One day, after six years of marriage to Jonathan, believing she would feel nothing and could happily dispose of them, she removed the letters from the box. Upon reading them, she felt a sense of irretrievable loss and grief that lasted for days. She never looked at them again, though she could not bear to throw them away.

Hannah questioned whether there was a reason for everything that had come to pass. Was it written in the stars that she was destined to marry first Jonathan, then Robert?

*

On the previous weekend in the country, Hannah had picked a bunch of crab apple branches covered with small buds and placed them in a tall, water-filled porcelain Chinese vase. Today the branches were blossoming, providing a brief preview of the promise of spring.

Shortly, the garden would be ablaze with the white, purple, and deep wine-red blooms of trilliums and wild dogtooth violets, wildflowers she had carefully transplanted from the woods of their country house. She wondered what wildflowers would be blooming in Waskaganish in June when she planned to visit.

As she had many times before, Hannah tried to imagine Waskaganish. Jonathan spoke only of his clinical practice. Robert seemed to avoid talking about Waskaganish, as if not to remind her of Jonathan. Kurt also said little about Waskaganish. What she knew of this small Cree community was from articles and books.

Hannah felt she had deferred travelling to Waskaganish for far too long. She could not understand how so many people she knew could die so violently with no resolution. Was there a connection, particularly with Robert's business? From all reports, June was the ideal month to go. It would be warm and inviting.

Today she was nostalgic for her old neighbourhood and wanted to experience it as she had when she first arrived in Montreal just over twenty years ago. It was a few hours before the afternoon hustle of children returning home. Hannah donned her long sheepskin coat and gloves and tall leather winter boots and dialled a taxi.

"Park and Mont Royal, please," said Hannah, getting into the taxi. Without a word, the cab sped down the boulevard, past McGregor, Pine to Park Avenue. At ten in the morning, most of the traffic had passed.

"Merci." She looked at the meter and handed the driver twelve dollars. Stepping carefully out of the cab onto the slippery sidewalk, she looked around to get her bearings. The small, smoky tobacco shop that once stood at the corner of Park Avenue and Mont Royal where she picked up her morning newspaper when she and Jonathan lived in the area was gone. She had heard it burned down.

A few doors east of the tobacco store, stopping in front of the naturopath shop, she heard her name.

"Hannah, I'm surprised to see you in my neighbourhood," bellowed Avrum as he approached her.

"This was my old neighbourhood. So much has changed here. I heard the small tobacco store I frequented burnt down. It was such an integral part of the neighbourhood. It was a place much like home. All the neighbours could drop by any hour of the day or night and always felt welcome," said Hannah.

"True. I recall when it burned down. At the time, everyone said it would be rebuilt. Instead, the pharmacy expanded and took it over." Avrum looked toward the pharmacy.

In 1967, it was here that Hannah, along with a small group of diverse Canadians from the area wearing badges with the likeness of Pierre Elliott Trudeau, congregated to talk while purchasing their morning newspapers. Here they dreamed of a just society and a visit from Trudeau, who was to make their dreams come true when he became Canada's fifteenth prime minister.

"All over Montreal the landscape is changing, with low-rise, older buildings being demolished to make way for modern high-rises." Hannah appreciated that nothing in life remains the same.

"In a few years you won't recognized this area. Things are changing fast. I have lots of faith in this area. I love it here. I feel at home. Lots of people feel that way. I've lived here since I came to Montreal. I'll never leave this area. I just picked something up at the pharmacy. I've got an appointment with some Hasidic. It's cold to be wandering around."

"Unlike you, I'm very warmly dressed. There's nothing like sheared sheep skin to keep warm. I plan to walk around the neighbourhood. Strange how little I see of you. I think you're avoiding me."

"Let's get together soon so we can talk. I'm late. Keep warm." He kissed Hannah on both cheeks and said goodbye.

Back home, Hannah felt restless. Habitually, she leisurely soaked in a hot bath and mulled over the past. Today she had no patience or desire to. She wanted to escape her former connections. She craved change.

Hannah took off her clothes, letting them drop on the comfortable white wicker chair in the corner of the bathroom, turned the shower dial, and stood under the warm, pulsating stream. With the door closed, the steam built up and condensed on the arched ceiling, rolled down into a small trough, and then into the drain. Ideally, as in the baths of ancient Rome, after which Hannah had modelled her bathing room, the water would have been collected and reused.

*

Next morning, Helen was on the telephone. "How about lunch today? Your choice."

Without even thinking, Hannah said, "Eaton's Ninth."

"Okay, noon."

Hannah deemed Eaton's dining predictability a blessing, especially in times of stress and uncertainty, when a modicum of stability in one's life was imperative. Ninth-floor Eaton's décor remained the same, as had the menu since Hannah had first eaten there in the sixties. She knew she would take the buffet; she did not have to read the menu. She knew where she would sit; she did not have to think about it.

In a busy café, Hannah once observed a harried businessman look at his menu, then without thought say to the waitress, "I'll have the same as the man at the next table."

Five minutes later, Hannah did something she had never done before. She telephoned Helen back and cancelled her luncheon date. She was not ready to confront her friend with her confusion and pain. She needed time.

CHAPTER FORTY

For the twins' much-anticipated birthday party, Hannah chose a fine cotton periwinkle dress with a misty pink floral pattern from her closet crowded with clothes in various shades of blue.

She questioned if her irresistible attraction to blue was habitual or genetic. Her mother always wore blue, only blue, in all different shades, no other colour. It made Hannah grin when she thought of how the clothes of her childhood had a bluish tint from the bluing her mother used in the laundry.

Or was it a part of her religious culture? As a young girl, Hannah could recall asking her father why Jewish prayer shawls had a blue cord. He had replied, "The Bible says the Lord God had instructed Moses to tell the Israelite people to attach a cord of blue, tekhelet, to the fringe at each corner of the prayer shawl to recall all the commandments of the Lord and observe them." Israel's flag is also blue and white.

But the Israelites were not alone in their preference for blue. An old belief of the people of the Greek Cyclade Islands was that sky blue had the power to repel evil by forming an invisible shield thwarting the approach of bad spirits. Blue church cupolas, windows, doors, walls, staircases, fences and "belts" around buildings also protect against evil, as do blue-turquoise stones and the sky-blue scarf around the neck of Boy Scouts. The Chinese dye most of their fabrics indigo blue. And of course, everyone loves blue jeans. An azure blue field symbolizing heaven is seen on the Quebec flag.

Hannah closed her eyes and thought of her very favourite piece of jewellery, her necklace with the deep blue diamond, one she cherished more than all her white diamonds. If blue protected against bad things, conceivably it has done that for her all these years. She and the children were healthy and had avoided Robert's disease, AIDS.

Instead of wearing the expensive pearls Robert had given her, usually her necklace of choice since she had received it, she took out from their worn silver box the pearls she had purchased years ago from the dark-haired young man with the surprisingly light blue eyes and quickly fastened them around her neck. A few minutes later, she removed them and placed them back in their box, leaving her neck bare.

*

Anxiously waiting for their guests to arrive, the children were racing up and down. When the doorbell rang, they scampered to get the door with the butler running after them. For the children, greeting the guests was all part of the fun.

"Hello there, and happy birthday," called the distinct, articulate voice of Kurt.

"You remembered," said the children in unison, jumping up and down.

"Yes, how could I forget your birthday on May twenty-fourth?" Kurt had a big grin and an armful of presents for the children.

"You're the first here," exclaimed an excited Jonah.

"Then I'll have the most fun. Here are your presents. There's something for each of you." He handed each child a gift.

"Can we open them?" asked Sarah.

"If your mother says so."

Sarah ran upstairs to Hannah. "Mommy, Kurt's here. He brought us presents. Can we open them now?"

"We should wait until our guests arrive and open all the presents together."

"Okay." She ran downstairs.

"We have to wait," said Sarah.

Hannah came down just as Helen and Jeff arrived. Around her neck was her blue diamond necklace. No doubt everyone but Kurt took it for a sapphire.

Then the other guests arrived, and all joined the children.

After everyone had eaten their cake and the presents were being opened, Jonah quietly and thoughtfully said to the twins, "Your eyes, you know what? They look just like Kurt's. You both have Kurt's eyes. They are the same blue."

"Many people have blue eyes," said Helen as casually as she could muster.

"I know," replied Jonah quietly, walking away.

"Come," said Kurt, rounding up the children, "let's take the kite outside and see how it flies."

"Yes, let's." Jonah was happy to run outside, away from the silent pause his innocent remarks had made.

Hannah went into the kitchen. Helen joined her.

"I realize I've got to tell the children and get this straightened out. But it's not so simple." *Knowing Helen,* Hannah thought, *she no doubt knows the story.* There was no use repeating it.

"I know. I'm going outside with everyone else. Come on. It's a party. Let's not ruin it."

Helen went outside, followed by Hannah. The colourful kite was whirling through the air, with the children chasing after it. Then it flopped to the ground. They all ran to get it. This happened repeatedly as the wind picked up then died down.

Hannah was content to sit and watch the idealistic scene of Kurt and the children indulging in the simple pleasure of kite flying. Keeping the fragile paper kite from hitting trees and rooftops was challenging. Hannah thought it was like navigating life; one moment your heart and being are flying high, the next they're on the ground struggling to get up and emerge in one piece unbroken by elements you often have little control over — like the kite has no control over the wind.

By seven thirty, the children were totally exhausted. Everyone said their goodbyes, except for Kurt.

"I see you're tired. I've overstayed my welcome." Kurt was looking at the sleepy-eyed children, who were hovering around him.

"No, stay, stay. We can play tomorrow," exclaimed Jonah.

Maria came down to get the children. It was past their bedtime.

"Promise you'll stay." Jonah reached over to Kurt and put his arms around him.

"If I don't see you tomorrow, I'll see you very soon. Goodnight." The children ran over to Kurt and kissed him.

*

"I was surprised that Avrum, Avrum Wood, wasn't at the party," Kurt said to Hannah when the children had gone upstairs.

"He left his presents. He had business abroad. He'd also decided it would be a good time to take a break, a well-deserved vacation."

"You must miss him." Kurt might have been thinking of how he was close by Hannah at Robert's funeral, and the last time he visited Hannah he was at the door as he was leaving.

"I do. He's a good friend. Come. Let's sit in the garden. It's such a perfect night."

Lighting up the sky, a full moon cast a warm glow over the garden, pleasing Hannah as she poured sweet red liqueur into crystal glasses. Sipping her sweet beverage, relaxing on a low, teakwood daybed, brought her back to the time they met and sat on pillows in a Japanese restaurant, eating sushi and drinking sake. Unlike when they were strangers cloistered together, with no past connections, today they had a shared history.

"I remember this house. It's where I stayed with the Steinman's years ago. It has so many memories." Kurt looked back at the house and then at Hannah.

"Good ones, I hope?" Since Hannah had heard Kurt stayed with the Steinman's, she often wondered how he interacted with them.

"Good and bad, and strange," Kurt reflected as he sipped his beverage.

"I've tried to escape the ghosts by redecorating." Hannah thought they would always be hiding in the rafters and was periodically reminded of them.

"I see. You've done a wonderful job," Kurt tried to assure her.

"But now I've created my own ghosts. Unfortunate circumstances robbed Robert of his health and of Rebecca. I felt so helpless. I don't even know if I was the slightest help. I often wonder what more I could have done to ease his pain and help him." She was haunted by the thought that she should have accompanied him to his doctor's appointments and his last trip to Waskaganish. She tried to comfort and reason with herself that she had the children to care for, and he had never asked her or even encouraged her in the slightest way to join him. Also, like Jonathan, he must have had his reasons.

"I'm sure it was a blessing for him to have you and the children. Children make you feel so alive. They see the best in everyone and everything. All the birthday parties and holidays, all the fun and laughter, all the pride. Children are so precious." Kurt sounded like he'd given a lot of thought to the pleasures of parenthood.

Then he paused, as Hannah had noticed he often did when he had something difficult to say. "I never heard how Robert died."

"No one was told. Only Avrum and Lionel, the police, and obviously those involved in the act know what happened. He was alone when he was beaten up and left to die. He was very weak, so it wouldn't be hard to tackle him."

"How sad. Do they have any suspects?" said Kurt.

"I haven't heard. It's like a nightmare. I must find answers. First there was Jonathan, then Rebecca, now Robert. Who will be next? There must be a reason." Hannah did not want to speculate. She was determined to find out. With Robert gone and the children older, she would have the time.

"Maybe there is a common thread. The police will find it, Hannah. We've talked a lot, but you haven't mentioned your work. Are you still struggling with ethical concerns?"

"I think about ethical issues. Few things have changed. There's still so much false nutrition and diet information in the media. It would be a full-time job to try to tackle them all." Hannah's frustration continued. She had vowed to herself that she would let others tackle the thorny problem.

"I imagine the children take up a lot of your time. They're pleasure to be with. Each is so different. Jonah is his own person. It will be interesting to see how he develops," reflected Kurt. "Apparently, he's very much like his father."

"You know who his father is?" Hannah wondered why she asked. It appeared it was common knowledge.

"Yes. I'm sorry. It must be hard for you. Hannah, you're so secretive about everything. Why?"

"I think it's partly the way I was brought up. My mother said, 'Never explain or complain.' I carry her words with me."

"As a child, how painful that must have been."

Kurt put his arms around Hannah. Tears flooded her eyes.

"I was also taught not to cry." Then Hannah started to laugh. "If I coughed as a child, my mother said, 'Control the cough.' Don't let it come out and get the better of you. I also had a weird upbringing. Maybe everyone does. What have you been doing recently?" Hannah was struggling to turn the conversation around to Kurt.

"Lost and found in my filmmaking. It's my salvation," Kurt said tentatively.

"What do you mean by lost and found?"

"I lose myself to escape my reality and find myself in the process." Kurt stood up and looked down on the city lights below.

"I see. How'd the film shot in Waskaganish go? The one you were eager to make when I saw you before your lecture in Montreal." Hannah recalled there was such a rush to shoot it.

"Strangely, it's still on the editing table. It's painful. It portrays the Cree people of northern Quebec, including Waskaganish, with all their problems relating to today's society. There was hope when I started the film. A hope which was hard to realize after spending time there, the death of Rebecca, and other nameless faces. So many unanswered questions."

Hannah wanted to talk more about Waskaganish. Seeing the sorrow on Kurt's face, she hesitated. Was the pain connected to Rebecca's death? "I have something to tell you. I don't know how." Then she added, "It can wait until tomorrow."

"I might be gone."

"Now you'll have to stay to find out," Hannah teased.

Talking to Kurt, the years faded away. She craved him in the same carefree way she had when they had first met. Nothing else seemed to matter. She felt selfish.

For so long, Hannah had thought of this moment. It kept her going when Robert's disease had consumed her. She was thankful she had not allowed it to annihilate her spirit and her life. Hannah had the ability to compartmentalize her life, something she realized early in her marriage she had in common with Robert. He and the sadness and pain it evoked were but a small part of her being. The rest was her world of children, friends, home, work, and other pleasures conjured up in her mind to fill the voids in her day, usually at night when others slept.

Wind blowing off the mountain cooled the balmy night air. Walking indoors up to the second floor, past the numerous paintings revered by Robert, they entered her bedroom overlooking the lights of Montreal. Kurt took Hannah in his arms, looking at the face of the woman with the astonishing amber eyes he had met long ago. The pupils of her eyes dilated; the circling amber irises sparkled like gold as they combed Kurt's deep blue eyes, mirroring the colour of the diamond resting at her throat. Her warm body fell into rhythm with his as they made love in the house Hannah had tried to make her home. It was also the house of Kurt's turbulent late teenage years.

*

Awaking, Kurt turned to Hannah and said, "Hannah, now what is this secret you promised to tell me?"

Hannah was half-hoping Kurt had forgotten. "I don't know how to say it."

"Then just say it. Nothing can be that bad."

She hesitated and quietly said, "The twins, they were conceived when we were together in New York. The first time we met. They're yours."

"When I saw them, I felt a distinct connection. You've confirmed my suspicions."

"They are in so many ways like you." Hannah put her arms around his tense body. Looking into his downcast, sad eyes she felt his pain. She knew he had every right to feel cheated.

The children must have heard them talking and ran into the room.

"You're here. You're still here." Jonah ran up to Kurt and grabbed his hand.

"Yes. Good morning." Kurt was taken back by the children's affection.

"Let's have breakfast," Sarah said gleefully. "Come on."

"I'll be down in a minute," Hannah called from the top of the stairs.

"You look sad. Do we make you sad?" Sarah asked Kurt.

"No. No. You make me unbelievably happy."

Hannah joined them at the table. The gusto with which Kurt had eaten his breakfast when they first met in New York had disappeared.

"The children are off to kindergarten. They must say their goodbyes now." Hannah kissed the children goodbye and joined Kurt inside.

After they left, they were alone once again. He took Hannah in his arms. "What can I say? Why didn't you tell me?"

"I wanted to, but…"

"I'm at a loss. I want to stay and sort out my new world, but I can't. I must be on the set. Everyone is waiting for me. I'll phone you. We'll see each other very soon. I really can't think ahead until I finish this movie. It's way overdue. I love you." Kurt stepped back, as if he was ready to leave.

In the past, Hannah would have said goodbye without a word. Today she felt strong and assertive. "You know, Kurt, I hate to see you go. Be alone with all I've told you. We should spend a little more time together. It's important to us both. Schedule your flight for later today, even tomorrow. This is hard for you. It will take a while to get used to the idea you have children. Let's walk downtown and stay for lunch. Then we can talk along the way. It is such a gorgeous day." Hannah turned and looked directly at Kurt. "I won't take no for an answer."

"I haven't explored Montreal for some time. I'm always in such a rush when I visit. To walk from place to place is a luxury and pleasure."

*

Walking down the boulevard, the last four years of their lives unfolded.

"I haven't been here in years," exclaimed Kurt as they got off the elevator at the ninth floor of Eaton's. "Robert's mother and his aunts used to come here. Occasionally, we'd come with them. I feel like I've been transported to another era."

"Here, time takes on a different tempo." Hannah was hoping Kurt appreciated each day was precious as they were seated at their table.

"It's good to reset our clocks. I believe that's how I've survived." Looking up at the pastoral scene in the long mural over the fountain, Kurt settled back in his chair.

"It's called *The Pleasures of Peace*." Hannah removed her long-sleeved cotton cardigan and placed it alongside her straw hat on the back of her chair. She felt comfortable in her sleeveless floral cotton dress as she sipped iced tea.

"The scene is complex. It looks like a gentle river running through an elaborate garden of sculptured trees, fountains, and flowers, with lovely young women engaged in various activities," Kurt observed.

"And all the women are dressed in different clothing styles. The one with bobbed hair, stroking a fawn, is wearing a dress to her knees, while the woman with shoulder-length hair holding the chubby, fair-haired child is in a long dress with a dropped waist. The others sitting near a fountain or looking at a sculpture of an angel wear long, fitted dresses and their hair is in chignons." For Hannah it was curious how the artist had incorporated into the mural such an array of styles. "If you look closely, you'll see the signature of the artist, Natacha Carlu, on the lower stone sculpture. She was the wife of the architect who designed the ninth floor in 1931. It and the one at the other end of the room were painted in Paris."

"It's complex, yet peaceful. Like this room." Kurt looked around.

Hannah sensed he wanted time for himself to pause and enjoy his lunch.

The buffet, with its assortment of hot and cold dishes, was better than mulling over a menu and having to make a choice. On the cold table, Hannah enjoyed the pickled beets, devilled eggs, and wide variety of cold fish and salads. There were also the hot dishes and fancy desserts.

Hannah was about to ask Kurt how the menu had changed since he had eaten there as a youth in the late forties but thought it might be too painful for him to recall.

Looking up, he seemed far away. Was he remembering his visits here with the Steinman family? How difficult it must have been for him, a young man who had lost his entire family and everyone he had ever known, everything he had ever possessed, to a brutal, unjust war. His German accent, now difficult to detect, was no doubt strong as he struggled to fit in and emulate the habits of his peers, striving to find his identity in a world that also was at odds with itself. How different he was from Robert.

"It seems so peaceful here, almost surreal, like the paintings. One would think nothing bad happens here," Kurt remarked. "But we know this isn't true. Look at the lady at the next table bent over, attentively listening to the younger woman. What do you think they're discussing that appears so serious?"

"It's hard to say. But it definitely looks important."

"Maybe a wedding."

"Or a divorce, or any number of things." Hannah wondered if Kurt was thinking about weddings. "Look at us." She was trying to get back to their situation.

"I know. You and the children mean a great deal to me. But I must go."

Hannah took his hand and said, "Wait. We will get together soon. There's nothing that can't wait. The children and I will be here."

"I don't want to leave. Leave the only family I have behind. Finishing this movie seems so mundane."

The next morning, Kurt left for Los Angeles amidst protests from the children.

Hannah had no choice but to explain to the twins that Kurt was their father.

CHAPTER FORTY-ONE

Leaving the small Waskaganish airport with the children and Maria, Hannah felt apprehensive. The driver was waiting to pick them up. Proceeding along the dirt road, Hannah could see no other vehicles.

"Jonah, is it always this quiet?" she asked.

"Yes, always. That's why it's so safe here, not like Montreal. I'm not scared of cars here."

Hannah thought there certainly were no cars to fear, but what about the other rampant problems, particularly the brutality? It distressed her.

"There's the house," declared Jonah with a wide grin. He looked so happy Hannah could have cried.

Jumping out of the oversized four-wheel drive, Jonah ran to the front door of Robert's sprawling wood-clad house.

A short, stocky Cree lady greeted them. Quickly, the children removed their jackets and shoes. Led by Jonah, they raced ahead into the large front room overlooking the river.

Sitting at the junction of James Bay and the Rupert River, the front windows looked out on the panoramic span of water beyond the meadow, which at this time of year was covered with large yellow dandelions growing in the sparse patches of soil.

Hannah was transfixed by the sight of the dandelions and her thoughts of how, like the people of this remote area, they were tough and resilient. Try to pull them out, and they will return the next year with bigger, bonnier blooms with seeds that parachute off to propagate beyond. Harvested, they were said to be a nutritious part of the Cree diet and medicinal ingredients.

Looking around the great entrance room of the old house, Robert's collection of paintings and Indigenous Canadian artifacts caught Hannah by surprise. He had mentioned it, yet she never imagined it would be so extensive.

*

Hannah left the house early next morning, leaving the children in the care of Maria and the Cree housekeeper. Along the gravel road bordered with dandelions, she walked the short distance to the medical clinic where Jonathan had practiced. There, her guide was waiting in his truck.

From there they went to the site where Jonathan's body was found. Hannah tried to imagine what it was like that stormy day. Her eyes welling with tears, she lingered a long time, absorbing the scene. She could not erase Jonathan's cautious nature from her memory.

Why was no one held responsible for Jonathan, Rebecca, or Robert's deaths? What went wrong? Were the police bribed?

Along the road, they came to an inviting cedar log house.

"Was that where Rebecca Stone lived?" Hannah asked her guide, who was lighting up a cigarette.

"Yes," the guide replied.

Her head spun as she visualized Jonathan leaving Rebecca's house early in the morning. Pain, sorrow, and sadness overtook her. She had to pull herself together before returning to the children.

"I'll walk back. You don't have to wait."

"Okay." The driver lingered for a while then added, "It's not a good place to be alone. Are you sure?"

"Sure." Hannah felt a detour through the woods would calm her.

Running parallel to the Rupert River was a trail lined with stunted black spruce, their roots clinging to a bed of hard rocks. Engrossed in carefully stepping along the hard, uneven surface as she proceeded pushing back the hanging moss, she lost track of time. Coming upon a clearing robbed of trees, only low vegetation, she was perplexed. What had happened here? It was like a bomb had struck, or more likely a bulldozer.

The clearing prevailed for a long distance beyond. Looking at her watch, she saw it was one thirty, past lunch. She must get home.

Turning around, she was confronted by a tall, heavy-set man.

"May I help you? It is dangerous here to be wandering around."

"I'm lost. Could you help me back to the main road?" Hannah was frightened.

"Yes, I can," he replied.

"I'm Mrs. Steinman. My late husband spent a lot of time here."

"You are Robert Steinman's wife?" His face lit up as he stepped forward and shook her hand.

"Yes."

"I am so sorry for your loss. He was a good man. He helped our people. Let me get you to the road. Then would you like a ride back?" He paused and led the way forward.

"That would be kind of you." Hannah wondered how she would have found her way back if he had not come along.

"I am Billy Cheechoo, a supervisor of operations." He held out his hand.

She took his rough hand. "Nice to meet you. What do you do?" Hannah had a million questions.

"Your husband didn't tell you?"

"No, he told me little about what he did in Waskaganish."

"We're building a pond for farming fish," he replied with downcast eyes, flicking the ashes off his cigarette.

"Fish. I never imagined." Hannah was dumbfounded. It seemed so far-fetched.

Entering the house, she hesitated at the door to watch the children sitting on the floor, sorting through Jonah's remaining belongings.

"Here's a photo of my mom wearing pearls. My dad gave them to her for her birthday. Here's my dad," said Jonah proudly to Hannah. "He was a doctor too. He died before I was born."

It was a photo of Jonathan.

"My mother said I look just like him. Do you think so?"

"Yes," Hannah said, then paused and added, "Yes, you do. You have the exact same steel-blue eyes." She struggled to stay calm.

"We have all been invited to dinner. The guide has arranged for us to join the Diamond family for a traditional goose roast." Hannah had read about goose roasts and felt the children would enjoy it.

"It's going to be so much fun. I love goose roasts," said Jonah.

Maria took the children to get dressed. Hannah went to Robert's large bedroom and collapsed on the bed. She was distraught. Hannah understood Jonathan's longing for a former love, but this did not justify him ruining ten years of her life. She could not forgive him, or herself for being so blind. Now all seemed so obvious. What husband in love with his wife would not understand her longing for a home and children?

*

Watching the goose cook over the open fire, Hannah felt an inherent sense of belonging she never experienced in Montreal. No doubt it was evoked by the sincere friendliness of the people and the longing look in Jonah's eyes.

In a hut with a smoke venting hole over an open pit wood fire, slowly roasted geese, *sakapwaan*, hanging on cords that were spun around occasionally so they cooked evenly. Roasting along-side the goose, the children watched the bannock dough they had helped wrap around wooden sticks, turn golden brown.

Hannah sat silently by listening to the children.

"Did you know mother and father geese stay together for their whole lives, unless one dies?" said Jonah, "Even then they often stay alone."

"Do you think Mom will stay alone?" said Sarah.

"I don't know. She could meet someone," said Jonah.

"Like Kurt?" said Sarah.

Joined by a group of friends, the children happily shared the feast.

Looking at Jonah, Hannah realized what a shock it had been for him to leave his home to live in Montreal. How he must have missed the great love his people shared in this tight-knit community.

CHAPTER FORTY-TWO

Walking around her neighbourhood high on Mount Royal, Hannah absorbed every detail of the landscape as if she was seeing it for the first time.

She noted most of the houses, sitting amidst their well-manicured gardens, still proudly carried their original slate roofs, whereas due to the expense of replacing broken tiles in less affluent neighbourhoods slate tiles generally were replaced by asphalt tiles. To Hannah, a stone house with an asphalt tile roof looked like a lady in a fine silk dress wearing a denim baseball cap.

Like carefully placed accessories, uniformed nannies walked in front of these grand houses, and the occasional gardener, housekeeper, or butler. On weekdays, boys in grey flannel trousers, white shirts, ties, and navy jackets, and girls in navy blue tunics or plaid skirts with white blouses joined them. Great order appeared to prevail. Yet Hannah knew how deceptive appearances could be.

Children from these mansions attended English and French private schools, as well as Jewish parochial schools. Hannah read that about eighty percent of Quebec children were registered in private schools. The Quebec government highly subsidized the French schools, making them affordable for a large number of families. When considering schools for the children, she learned the choice of schools was mind-boggling.

Hannah missed the energy and excitement of downtown Montreal where she had lived with Jonathan, a place where neighbours were going about their everyday activities, chatting, taking care of their gardens and walking their children and dogs. She ran back to her house, grabbed her purse and put on her leather jacket. Just as she was about to leave, she removed her diamond ring.

Running down the hill to the bus stop, she felt invigorated. She could have taken a car or a taxi but enjoyed the company of her fellow travellers. Placing her fare in the box, she smiled at the bus driver and reminded herself she must purchase a book of tickets.

To friends who had never ridden the bus, she often tried to explain what they were missing. They simply nodded politely.

At about ten in the morning, there was merely a handful of people on the bus. Students and the nine to five crowd had passed. Echoing through the almost empty bus were the high-pitched voices of two young women in their late teens or early twenties.

"I come this way when I can take my time and don't have to work. I come to see the houses. Oh, how happy all those people must be living up here," said the dark-haired young woman with the low-cut T-shirt under her bulky cardigan.

"I've always dreamed of living here, married to a rich guy," added the other young woman with bleached blond hair, peering out the window.

"I wonder what these houses are like inside?" said the dark-haired girl, pushing up the sleeves of her bulky sweater.

"If you take the bus at night, sometimes you can see right in, if the curtains are open, all the fancy furniture," explained the blond young woman, peering out the window.

"Think of having someone to do all the housework. The clothes. All those fancy clothes you see in the windows of Holt Renfrew's when you walk by. Imagine having them." A grand smile spread over the dark-haired young woman's face as she leaned back in her chair, oblivious to other passengers.

"And not having to worry about how much they cost. You don't even look at the price tag. You'd buy what you want, having nothing to worry about," cooed the other young woman.

Hannah recalled when she had also imagined what it would be like to live in one of these mansions. Like the young women on the bus, in those days she was bursting with dreams and expectations.

As the bus raced along the boulevard, the remaining few people on board sat silently listening to the two young women chat on and on. Hannah got off at Sherbrooke Street. Everyone else stayed on.

Her first stop was Holt Renfrew's. She rightly knew she should look for sandals before she was tired. Otherwise, she might settle on any shoe, even if it did not fit properly. She had bought many shoes too uncomfortable to wear. The shoe salesman, attired in a fitted dark suit, white shirt, and grey tie, looked more like an undertaker than a snappy salesman. He brought out piles of sandals and placed them at her feet.

"Now we have a large selection, don't we?" he remarked as he bent down to help Hannah buckle the straps.

Hannah could not decide which pair to choose.

"Take them home, try them on, then decide. Return those you don't want. It's as simple as that. I insist," he said. "I'll pack them up."

Hannah left armed with three pairs of sandals.

Just to reconfirm its existence and hers, she walked up the hill to visit the Tudor-style house she had shared with Jonathan, now rented to a professor from France. She did not go in.

Everything in the neighbourhood appeared the same until she looked toward the Saint Lawrence River. There were towering condominiums in place of the familiar parade of tall poplar trees standing directly across the boulevard from her sunroom.

It was no surprise. Driving quickly by, she had seen the condominiums. She now noticed how they robbed her house, and all the other houses north of it, of their views of the city and the river. Views that had inspired so many of her dreams and adventures.

The developer who had built the condominiums had bought from the Sulpician Order the northwest part of the grounds with the row of large, majestic poplar trees. Hannah felt a tug at her heart. She had been too busy with her own life to join the protesters, who insisted it was a part of Montreal's heritage.

In the past, Hannah would have directed all her anger at the developer. Recently, she had sadly realized that elected officials, the ones she had placed her trust in and helped elect, had permitted it to happen.

Once home, Hannah jotted in her diary a stream of notes

June 19, 1987

How did the developers get around the zoning code? How did the city allow it? They were elected to help make the city a better place, not thoughtlessly hand it to over to developers. Sell our past to the highest bidder. I miss old familiar things, places, and people. Now I know how elderly people feel when so many of their past connections are gone.

CHAPTER FORTY-THREE

"**D**o you have everything you want to bring to the country packed?" Hannah hollered to the children. There was no answer. She found the children in the back garden.

"We'll miss the parade," Sarah moaned.

"Tomorrow is Saint-Jean-Baptiste Day. Our neighbour gave us these flags." Jonah had a handful of small blue and white Quebec flags.

"I know, but we'd planned to go out to the country today with Helen. You can bring your flags and celebrate out there."

Just before arriving at the country house, they stopped at the corner store in Austin.

"I'll take the *Gazette*." Hannah handed the newspaper to Adele, the store owner. Jonah placed a block of Frère Jacques cheese on the counter next to the newspaper. This mild cheese made just down the road at Abbey Saint-Benoît-du-Lac had become the children's favourite.

"It's a long time since we've seen you. We're sorry to hear about your husband. Our condolences," said Adele.

"Thank you." Hannah knew Robert was a long-time customer.

"Howard Roper was in for his paper a few days ago. He looks terrible. You know he has bad cancer," said Adele as she placed the cheese, along with the newspaper, in a brown paper bag.

"How sad," replied Hannah.

"I don't think he'll last much longer," Adele said.

Howard Roper was a well-known political figure and writer who had a house on the lake, the next road over from the abbey. He was renowned for his caustic writing opposing the present Parti Québécois separatist Quebec government.

"The annual fair is this weekend. Come along, bring the children." Then Adele added, "I don't think we ever heard what caused your husband's death."

"It was sudden. Too sad to talk about. Thanks for telling us about the fair. We'll try to make it." Hannah thought the children might enjoy it.

"Well, remind me not to tell Adele anything I don't want the whole countryside to know," said Helen, who had been silently standing by, scanning the latest magazines on the rack.

"I never knew Howard Roper's cancer had returned. The papers said he was fine." Hannah thought Adele must know she saw him nearly every day.

"The family didn't want it known. Jeff knows."

"You know," proclaimed Hannah.

"Yes. It was hard not to say anything when everyone was saying how well he was doing lately."

"I know how difficult that is. Jonathan would tell me, or I'd hear things about patients, and I had to keep mum about them." Hannah understood.

"If anyone wants any extra publicity, they should visit the corner store and talk to Adele," said Helen, laughing.

"Come to the house. We'll have lunch on the deck," said Hannah.

"Isn't it wonderful to be in the country? Now you can relax. You look tired. Are you all right?"

"Yes. The country is a wonderful place. I need the quiet and fresh air."

"Enjoy it now while the children are young. When they're older, they'll have minds of their own and might not relish the quiet as much. They often want to be in the city with their friends. It can be difficult." Helen recalled the arguments she had with Jeff about the country house.

"I can imagine. Many times I didn't want to go to the country, there was so much going on in the city. Jonathan wanted to go. I resented it."

For some time, Hannah was unusually quiet. She was thinking of those arguments with Jonathan. She did not want the country to become a burden for her children.

"Have you heard from Kurt, or is he lost again?"

"I have. He has asked me and the children to join him in Nantucket in August. He has a house there."

"That sounds good. But don't hold your breath. He could get behind on shooting and never make it."

Though Kurt had been calling regularly, Hannah understood the anger and pain he harboured for the years he had been robbed of being with Sarah and David. That was understandable. They were his children. Could their love surmount the past, or were the wounds too deep?

"I'm surprised you decided to stay at your country house, not Robert's large estate," said Helen as they approached the house.

"I feel it's more fun."

Standing high on a gentle knoll, Hannah's house gave the illusion of being much grander than it was in reality. It was more like a big playhouse. Children loved to climb up the steep, winding stairs to its octagonal central tower room and pretend they were on secret adventures with mysterious missions. Presiding over meadows, mountains, and lakes, surrounded by forests and miles of sky unfolding before their eyes, with the bells of Abbey Saint-Benoît-du-Lac periodically chiming in the distance, dreams came true, just like in their familiar fairy tales.

Hannah yearned to recline beside her bedroom window on her blue velvet chaise-longue and look up at the ceiling rising to a lofty peak, reminiscent of an alluring desert tent, and, like the children, be transported to another place and reality.

*

Shortly after arriving, the children ran through the fields beyond the house. As the clusters of well-camouflaged, small, sweet berries were crushed beneath their feet, the perfumed scent of ripe wild strawberries filled the air. The Abenaki Indians called them heart berries because they believed they strengthened that organ.

Unlike at Robert's country estate, there were no unnecessary, ecologically unsound, manicured lawns, only wildflowers, tall grass, and large, leafy trees providing shade.

In late July there would be wild raspberries and in August wild blackberries. A favourite snack was berries simply mashed with a fork and eaten on crusty homemade bread.

*

Toward the end of July, after taking a late afternoon dip in the cool pond nestled in the forest beyond the house, Hannah began to climb the knoll toward the house. Looking up from a profusion of wildflowers scattered amongst the grass, she saw a tall figure approaching. A straw hat covered his face. Coming closer, she realized it was Avrum. Wrapping a towel around her waist over her bikini, she ran to greet him. He reached out his arms and embraced her tightly.

"When did you get back?" asked Hannah as he held her hands.

"You're shivering."

"I've been swimming. The pond's always cold." That was something Hannah could never get used to.

"I got back about a week ago. I've bought a small house just down the road. I hope to expand it."

"We'll be neighbours." Hannah was elated.

"I suppose so. You're not going back to Robert's big house?" Avrum was shifting from one foot to the other, trying to keep his balance on the steep slope of the knoll.

Then he added, with a twinkle of his eye, "I see your house is decorated with Quebec flags. Quite a sight to see, all those blue flags

236

with a large white cross and fleurs-de-lis. What do the neighbours say?" He must have known the neighbours were staunch supporters of an undivided Canada.

"No comments yet. The children hung them up and are thrilled." Hannah was happy that the children were happy.

"Do they know the fleur-de-lis represents the early French settlers?"

"Oh, yes, the neighbour in the city who gave them the flags told them all about them."

"I doubt if he told them the flag is hung by those who advocate a separate Quebec. I imagine they are too young to understand. The political unrest continues. There's talk of a second referendum." Avrum added, "It's bad for business. Something we don't need."

Hannah spread her towel, sat on it, and put her sandals on. Avrum sat on the grass beside her.

"You look different," he said pensively.

"Is that good?"

"Yes."

He hesitated and added, "You look so carefree."

"So do you."

"But how did your legs and arms get so scratched up?"

"Oh, that, it's the brambles. I was picking berries and looking for mushrooms. There are not only brambles, but you can also trip over fallen trees and rocks. But the forest air feels almost therapeutic. I feel so good wandering through the tall trees," explained Hannah.

"And the mushrooms, how do you know they aren't poisonous? Do you know out of the thousands of mushrooms in the world, only a few hundred are edible? Many might not outright kill you, but they can make you extremely sick."

"Avrum, don't be so concerned. I only pick those I know. Right now, it's golden chanterelles. They are easy to spot. A Czechoslovakian lady, who was surprised by Canadians' lack of interest in mushroom hunting, unlike foragers from her homeland, showed us which mushrooms were edible."

"There are so many tales of deadly fungi. Particularly in Britain, where nearly all mushrooms are considered poisonous and are derisively called toadstools."

"In Roman times, mushrooms were referred to as the food of the gods," said Hannah.

"Claudius's fourth wife, Agrippina, with her son Nero's help, was poisoned by a plate of deadly mushrooms." Avrum was now lying back on the grass.

Enjoying the late afternoon sun with Avrum beside her on the grassy hill, she thought of how she would love to bare her body to the sun. Alas, that was a luxury she could not indulge in without damaging her fair skin, and even worse, developing skin cancer. Accordingly, unlike "wild dogs and Englishmen," she and the children wore hats and lightweight clothing to shield from the midday sun.

Hannah never worried about the children getting their vitamin D. Plenty of times on a sunny day they ran outside unprotected or swam in the pool. Ten minutes a day in the sun would provide them adequate amounts. They also drank milk. Like all milk in Canada, it is enriched with vitamin D.

"Would you like some raspberries? They're the first of the season. There's been plenty of rain, so they're extra juicy this year."

"Thanks." Avrum reached into the pail for a handful.

Hannah watched him carefully crush them, one by one, under his tongue to let out the sweet juices before slowly swallowing them.

After a moment, he looked up at Hannah and said once more, "It's so good to see you."

"You too. How long are you staying? Can you come for supper?"

"I wish I could. I'm on my way to have dinner with a friend on the other side of the lake. I just dropped in as I was passing by. Another time."

"Oh, you must stay for afternoon tea. The children have run ahead with the rest of the raspberries. They would be so disappointed if you didn't, and so would I."

"Are you free tomorrow afternoon?"

"I am."

"Then I look forward to seeing you."

That night Hannah scribbled in her diary.

June 24, 1987

It was so good to see Avrum. He made me feel alive. He was so full of life, so vigorous. So unlike Robert. Twenty years is a lot of difference in age. Kurt is also twenty years older than Avrum. Should my heart rule my head? Time, time. I need time. This time I will take it, regardless.

In the country, she felt she had all the time in the world. Here, everything could wait. The world stood still. There was time to ponder and think.

Hannah recalled making love to Jonathan on hot summer days in the country.

After long hours in the forest gathering golden chanterelle mushrooms and prized King Boletus mushrooms, as the sun lost its glow behind the towering trees, they would lie down on a thick bed of moss blanketed with pine and spruce needles clothing the damp earth, Jonathan would take her in his arms, and they would make love. Before returning home, they would search the sky through the branches of the gigantic evergreens for glimpses of the setting sun and the slowly emerging moon.

They were grateful for the umbrella those aging trees provided from the sun, and also for the sugars they produced from photosynthesis to nourish the mushrooms. In return, the mushrooms helped the trees' roots absorb nutrients from the soil. An abundant network of water from artesian wells and rain that ran off the mountain into streams provided the ideal environment for vegetation, also for a freshwater pond, into which they would jump on hot days to cool their naked bodies.

A feast of chanterelle mushrooms followed those ventures into the woods. Hannah closed her eyes and could see the golden plates of mushrooms and imagine their sweet aroma and smooth, sensual texture under her tongue. She well appreciated why they were fondly called the queen of the forest.

CHAPTER FORTY-FOUR

Hannah spotted Avrum coming up the hill. She ran down to meet him.

"You're early. Which is good. We'll have more time to talk."

"It took me less time to get over than I imagined it would." Avrum looked so pleased.

"Let's sit under the umbrella in the shade and talk before the children return from swimming classes. How're you enjoying your new house?"

"Very much. I have a lot of renovating to do before my family visits."

As Hannah poured the tea, Avrum said, "I know you have lots of questions."

Hannah laughed and replied, "You're right."

"I can imagine how frustrating it must be not to know about your husband's business. What I don't understand is how you've been so patient so long."

"Robert was away a lot. When he was home, there were so many other concerns that were a priority. His health was my main concern, and then there are always the children. There's never enough time." Hannah thought this really did sound like a lame excuse.

"I understand. You sound like my mom," Avrum replied with a grin.

"How's your family? They're in Queens. Did they always live there?"

"In the 1870s they came from Poland and settled in Eagle, Wisconsin on a farm. They prospered."

"My family left Poland for England around that time. A lot of Jews left then. What brought you to Montreal?"

"Opportunities. I had a dream." Avrum had a distant look in his eyes.

"That's fascinating, following a dream. Did you find your dream?"

"I did, to a certain degree. I was looking for diamonds. I studied geology before I studied business and gemology."

"Diamonds!" Hannah could hardly contain herself.

"My connection with diamonds and Robert started with the Eagle Diamond. My great-grandfather found the famous Eagle Diamond while digging a well on his farm in Eagle, Wisconsin."

"I've heard of the Eagle Diamond. I read an article about its theft. According to the newspaper, it was a daring heist by three guys from Miami." The story had caught Hannah's imagination. It seemed so surreal.

"Actually, there was a fourth guy no one heard about," Avrum divulged.

"How's that?" From the article, it had sounded to Hannah like the police had the robbery all sewn up.

"It's a rather long tale. Would you like to hear it?"

"Yes, yes, I would, very much. I love tales of jewels. My father was in the antique and precious gem business. I miss all the tales I heard."

"Where to start? I was visiting the American Museum of Natural History, my second home, when saw I these guys who really looked out of place standing around surveying the place." It sounded like

Avrum recalled the scene exactly, even though it must have been about twenty years ago.

"The guards never noticed them?" asked Hannah.

"I suppose not. They didn't appear very diligent. They were used to me roaming around. I was like a fixture there. The guys looked up and saw me, and asked, 'What do you want?' I replied that I believe I could help them. They asked, 'What do you know about this place? Do you know about these stones and where to find maps of the museum?' I said I was studying gemmology and knew all about the place. I really hadn't heard enough to know what they were up to, but I think they thought I'd heard their entire plan to rob the place."

"Wow! I don't know what I would have said." Hannah was enthralled.

"I had to think fast. I said I could help them with their project. I could definitely get the maps and identify the stones. What else?"

"You never mentioned about stealing them?"

"No. I was waiting for their response. They asked, 'If you help us, what do you want?' I answered, what can you give me?" related Avrum.

"You were the fourth person?" Hannah said in disbelief.

"Yes."

"Oh my gosh! I'm speechless."

"We ultimately settled on a deal. I get the info. I'd meet them at the museum the night of the robbery and help them remove the stones properly. I convinced them I knew exactly what to do to pull this caper off. I could sense it was a challenge for them, like it was for me. I told them I really just wanted to see the jewels outside the glass cabinet. Also, a minor cut on the haul. They agreed. They said, 'We'll call you from Miami when we get there, and we'll meet up at the Fontainebleau Hotel.' I knew after the robbery I'd never hear from them again. I'd seen too many movies. I acted naïvely. I had a plan. What I really wanted to do was get my hands on the Eagle Diamond. I thought my family were cheated out of it. These guys weren't the brightest bunch."

"Sounds dangerous." Hannah reasoned that any theft is a gamble, a dangerous one.

"I suppose it could have been. Next day I met them at a café with the info. We parted. I think they thought they'd never see me again. I was a cocky college student who was bluffing when I said I'd meet them at the museum. I went to the museum the day of the robbery, stayed all day and hid waiting for them, as I had done a few days earlier, so I knew the security at night was lax."

Avrum looked up for a moment, then continued. "In reality I never thought they'd show up or would get caught before they could make the haul. Around midnight, I watched them go to the case with the Eagle Diamond in it. I popped up and surprised them and asked if I could see the jewels as we had agreed. They said, 'Okay, kid, hold them for a second, look at them, and get lost.' I looked at them. Held them, and put them all back in the bag, all but the Eagle Diamond. I put it in the lining of my coat. Then I disappeared back to my hiding place. I later sneaked out through one the open windows."

"Was it that easy?" It sounded unbelievable easy to Hannah.

"Maybe it was just luck," responded Avrum.

Hannah laughed and added, "My mother would say it was meant to be."

"The stones were almost there for the taking. As newspapers reported, there was little security. The building's alarm system wasn't working properly, and there was no alarm to protect the jewel display case; the battery was dead. The second-storey windows were kept open for ventilation. On top of this, I knew from my observations that the security guards didn't make proper routine rounds. The jewels were left unwatched for hours."

"Yet it was daring." It was hard to imagine Avrum being involved in a robbery.

"Anything could've gone wrong. Actually, I thought the police would track me down. I had to get rid of the Eagle Diamond." Avrum continued, "That day there was a meeting of the New York Mineralogical Club. Robert, who I'd met at a previous society meeting, had given me his business card and told me he always stayed at the Waldorf Astoria on Park Avenue."

"That's right. He always stays there." Hannah recalled from her stay what a luxurious hotel it was.

"He said he'd be at the October New York Mineralogical Club meeting. When we first met, we had talked about the Eagle Diamond. Instinctively, I thought I'd met a soul mate. I called him. He met me in his hotel suite. We struck a deal."

"Way back then?"

"Yes. He bought the diamond. We agreed we'd work together to find the source of the diamond, based on the findings of Tiffany mineralogist Dr. George Kunz. We were both familiar with his work. Dr. Kunz had actually purchased the Eagle Diamond for Tiffany, who sold it to J.P. Morgan. Morgan donated it to the museum."

"That's a great story." Said Hannah enthusiastically.

"Since 1830, about two hundred small diamonds and the Eagle Diamond had been found in the United States in glacial moraines. So the glaciers must have picked them up and deposited them. Dr. Kunz realized there must be a source of diamonds in Canada from where the glaciers originated. He referred directly to one glacier coming from James Bay."

"How fascinating. Jonathan might have also known this information." Hannah recalled he was always reading articles on geology.

"Jonathan could very well of known of Dr. Kunz's findings. That might have been the reason he took a position at Waskaganish,"

Hannah wished it truly was his reason.

Avrum continued, "When I finished my studies, I worked with Robert to find the diamond deposits. I needed someone with the interest and the backing. He had both."

"It must have been the business dealings Robert alluded to shortly before his death. In Waskaganish I saw the clearing in the forest when I visited. One of the workers said it was a fish farm."

"The diamond business can be dangerous. Robert always said he didn't think it was wise to get you involved. He wanted to protect you. I must admit it was difficult for me not to talk to you about it."

Now Hannah understood the reason Robert had never encouraged her to visit Waskaganish.

Seeing the children happily running up the hill after their swimming lessons, she ran down to greet them.

"We'll talk more after your trip to Nantucket," he said. "I'm sure you'll be pretty busy until then. Summer will be over soon, and the children will be back at school."

"Yes, let's enjoy the remains of summer. It's so short. The children are excited. I told them you were coming for tea, and they picked watercress from the stream for sandwiches."

CHAPTER FORTY-FIVE

"**W**e're going to see Kurt," announced Jonah.

"We'll have a wonderful time," Hannah assured them. "We'll fly from Montreal to Boston. Take a bus to the ferry, which will take us to Nantucket to see Kurt. We could fly all the way, but I think you'll enjoy crossing over the water."

"I love the water," said Jonah.

"Tomorrow morning we'll leave for Montreal right after breakfast. After I do my errands downtown, we'll pack up for Nantucket." Hannah was thinking of all the things she had to do before her trip.

Blazing August sun beat down on Montreal as Hannah went about her numerous errands. When leaving the comfort of air-conditioned shops, she was uncomfortably hot, even though she was wearing a fine cotton summer dress with open sandals and a large-brimmed straw hat that shaded her entire face.

Sensible people were no doubt indoors enjoying a leisurely lunch. Hannah had no time to stop to eat. She was focused on shopping expediently and returning home to pack. Her main concern was replacing her pearl earring she had lost in the country. Those earrings were the sole gift of jewellery Jonathan had given her.

Cool, refreshing air greeted her as she stepped inside Spear's jewellery shop on Mountain Street. She quickly removed her sunglasses and hat, placing them on the long glass counter. As she was transfixed by the gleaming gems displayed on velvet stands, a tall gentleman with downcast eyes appeared from an adjoining room, "May I help you?" he asked gently.

"Yes, I lost an earring." Hannah reached into her purse to find the other one. "Can you match it?"

"I hope so. My uncle died eight days ago, and I am watching over the shop today. Just until his family feels up to coming back. Excuse me if I take a little time to find the earring."

It was the same voice she had heard many years ago. It was also the same surprising light blue eyes.

"I think I remember you," Hannah said, hesitating. "You once sold me a pearl necklace."

"Yes, I recall. It was when I was a student. I worked here during my summer breaks from university."

"Now what do you do?"

"I teach and do research," he replied as he handed her an earring. Looking from her throat up to her face he quietly said, "This looks like a match. Let's see. It also matches your necklace."

"My late husband bought these pearls for me when my twins were born. I think he bought them here. They came in your signature silver box."

"I'm sorry to hear of your loss. How old are your twins?"

"Nearly five."

"My children are much older now." Then he added, "But when my wife, their mother, died about ten years ago. They were young. It was hard on them."

"And you?" Hannah asked.

"I have a wonderful mother who has helped me. I also have always had loyal help."

"I understand how hard it must have been. It's getting late. I must get home. I'm going on a trip tomorrow. I'll take the earring. It's perfect."

"If you'd ever like to get in touch with me, you can reach me at this number." He wrote his name and number on the back of one of the store's business cards and handed it to Hannah.

"Thank you. Thank you very much." Hannah read what he wrote on the card and placed it in her purse.

"Thank you." He reached out his hand, and she took it. For a moment, her mind flashed back to their first encounter.

Outside, it was still sweltering hot.

*

Departing the ferry at Nantucket, Kurt was nowhere to be seen. Fellow passengers dispersed, and Hannah and the children, their baggage piled beside them, stood alone at the dock as the seagulls swooped down, searching for leftovers.

Trying to compose herself, Hannah pushed her hair back from her face, adjusted the large brim of her beige straw hat, and took a deep breath of the salt-saturated air. She was hoping to catch a whiff of the unforgettable, intoxicating perfumed profusion of honeysuckles and roses creeping up the walls of the traditional, weathered, grey-shingled Nantucket cottages on this prosperous island. During the late eighteenth and nineteenth centuries, when whale oil was used for lamps and whale bones for women's corsets, it was the whaling capital of the world.

"We must be patient. He'll be here. Stay together." Hannah was struggling to sound reassuring. As she straightened her new moss-green, patterned cotton Laura Ashley dress, she was thinking of a back-up plan if Kurt did not show up.

"Doesn't it look wonderful here? There are long beaches to roam along and shells to collect." Hannah looked out across the harbour, then back to where they were to meet Kurt.

"Shells we can make things out of," said Sarah.

"I once covered a box with shells I took from this beach. Then I kept all the shells I gathered in it. I think I still have it. I'll try to find it when we get home." It was years ago, when she studied in Boston, shortly after Mr. Levy had told her to visit the island.

Hannah looked up to see Avrum running toward her. He was casually dressed, carrying no luggage. "I flew down as fast as I could. As soon as I received word that Kurt couldn't make it."

Stunned and speechless, Hannah flung her arms around Avrum. Her uncontrolled tears streamed down her cheeks onto the front of his pristine white linen shirt. Clinging to him, she searched for the strength to regain her composure. After a few minutes, she slowly pulled away.

"I think I would have stood here forever if you hadn't come. Do you know where he is?" she asked anxiously.

"He's in Waskaganish." His office had heard word.

"Then I'm going there. I must go. I don't care if he wants me or not. I'm going." Hannah was adamant.

"We'll all go," said Jonah.

"Yes," echoed Sarah and David.

"Please, Hannah, come back to Montreal, think about it," implored Avrum.

"No, I'm going, now. I must see him. Talk to him myself. Find out why he was in Waskaganish when he was supposed to meet us in Nantucket." Hannah was resolute.

Avrum convinced her to take the next flight to Boston then decide.

Once they were in flight, Avrum explained, "Apparently Kurt has been injured in some kind of brawl."

"Do you know the extent of his injuries?" She feared his injuries must be bad if he was still in Waskaganish. She was frightened.

"No, nothing more. When we get to Boston, I'll make some calls." Avrum was trying his best to keep her calm.

Arriving at Boston's Logan Airport, Avrum slipped away to find a telephone. When he returned, Hannah was at the food counter ordering refreshments for the children.

"I was unable to get any information on Kurt. I suggest we fly back to Montreal and get a good night's sleep."

*

Next morning, Hannah and Avrum boarded the flight for Waskaganish.

"You look familiar with this flight." Hannah was observing his easy-going manner as they took their seats.

"When I first came to Canada, I spent a lot of time in Waskaganish exploring the terrain. It's been about ten years since I've been back."

"Why the change?

"It was a time of exploration for the diamonds. Now the mine is operating. After the diamonds are extracted, they have to be graded and cut and distributed. I assembled a team of mostly Hasidic diamond sorters and cutters. That's where my interests are now." He was pleased at last to be free to discuss his business dealings with her.

"That's how you've gotten to know the Hasidic?" Hannah was intrigued by the connection.

"Yes. When we met on Park Avenue, I rushed away because I had a meeting with them."

"There must be a lot more sites for diamond exploration in northern Canada." Hannah was slowly getting a clearer picture of the business Robert alluded to.

"There are. As I mentioned before, a fellow named Chuck Fipke has for some time researched the possibility of Canadian diamonds. In 1983 he founded Dia Met Minerals. It's listed on the Vancouver Stock Exchange. It's just a matter of time before everyone will be staking claims. and that includes the deep pockets, De Beers and Tiffany. Hard to compete with. It's a vicious business. There'll be a need for sorters and cutters. Right now all this is mostly done in other countries — Antwerp, India, Israel." Avrum's enthusiasm was energizing her.

"You want to do it in Canada? It sounds like a good idea."

"It will cost more, but the more diamonds change hands, the more security they require. Even then, there's always a chance of loss and theft and hazards." Memories of Rebecca's burglary and death were no doubt still fresh in his mind.

"I understand stolen diamonds are easy to transport and sell." Since Avrum had told the Eagle Diamond story, Hannah had been more attuned to any news relating to diamonds. It appeared diamond thefts happened more frequently than one would imagine.

"Yes, diamonds cut or uncut are easy to transport and sell." Avrum paused and added, "The diamonds from here will be special. They will be certified as genuine Canadian diamonds, mined and cut in Canada, not war-torn areas of the world."

"One would rather not have blood diamonds. It's a big selling point. One that most people I think would be willing to pay extra for." Hannah knew everyone hated to be associated with blood diamonds. She recalled how Jonathan had deplored them.

"Ideally, another team of Hasidic sorters and cutters living close to the mines in northern Canada would be a big bonus. It's a fabulous opportunity. If I don't do it, someone else will." It seemed he could not wait to get started on the project.

"Do you think the Hasidic would live up there?"

"That's the big question. It might depend on what we could offer them. Right now it remains to be seen." Avrum sat back. It looked like he was pondering what he could offer them to entice them to move to a frigid land far away from the comfort and security of their Montreal neighbourhood, their families, and friends. They were a tight-knit community. History told him they had descended from families that had left their roots behind before for better lives. What possible reason would there be for them to leave? Was there enough of money to entice them away?

"Something else to think about." To Hannah it sounded more like a fantasy. She was trying hard to picture Hasidic with their ever-expanding families living far up north.

"This kimberlite pipe we're extracting diamonds from now as we dig deeper will be harder to extract diamonds from. Then we'll have to find other deposits. That's before the rest of the world catches on. Then there will be a stampede, which will put the gold rush to shame."

"I'm shocked word hasn't spread yet." Hannah could not see how one could keep something like that a secret.

"The Cree community benefitted with jobs and payoffs. A small, close-knit group benefitted most. They became wealthy. The James Bay hydro-electric project has occupied most people in the area. Even if they saw equipment and digging, they assumed it was related to that project. Outsiders who got too close to the mining operations weren't welcome. If word had spread about the diamond deposits, prospectors would come from far and wide."

"One of these could have been Jonathan? What about Rebecca?"

"Through Yvon, she got involved in the diamond business. The day she was beaten up, she was preparing to make a delivery to Montreal. She had a stash of uncut diamonds in her possession. That evening, Jonah was staying over at a friend's house and the housekeeper was given the day off. Rebecca tried to stand up to the thugs. There was supposed to be protection, guards. They were in on the haul, an inside job. They were recently arrested."

"Good news they were arrested. One can see why Robert was so upset." Hannah was abruptly brought back to reality. Now she was trying to prepare herself for another reality as the plane came into a landing, one she could never have imagined facing.

*

Once at the small Waskaganish clinic, Hannah's anxiety heightened.

"Sorry, you can't go in. Only family," the nurse informed her.

"How is he?" asked Avrum, who was once again taking control.

"We're monitoring him," replied the nurse.

"How bad is he? Can he speak?" Hannah asked anxiously.

"Right now he needs rest. We're getting ready to fly him to Montreal. They have the facilities there," the nurse said hastily as she filled in some papers."

"I must see him. I'm his fiancée, the mother of his children."

His face was bashed up and bruised, nearly beyond recognition. When he saw Hannah, he tried to sit up.

"I'm sorry, Hannah. So sorry. I was ready to leave for Nantucket to meet you when I was attacked by a bunch of thugs," murmured Kurt in a barely audible voice.

Hannah took his hand. "Please rest now."

"I must tell you. Before going to Nantucket and seeing you as planned, I went to Waskaganish to get a few missing shots for my long-delayed movie."

"Waskaganish seems more dangerous than I could imagine. So sad," Hannah said in disbelief.

"These thugs were sicked on me by this Yvon character. I have the proof that he was involved in the deaths of Jonathan and Robert. As a filmmaker, everyone wants talk to you, tell you their tales. My movie is about the harsh, brutal life of the Cree country. I found someone who heard Robert saying to Yvon the night Jonathan died, 'Do what you have to do.'"

Hannah felt devastated, speechless.

Kurt continued, "The word is Robert and Yvon were heard arguing. It appeared he wanted to be a part of Robert's business. He was tired of being his go boy." He paused again. "Yvon was also terribly upset by Rebecca's death. He remained emotionally attached to her, obsessed by her. He got her involved in the diamond business. It was up to Robert to protect her. I think Yvon thought Rebecca ultimately would come back to him." Kurt leaned back, exhausted.

"Please, we'll have lots of time to talk. Rest," Hannah said, clutching Kurt's hand.

But he continued, "Apparently, in a fit of rage he came to see Robert when he was alone. I know Robert usually has people around him. They argued. Yvon beat up Robert. I don't know if he meant to kill him. Robert was too feeble to defend himself." He leaned back, exhausted.

Hannah wondered how Robert could have kept quiet all these years about his involvement in Jonathan's death. But it was understandable. If he had said anything, he could have been drawn into Jonathan's death and questioned. He seemed to give Yvon permission to do what he had to do.

Hannah recalled an Agatha Christie Poirot mystery in which one is asked to decide who is guilty — the killer or the one who egged him on.

She knew Robert had others do his dirty work. He kept his hands clean. She also realized he probably paid everyone off to keep quiet.

"It's time," the nurse quickly said on entering the room. "We need to get him ready to be flown to the Montreal General Hospital for surgery."

"Can we come along?" pleaded Hannah.

"I wish you could. There is no empty space on the plane. You will have to wait for the next flight. I'm so sorry."

CHAPTER FORTY-SIX

By the time they had boarded the next four-hour flight to Montreal, Hannah was weary and worried.

"Kurt is strong. He'll heal," Avrum tried to assure her.

"I hope you're right. Since I met him, I've fought to deny my feelings for him. I've tried to convince myself it was a fatal attraction, not to be. He was forbidden fruit." Hannah was at a loss.

"Then you married Robert," said Avrum, looking rather puzzled.

"Yes. His kindness and caring made it difficult not to care for him. It was a special kind of relationship. I know he had his weaknesses." She also unfortunately realized he had a brutal side. A side she hated to acknowledge.

"Who wants perfection? But we do crave kindness and caring. You said you were Kurt's fiancée?"

"It was the only way they would let me in to see him." She would have said anything to see him.

"I thought so."

"I don't know what the future has in store." Hannah was still trying to get a grasp on the situation. All she understood was that she had to remain optimistic.

Once home, she phoned the hospital. "He's waiting for surgery. No news." Hannah turned to Avrum as she slowly put the phone down.

"You need a good night's sleep. I'll see you in the morning. Good night. I'll let myself out."

Hannah was thinking of what Helen would have made of the situation. The evening before Hannah and the children left for Nantucket, Helen and Ted had flown to Sapporo, Japan for a cardiology conference.

*

Early the next day, Hannah and Avrum went directly to the Montreal General Hospital surgery floor.

Hannah approached the nurse. "We'd like to see Kurt Garner."

"I'm sorry, he can only see one visitor at a time. His son just arrived from Waskaganish. He'll be going in shortly," replied the nurse, who looked up from a chart she was writing in.

"His son? I never knew he had a son," said Hannah in astonishment.

When Avrum walked toward the recovery room, he spotted Yvon Stone standing in the hallway. Then he turned around, and Yvon was gone.

"You may go in now. The other visitor has left," the nurse said hastily to Hannah, then added, "Don't stay too long. He's still unconscious."

It was hard for Hannah to see Kurt looking so helpless. She missed his bellowing, articulate voice and his long, graceful strides. She understood the tremendous healing powers of the body. The quote of the world-famous neurosurgeon Wilder Penfield consoled her: "Mind, brain, and body make the man, and the man is capable of so much!" She had faith Kurt would recover.

Hannah was deep in thought when the nurse interrupted her visit. "I have a procedure to do. I suggest you come back later. He should be awake."

"Yes. Thank you. We'll be in the waiting room," Hannah said, getting up from her chair beside Kurt's bed.

Then the nurse added, "By the way, there's an envelope for you at the nurse's station."

Hannah took the manila envelope and settled down in one of the comfortable armchairs lining the walls of the small waiting room. She stretched her legs out and tried to think logically. She wondered whether it was true that Yvon was Kurt's son. The years had taught her anything is possible. More disturbing and potentially fatal was that perhaps he was an intruder, hoping to silence Kurt?

When she opened the envelope, out fell a small silver box and her gold-linked charm bracelet, from which dangled her treasured compass mounted in whalebone. She turned the compass over and for some time looked at the engraving on its back — a scrimshawed bird in flight carrying a heart. On her wrist she placed the bracelet she had left behind years ago when she first met Kurt in New York's Waldorf Astoria Hotel. An intense pang of sadness engulfed her.

In the silver box was a gold ring with a central deep-blue gleaming gem. On each side of it was a brilliant, clear diamond. Scrawled on a small piece of paper was, *After I saw you in your exquisite blue dress at the presentation I gave in Montreal, I had this ring designed for you, hoping to give it to you when we next met, which I was hoping would be shortly. The blue diamond matches your necklace. I will love you forever, Kurt.*

Refracting the sunlight streaming through the windows overlooking Montreal, the ring sparkled and glistened as only a blue diamond and true love could in spite of challenges, pain, and time. No surface dirt can tarnish a diamond, just as one hopes none of life's trials can dull true love or break it apart.

"It's an amazing view from here. One of the best in the city," Avrum noted as he sat down. "It's going to be a while before we can see Kurt."

"I'll wait." Hannah had no intention of leaving Kurt alone in the hospital.

"That's a magnificent ring you're holding." Avrum could not take his eyes off the central blue diamond.

"It was in an envelope from Kurt the nurse gave me." Tears flowed down Hannah's grief-stricken face.

Avrum handed Hannah a white cotton handkerchief. She wiped her face and tried to compose herself as she continued clutching the ring. "May I see it?"

"Certainly." Hannah handed the ring to him.

Avrum inspected it closely. "It has the sparkle of a real blue diamond."

Out from under the collar of her blouse Hannah pulled her necklace with an almost identical blue diamond. "When I wear it, most people think it's a sapphire or any blue gem."

"You can tell it's a diamond. It has the fire and brilliance. Tested, it would have the hardness of a diamond, ten on the Mohs scale; sapphires are nine. It can scratch a sapphire. It also refracts more light than a sapphire. Even when it has surface dirt, it glitters," explained Avrum.

"I know you must be wondering how I came by it, or probably if it was Robert who gave it to me. Though Robert gave me some lovely jewellery, my father gave it to me as a wedding present," Hannah said with a distant look and longing in her eyes.

"It's an exquisite gift." The unusual gold chain the blue diamond hung from caught his attention.

"I cherish it. My family's business started in England in precious stones, gold, and silver. We came to Canada with drawers full of gems." Hannah could still picture the long trays they were kept in.

"What happened to them?"

"We gradually sold them to survive in Canada." By the time her and her brother had grown up, they were nearly all sold.

"Did your father tell you where he acquired it? Blue diamonds are rare and expensive." Avrum must also have been thinking of how Kurt had purchased a blue diamond and why he was not more cautious with it. He appeared to be carrying it around with him. Avrum had witnessed numerous robberies of precious gems.

"He bought the necklace from Kurt when we were living in Bournemouth. At the time, I was a child. Kurt was a high school student studying in Bournemouth," explained Hannah, knowing, understandably, that Avrum would have questions.

Avrum looked astonished.

"It's a long story. I first met Kurt when I was three years old." Then Hannah proceeded to tell the tale.

After about five minutes, Avrum said, "That's an astounding story."

"Your stories are also," said Hannah with a grin. "I'm interested in the diamond mines of Waskaganish."

Avrum knew Hannah well and no doubt understood she sought a diversion. "The mine in Waskaganish is unique. It has high-quality ore, which means there are more diamonds per ton than usual. It requires less digging to extract diamonds. Mining in Waskaganish left a comparatively small footprint."

"And this all started with the Eagle Diamond. Do you know where the Eagle Diamond is now?" inquired Hannah.

"We have it in the safe. We've actually considered returning it to the museum."

"It would be difficult to rationalize how you acquired it." Hannah imagined all kinds of scenarios, some with unfortunate endings. The worst was Avrum being charged with its theft and ending up in jail.

"It would. More people could enjoy it. It's the most famous di-hexagon diamond in the world," Avrum said with pride.

"Mr. Garner is awake now. You and his son may visit. One at a time," said the nurse firmly.

"I'll be waiting here for you." Avrum stood up. He pictured the painted photo, set in an ornate gilded frame, that sat on the mantle in his parents' Queens home. It was a photo of his great-grandmother on her wedding day. In it she was wearing a blue diamond necklace with an unusual gold chain. It was the same chain he had just seen on Hannah.

When Avrum had once asked where the necklace was now, he was told it was sold to a Polish Jew fleeing to Vienna. That must have been Kurt's family.

THE END

WASKAGANISH

After *Waskaganish*, follow the lives of Hannah Epstein Star and other characters in the up-coming novel *Montreal.*

In the new study, scientists estimate that cratonic roots may contain 1 to 2 percent diamond. Considering the total volume of cratonic roots in the Earth, the team figures that about a quadrillion (10^{16}) tons of diamond are scattered within these ancient rocks, 90 to 150 miles below the surface. July 16, 2018 by Jennifer Chu, Massachusetts Institute of Technology.

WASKAGANISH

About the Author, Sandra Cohen-Rose:

To Waskaganish, Sandra Cohen-Rose's first novel – the author of the Canadian Best Seller, *The New Canadian High Energy Diet*, and the first book on Canadian Art Deco architecture, *Northern Deco - Art Deco Architecture in Montreal* – brings her passion for storytelling.

Interwoven into her historic love story and fantasy world are her deep-rooted ethical concerns honed from 15 years on the McGill Medical Ethics Committee and her advocacy work as chair of Dietitians of Canada, Consulting Dietitians group, and President of the Montreal Council of Women and the National Council of Women of Canada, and Art Déco Montréal.

With her family she immigrated from Bournemouth, England to White Rock British Columbia on Semiahmoo Bay. Here her family continued their gem and antique business.

After graduating the University of British Columbia, she lived and worked in Boston then Montreal as a Consultant Dietitian-Nutritionist and Home Economist. She and her husband, cardiologist Colin Rose, divide their time between Montreal and the Eastern Townships of Quebec where their daughters and grandchildren frequently join them.